DISCARDED

NOTES FROM
MY CAPTIVITY

NOTES FROM

MY CAPTIVITY

Kathy Parks

KT KATHERINE TEGEN BOOKS
An Imprint of HarperCollins Publishers

DISCARDED

Katherine Tegen Books is an imprint of HarperCollins Publishers.

Notes from My Captivity
Copyright © 2018 by Kathy Parks

Library of Congress Control Number: 2017962569
ISBN 978-0-06-239400-2 (trade bdg.)

18 19 20 21 22   PC/LSCH   10 9 8 7 6 5 4 3 2 1
❖
First Edition

To Michael Parks,
My Vanya

I have a family.
And they have me.
They have me.
They have me.

part one

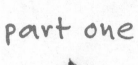

Grigoriy and Nika Osinov were young university professionals when they vanished from Moscow in 1987. They did not lock their door on the way out. Mrs. Osinov neglected to even take her purse. The landlord at their tenement building, which overlooked Tverskaya Street, found the apartment eerily pristine. The table was set. Food still in the refrigerator. And something that, in light of the rumors of sorcery, terrified him: the startling movement of a crow, which had been sitting on the table, suddenly flying out the open window.

Dr. Daniel Westin
New York Times article

one

My mother puts a lot of stock in dreams. She says she dreamed of me before I was born, knew the color of my eyes and hair. She named me Adrienne in her sleep, and that's the name she gave me when I came along, blond haired and blue eyed just as she'd predicted. The night I lost my father, she dreamed a heart-monitor line went flat. But I'm not a superstitious person, or one inclined to believe in the magical or the supernatural. So I'm not alarmed, just annoyed, when, the morning my stepfather and I are leaving on our trip, Mom wakes from a nightmare about what will happen to us in Siberia.

She's talking about it, totally agitated, when I wander in for breakfast. She's flipping pancakes as she speaks. The pancakes are falling apart. Dan, my stepfather, watches her. He is on the tall side, thin, and his teeth are a tiny bit too big for his mouth, giving people the perception he is smiling.

But he's not smiling right at the moment. The look on his face says, *Oh shit, we were almost home free and now this stupid dream.*

Jason, the stepbrother who was foisted on me seven years ago, lounges at the breakfast table in an old T-shirt and board shorts, looking amused. He's just jealous because he wanted to go on this trip—if only to meet some Russian girls on the way to Siberia—and I'm going instead. Or, I think I'm still going.

"It was terrible!" Mom exclaims.

I glance at Dan. "Let me guess. Mom had a dream."

"Just a dream," Dan says quickly, directing that at Mom more than at me, his tone reassuring and just a little dismissive. "Dreams mean nothing. They're just chemical reactions in the cerebral cortex that occur during REM sleep. . . ."

Great, Dan. Calm her right down with geekspeak.

My real father was a quiet district attorney, a man of few words, with body language that never gave away his game. Dan is a frenetic anthropologist with jazz hands. His hands are busy right now, in the air, helping form his nonsense about REM sleep.

"Nothing's going to happen to me, Mom." I go to her

and touch her shoulder, feel the tension there. She flips another pancake. It tears in half. I'll be having scrambled pancakes for breakfast, with a side of nightmare.

She shakes her head. "You and Dan were sleeping in tents, and then they came through the woods with knives and sliced your tent open."

They. She's talking about the Osinovs, the family of mysterious Siberian hermits Dan has been studying for years. He's an anthropologist at the University of Denver, and a very well respected one—at least he was . . . until last month.

"Then what?" Jason asks. My stepbrother seems eager to hear about horrible things done to me even in my mom's subconscious. He's thoughtful that way.

"I woke myself up screaming."

"Sorry, Jason," I say. "She didn't get to the beheading part."

"Stop it," Mom orders, shooting me a fierce look. "This isn't a joke."

I roll my eyes. Some girls are stricken with Resting Bitch Face. I've got Argument Bitch Face, in which my mild features turn into an unconscious embodiment of Teenage Attitude when I'm about to state my case. And my voice. I can't keep the sarcasm out of my voice at such times. It's like trying to take the calories out of a cupcake. What I want to say out loud but cannot is that the crazy, possibly murderous Osinov family won't sneak up on me with knives because there is no family. They're just another leg-end like bigfoot and the Loch Ness monster. But I can't say that out loud because Dan has based his entire aca-demic career on them. Dan's article "The Vanished: The Story of the Osinovs" was published three years ago in the *New York Times* and made him a star. That is until Syd-ney Declay, badass journalist and my own personal hero, wrote the now-famous article in the *Washington Post* last month debunking the whole thing.

"It's perfectly safe," Dan assures her, rising on his toes like he always does when he's excited, which is often, jazz hands going, words pouring out. "Remember I've done it twice, and Adrienne is a smart, responsible girl, and she'll be with me at all times, *please*, honey, this is a trip of a life-time. . . ." He lowers his heels to the ground, raises them again, as though performing an exercise to strengthen his calves.

"A trip of a deathtime," Jason chimes in.

I glare at him. "Shut up, Jason."

He laughs evilly. Dan pauses for breath. Mom shakes a dollop of butter onto my sad pancake, sloppy as an unmade bed. Her eyes are troubled. I've been begging to go for months, have finally gotten permission, inoculations, a ticket, everything, and now it's all going to hell.

It's rare that Dan and I find ourselves on the same side. Sure, he usually wants to be on my side. He's still trying to fill that void where my father used to be. It's weird to be allies with him. But I find myself drifting over next to him as though our argument will be more powerful if we are standing closer together.

"Adrienne wants to be a reporter," Dan says. "She needs to see the world." A wave of guilt rushes through me at his words. I wish I believed in his Russian family. But it's like belief in anything. I need proof, and wouldn't he have found it by now if it existed? Besides, Sydney did an amazing job of discrediting him with her article.

"I wouldn't bring her if I didn't think it was safe," he adds.

I join in the argument. "I'll be going with a whole crew." *Two people at least.* "And a guide."

"Dan, she's a seventeen-year-old girl!" Mom protests.

"Eighteen in three months," I say.

Jason's already halfway through his pancake. "I'm nineteen. And I'm a *guy*."

"What's that supposed to mean?" I ask. "Like, a girl can't make it in the woods? Besides, why do you want to go? You're not interested in Russia. You've never been out in the woods, and you're not a reporter."

"*You're* not a reporter," Jason sneers. "Editor in chief of the Rosedale High student paper means absolutely nothing."

"My article on fracking ran in the *Denver Times*, douchebag," I shoot back.

"Jason," Dan said severely, "stop making fun of your

sister. At least she has goals. She didn't flunk out of community college for missing half her classes."

Jason winces. I stifle a snicker.

"Whatever," he says. "Siberia sucks, anyway."

"It's freezing there," Mom says. She stares down at the new pancake, wanting to guard it till it grows up perfect.

Dan's getting annoyed now. It's two hours before we leave for the plane, and I can see the exasperation on his face. "We've been over this again and again. Siberia warms up in June." His hands rise in the air. Is he trying to communicate heat rising off the earth? Who knows.

"Unless there's a freak snowstorm," Jason pipes in. "You've mentioned that possibility, Dad."

"God, Jason." I'm exasperated now. "Don't you have anything better to do than ruin my trip? Go fail at something."

Mom's pancake is now burning, and she hasn't noticed. Dan reaches over and moves her pan off the burner.

"Are you packed, Adrienne?" he asks pointedly. "You need to double-check your supplies."

Mom gives him a look. She has a pretty mild appearance. Hair down to her shoulders, a heart-shaped face. But her eyebrows are monsters. They can take an argument and bend it like a pretzel. And now her eyebrows are slowly contorting.

"*The dream*," she says again, as though those two words are all she needs to keep me in Boulder all summer.

I let out my breath. "You can die anywhere. At any time. Out of the blue. Just minding your own business."

Mom gives me a look. I see the grief that never goes away. I shouldn't have said this.

"I'm sorry."

She shrugs. We're great communicators.

I quickly change the subject. "Imagine how this will look on my college applications. And you know I have to get a scholarship to go to Emerson. You know we can't afford it."

I realize that in trying to divert Mom's attention, I've accidentally slammed Dan and his habit of draining our money away on his fruitless wild-goose chases.

"You know what I mean," I add lamely.

"The university is providing a Thuraya satellite phone," Dan says, ignoring my remark. "That's the best there is. We'll be in constant contact with the outside world." He seems weary, dejected. His hands aren't waving anymore. They're hiding in his pockets. Maybe I've made him sad with the budget talk.

"Bears." My mother quickly moves on to other arguments. "Wolves."

"Osinovs," Jason pipes up.

"The guide will have a gun, and we'll all carry bear spray," Dan insists. One hand struggles free of his pocket, points a finger for emphasis. "This is not some crazy stunt."

"And this family?" she asks. "This group of hermits or lunatics or whatever they are supposed to be? What if Adrienne runs into them?"

"Based on all my research," Dan retorts, using the kind of professorial sentence structure that usually annoys me but now might bolster my case, "the Osinovs were a harmless yet eccentric couple when they disappeared thirty years ago. I don't believe these crazy tales of their being dangerous." He doesn't mention his source, Yuri Androv, and his tale of being captured and menaced by the legendary family before he managed to escape.

"Your source says the family kidnapped him," Mom reminds Dan.

"And if you read the article—" Dan retorts.

"I've *read the article*, Dan." Mom's getting pissed.

"If you read the article," he insists, "you'd know that I don't believe he was ever in any danger. Yuri exaggerates. But I do believe he was at their campsite. Too many details ring true. The Osinovs wouldn't have hurt him."

The Osinovs. He must have said that name ten thousand times. And I'm really sick of hearing it.

Mom flips the burned pancake onto a plate. I know she will eat it herself because she hates waste and because she's the mom. She tries one more time. "Okay, Dan, but something you've never explained is why *now*? What's the hurry?"

I study Dan's face to see the reaction. He looks flustered. He doesn't say anything at first.

I know a secret. I know why now. I know what's the hurry.

There's a very fine line between being a reporter and a snoop, and I crossed it last month, a few days after Sydney Declay's article came out. I got the mail that day and noticed a letter for Dan from the chairman of the anthropology department. That night, I watched Dan's face as he read it. Something was up. Something urgent and serious. That night, after everyone was asleep, I went into his office, found the letter, and took a photo of it with my iPhone. It began: "Dear Dr. Westin . . ." A sure sign that Dan was in trouble because he and the chairman had been friends for thirty years. Why such an icy greeting? As I read on, I found out why: Sydney Declay's article had not only humiliated Dan, it had embarrassed the entire university, and if Dan didn't find proof of the Osinovs, they were going to pull his grant.

He'd already taken out a second mortgage on the house. I had learned that from another midnight raid. So that's why now. I watch Dan's face go dark.

"Because," he says at last. "Next year it will be too late."

"Too late for what?" Mom asks.

Dan doesn't answer.

The look on his face makes me wince. But whenever

I start feeling too bad for him, I think of all the things he's ruined. Like my life. Like our well-built, well-balanced family that liked to hike in the woods and believed in very little except one another. Then my dad died and Dan swept into the house, bringing his dumb son and his belief in the Osinovs. It reminded me of a particularly fervent brand of Christianity, except the Osinovs weren't coming back; they were supposedly here already. Dan has the glassy-eyed stare of the true believer. He never misses a chance to tell me about some new detail he's found through his research—all word-of-mouth, legend, rumor. Things my father would have dismissed from any trial. The tool that Yuri Androv, his main source, claimed the eldest son used to cut firewood. The mystical powers of the father. The fishermen downstream who claim to get a glimpse of two brothers fishing from a crude boat. The shoe sole—Grigoriy Osinov's size—found at the remains of an old campsite, along with a charred biography of the life of Carl Linnaeus, the botanist with whom Osinov was obsessed. The letters Osinov wrote his cousin detailing his escape plan. Every tiny item in the proof of their existence has been discussed at the dinner table.

And I'm tired of that life.

Tired of Dan's religion.

Yes, I want to write the article and get into journalism school. But I also want to be free. Free of the Osinovs forever.

Jason doesn't go to the airport with us. He's got a very important *Call of Duty: Zombies* battle to fight in the rec room downstairs. Mom, of course, has to go with us to make me feel guilty every mile to the airport. Soon as we pull out of the neighborhood, she starts in again. Am I sure I'm going to go? Why don't I stay home with her this summer? In return, she'll take me to Montana. Haven't I always wanted to go to Montana? It will be just the two of us. . . .

From the back seat, I watch Dan's hands tighten on the wheel. I know they are dying to join the argument. "Martha, stop trying to bribe her with a trip to Montana. She wants to go with me!"

He and Mom start at it again, and I decide it's a good time to tune them out. I take out the Dictaphone I bought online—the same one Sydney Declay uses—and speak softly into it.

It's a bright, clear summer day outside as we set off for Denver International Airport, full of those plans and dreams and expectations that always happen before a trip, but this trip is bigger, deeper, darker, and more vast than any I've taken in my life. I wonder, What is the day like in Siberia? Will the landscape represent the one whose—

Dan gasps. The tires screech as the car brakes hard, out of nowhere, jerking me out of my reporting. I can hear Mom shriek as I'm jerked forward and back again. The

Dictaphone flies out of my hand. The car is still. A brief silence and then Mom whips her head around.

"Adrienne! Are you okay?"

"I'm okay, Mom," I manage shakily. I'm confused and disoriented and rattled. It's like Siberia reached out a paw from across the world and disrupted a simple thing like a car moving down pavement.

Dan peers into the road ahead.

"Dan!" Mom has a hand on her chest, breathing hard. "Why did you slam on the brakes? Are you trying to get us killed?"

He turns to her, eyes wide. "Did you see the little girl?"

"Little girl?" Mom echoes. "What little girl?"

My heart steadies. I look around us. We're alone.

Dan shakes his head. "I'm telling you, there was a little girl standing in the middle of the road."

two

By some miracle, there are no other incidents before we arrive at the terminal, although I'm still a bit rattled from the near-accident we had on the way to the airport at the hands of some jaywalking phantom. And I'm feeling a little whiplashed, not the best condition to be in when you've got such a long flight ahead of you.

Dan saw a ghost in the road, almost killed us, I whisper into my Dictaphone. *Good times already.*

Dan and I get out and Mom tells us goodbye. "It's so hard to be a parent," she whispers, holding me tight.

"We've got to hurry," Dan says, glancing at his watch. "There might be a line."

"It's okay, Mom," I reassure her, extracting myself from

her grip. "I'll text you when we land."

I watch her kiss Dan goodbye. He's dressed up in Anthropology Geek activewear: chino pants, flannel shirt, a Gore-Tex upland field hat, and Birkenstocks. He'd wear Birkenstocks to the moon. It's still hard to see him kissing her when my dad should be there instead. The two men have different kissing styles. Dad turned his head a certain way, used his hands more. Dan still looks awkward doing it, like he's on a first date.

After some final, tearful instructions, Mom takes off and we breathe a sigh of relief.

"I'm glad that's over with," Dan mutters. "For a minute there I thought she wasn't going to let you go."

"Thanks for helping me calm her down," I reply, trying to keep the guilt out of my voice. He wouldn't have been so eager to help me if he'd known the working title of the article I'm writing: "Wild-Goose Chase." Intriguing subtitle: "Crazy stepdad drags long-suffering girl into the Siberian wilderness in pursuit of the legendary hermit family." What journalism program could resist me?

Speaking of journalism . . .

"What did the little girl look like?" I ask.

"Little girl?"

"You know. The one in the road."

He shrugs. "It happened so fast. Maybe it was, I don't know . . ." He searches for the words, two fingers of his right hand spinning as though turning the wheel of his brain. "I barely slept last night, and the malaria pills gave me nightmares."

"Makes sense," I say. Dan does have a habit of believing in things that aren't there. He takes off for the ticket counter, and I hurry to catch up with him. I checked in this morning on my phone, but Dan is back in the twentieth century when paper tickets were all you used. I stand in line behind him as he fumbles for his itinerary. He's rising on his toes again. Kind of a perilous habit when you're wearing Birkenstocks. I'm hoping he doesn't topple over. I'm excited too, because I really feel that this last doomed trip of his obsessive quest will make a good story. Maybe even a great story. Maybe even a story featured in the *New York Times*.

Sydney Declay once said: "A great reporter can really feel a story in the air, know it before they even meet it. It's this intuitive response to what will be fantastic on the written page that distinguishes the pros from the amateurs."

And I'm going to be one of the pros.

My phone buzzes. It's a text from my best friend, Margot. Good luck finding that family. I've located the daddy. A picture of bigfoot appears on-screen. My thumb, which holds much of my sarcasm, locates a photo of Jim Morrison on the internet. Not the early Jim Morrison but the late version, hairy and bearded and wild-looking. I text Margot back.

No, this is the daddy. He was last seen doing heroin in Paris.

Just before we get on the plane, I make one more phone call.

"You've reached William Cahill," the voice says. "Please leave your message at the sound of the beep." I loved the way my father said his own name. He used to take me to his law offices when I was a little girl and he'd answer the phone: *William Cahill.* So authoritative and calm. My mother got rid of his clothes and his books after he died, but she let me keep his phone, paid the fee every month to keep it going even though money was tight. I've got to give her that.

This is my first trip ever out of the US. My first trip out of Boulder. My father would have been the first to cheer me on.

Dan glances at me. "Who was that?" he asks.

I click my phone off.

"No one."

Ten hours later, our Boeing 747 still has a way to go before we land in Moscow. From there we will fly to Abakan and then drive to a tiny settlement, pile into a boat, and travel up the river into remote Siberia. We're meeting the crew in Moscow. There are two of them. A man and a woman, both Russians. Dan has gone to Siberia twice before with them. I've heard all about this crack crew: Lyubov and Viktor. How smart and dedicated and knowledgeable they are, and how close they all thought they'd come the last expedition, until bad weather had slowed them down and their supplies had dwindled and they'd had to return. Lyubov, the woman, especially intrigues me. She sounds completely badass. I wonder if she and Viktor really believe in the quest or if they're just doing it for money or adventure. I figure I'll have plenty of time to ask them.

Dan thoughtfully got us seats side by side, so I can't use my trusty digital recorder. I've spent the last hours studying my English-Russian travel guide. I've been learning words and phrases the past couple of months and can now ask, "How much for salted herring?" or say, "I think I missed the bus." Essential communication in the Siberian wilderness. And if I am kidnapped by the Osinovs, I can say: "Please don't eat me. I am from Boulder and my flesh is inferior." Well, not that eloquently, but I can get the point across.

I close the travel guide, tired of learning, and look out the window. The cloud bank stretches out below us; pure blue sky is all I see above it. It's June, but up here, it's nothing. No time, no seasons. I suppose Sydney Declay would be already writing her article, and so wearily I open my laptop. "Even before I enter a foreign environment, I begin to put words on a page," Sydney once wrote. "Thoughts, feelings, bursts of conversation around me. Although I have no idea how an article will shape itself, I know that a story is like a tourist in a foreign land. Every bit of direction that you can give it is appreciated."

Since there are not a lot of newsworthy events here on the plane—*NEWSBREAK*: the baby in the seat behind us just let out a screech that I feel up and down my spine—I start typing my thoughts.

> *Those crazy Osinovs. Peaceful hunter-gatherers¿*
> *Cannibals¿ Sorcerers¿ Fairy tale¿ Depends on who you*
> *ask. Five years ago, the family supposedly kidnapped Yuri*
> *Androv, a reporter from Kiev, Dan's most trusted source, and*
> *according to Sydney Declay, a liar and a drunk. The story*
> *he told seemed to confirm all the pieces my stepfather had*
> *put together—that somehow this young, extremely religious*
> *married couple had fled Moscow thirty years before, had*
> *journeyed up the Erinat River, and had a family of their*
> *own—one that grew up with no known contact with any*
> *civilization. Dan's breathless recounting of Yuri's wild tale*
> *seemed hyperbolic even to me—a mere tween at the time*
> *I read it. But the colorful Russian's account of the ordeal*
> *was so detailed, so passionate, that I could understand how*
> *someone as dedicated to the story as my stepfather could*
> *believe it—minus the kidnapping theatrics. But what I don't*
> *understand is, after what Sydney Declay dug up, why does*
> *Dan still believe it today¿*

It's time for a little investigative journalism. I pause, close the laptop, glance at Dan, who is busily going over some notes, making little scribbles in the margins.

"What are you doing?" I ask him.

He puts down his pen. "Just checking a few things. Want to make sure I get the crew up to speed first thing. Lots of moving parts on this trip. The weather should be good, but you never know. You'll like them, Adrienne, those two. And I couldn't get the guide I wanted this time, but I got the next best thing, his son. He's supposed to be great!"

There it is, the patter of Dan's speech getting faster. He's supercharged, so confident. I don't want to kill his good mood so that he clams up, so I'm very careful when I introduce the subject.

"I can't wait to meet Lyubov," I begin. "She must be so interesting."

"She is! Just got divorced over the spring. I never met the husband, but I can't imagine anyone wanting to divorce such a fascinating person." His fingers are spread out, jabbing at the air, underscoring how dumb the ex-husband must have been.

"So Yuri Androv's invitation must have gotten lost in the mail."

A look of annoyance crosses Dan's face. His fingers fold up and drop into his lap. "What invitation?" he asks.

"You know, to go on the trip. Didn't he go on the last trip?"

Dan seems to deflate a little. "Yes, he did," he says guardedly. "But I haven't been in touch with him since . . ."

"Sydney Declay's article came out?" I ask. Despite Dan's apparent enthusiasm to discuss all things Osinov, he has never discussed the article with me. His eyebrows go up.

"You read the article?" he asks.

Of course I did. About fifty times. "Yeah," I say.

He's silent for a moment. He rips open a tiny bag of pretzels. "What did you think?" he asks, and then dives in with his own opinion before I can even answer. "It was a total hatchet job. She came into it with an agenda and it was evident in every sentence. She's always promoted herself on the backs of dedicated researchers. Just remember, Adrienne"—he shakes the pretzel at me like a lecture ruler—"being a skeptic is easy. It's belief that's hard, and her article did nothing to shake my belief in that family."

"But what about the part where Yuri made up that other story out of thin air?"

Dan bites the pretzel, chews, and swallows before he answers. "The one where he took enemy fire with a group of Chechen rebels?"

"Right. She proved he was in Kiev at the time."

He shrugs. "So, yes, he can tell a tall tale. I don't believe every single story he slung at me while getting drunk on vodka. The man thinks he's bigger than life. That doesn't mean he lied about the Osinovs."

"No, but I can understand that if you find out someone lied about one thing, it's harder to believe them from then on. He's lost credibility. My dad used to talk about that a lot when he'd put a witness on the stand."

Dan crumples the pretzel bag and stuffs it in the seat pocket in front of him. Maybe I shouldn't have brought my dad up and how awesome he was. "I still believe Yuri," he says, a bit defensively. "There are too many things that match the accounts of Grigoriy Osinov's cousin in Moscow. Physical descriptions, items that were missing from the original apartment, books and tools . . ."

"She explains how Yuri could have faked all that by tracking down original source material."

"I know, but the campsite I found, the shoe, the *book* for God's sake . . ."

"But that book— "

He cuts me off with a look as frozen as the tundra. I've gone too far and I know it. Because the most damning thing Sydney Declay wrote in her article was her theory that my stepfather, desperate to hold on to his academic credibility, had planted that charred book in the old campsite.

That was the shot heard round the world. An attack not only on Dan's theories but his character, as well.

I should have been outraged on his behalf. But I have to admit, I couldn't say for sure that he hadn't faked the evidence he claimed to find. He seemed like a generally honest guy. But he'd been so obsessed with the Osinovs, so increasingly desperate for others to believe what he did— was it possible?

Dan has stopped talking to me. His knuckles stand out as he scribbles in the margins of his notebook. His annoyance, at me or the situation, has made his handwriting a little wilder so I can't really read it. Probably: *stepdaughter, traitor.*

"Hey, Dan," I say placatingly. " I'm a reporter. I have to look at things from all angles."

He doesn't answer me. I think he's gone radio silent, which is rare from Dan. But suddenly he drops his pen, pipes up again. "Wait and see. I'm *this close*"—he moves his thumb and forefinger an inch apart—"to finding their live campsite. And when I do, I'm not only going to write another article for the *New York Times*, I'm gonna write a book about it. It's going to be called: *Hiding in Siberia: The Story of the Osinovs.* And I'm going to sell the film as a documentary to the Discovery Channel. Won't that be remarkable?"

The religious tone is back in his voice.

"Remarkable," I say, trying to keep my own voice sincere.

Hiding in Siberia. "Wild-Goose Chase." Our expectations, outcomes, plans, and articles are completely at odds with one another. If my dad had believed in this family, if he was taking me to Russia, I would have been all in. I had faith back then. Faith in him, faith in magic. Faith in everything. All that went away the night he died.

"You're going to be proud of your dad," Dan suddenly declares.

I'm momentarily confused. Then I realize he's talking about himself.

I fold my arms. *Stepdad*, I think.

Finally we land in Moscow. The plane bumps hard. A startled gasp from the passengers as we feel a lighter bump and then the smooth runway. The passengers applaud.

I turn on my phone, wait for the connection, and text my mother.

Alive so far.

Relatives of the Osinovs—of whom there are many, although few are inclined to speak of them—are divided on the subject of whether Grigoriy Osinov was truly a victim of persecution or only imagined he was before he fled with his wife and infant son up the Erinat River in a dugout canoe. Rumors among hunters and fishermen persisted for years, of sightings of not just the Osinov family but of several more children. One local man claimed to have, but could not produce, the jar that, fifteen years ago, was supposedly discovered floating in the river. The label on the jar was a brand of sauerkraut that was discontinued in 1992. In the jar was a single piece of birch bark. And on that birch bark, one word had been scratched. *Salt.*

Dr. Daniel Westin
New York Times article

three

We're in the airport in Moscow, sitting in a bar waiting for the crew to get in and meet us. I'm a little disappointed so far. My surroundings remind me of Denver: big shiny corridors, stores everywhere, girls dressed like supermodels. Gate numbers and store names are written in English and Russian. Even what looks like Burger King is helpfully translated into something I could never hope to pronounce.

Dan's talking to me again in his patter: *They should be here any minute, look for a young guy with dark hair, was kind of longish last time but maybe he's cut it, and Lyubov has shoulders like a pro wrestler, she's an extreme skier too, did I tell you that?* I've decided to shut my yapper about Yuri, for the next little while and possibly for the remainder of my trip.

At least with Dan. I can always hit up one of the crew and see what they think.

The bartender comes over. He's big, with a black, thick beard, and looks like the kind of Russian man I'd expect to see. Dan orders, in fluent Russian, something that I know must be nonalcoholic, because Dan doesn't drink. I don't drink much either, but I've decided that I need to stretch my comfort zone, and after quickly perusing the menu, I order French fries and one of the Russian beers on tap. I order in part English, part Russian, with just a touch of millennial slang. Hardly the universal language, but the bartender seems to make sense of it all. He takes out a glass and starts drawing a light brew from the tap.

Dan raises an eyebrow at me. "Beer?" he asks. "Since when do you drink beer, Adrienne?"

"I drink beer from time to time," I fire back. "I'm an adult."

"You're seventeen."

"Almost eighteen. Come on, Dan, I'm a reporter. I need a beer and a cool hat."

"That's not what makes a good reporter." He taps his head. "Keeping your wits makes you a good reporter."

"Sure, Dan," I say. The bartender comes over with our drinks. I take a sip. It tastes warm and mysterious. The froth sticks to my upper lip. I dab it off with a napkin while Dan nurses a seltzer water with a single lime.

He looks at his watch. "Where are they?" he asks to no one in particular.

"Jeez, Dan, they're five minutes late." He gives me the eye. Dan's obsessions with time and schedules are just another reason he's the life of any party, even a Russian one.

I look around and drink my beer. No one looks remotely interesting. There's a tired-looking young couple—American or otherwise, I don't know—and an old man in a business suit muttering something in French into a cell phone.

"Did you text your mother?" Dan reminds me.

"Right when we landed."

"Easy on that beer."

"I'm *fine*." Jeez, the man is a nag. If he ever did run into the Osinovs, he'd probably harp on them for not getting in touch with him in all these years, and they'd rue the day they were ever discovered.

The beer is unusual and easy to drink. I'm already halfway through when Lyubov and Viktor arrive a few minutes later. Dan lets out a long, relieved breath and stands to greet them.

Lyubov, what a woman. Looks about midtwenties; dark red hair; almost black eyes; bushy, untamed brows; and a body to kill for. Or to run from, depending. She's got on a tight sweater and I can see the bulge of her biceps. Her jutting boobs look firm enough to hypnotize any man, even one who's been hiding in the woods for thirty years.

She could crush me with a hug. Her handshake is a vise. I wonder if she threw discus as a child and pushed around baby oxen in an enormous doll carriage.

Viktor looks more typical. Young guy, scruffy beard, playful eyes, an earring through one lobe, and hair that reaches his shoulders. The Russian equivalent of Bob Dylan must play on his iPod, which sticks out of the front pocket of his faded jeans.

Dan makes the introductions. "This is Adrienne, my daughter," he says proudly.

"Stepdaughter," I say before I can help myself.

Dan doesn't miss a beat, though. He's up on his toes. "She's the one who wants to be a reporter!" he exclaims, sweeping a hand toward me. If Dan only knew my real mission, he wouldn't have shared his frequent flier miles so readily.

"Great!" Lyubov enthuses. "I am so tired of the men."

"Well, now there's one man you don't have to put up with anymore," Viktor says with brotherly affection.

"Your husband?" I ask her.

"Ex-husband," she answers. "He is no more. I— How do you say it in English? Ditched him."

"Sometimes we also say 'punted.'" I shoot my foot out like I'm kicking a football.

"I should have punted him in the ass," she says. "Always telling me what to do. Lyubov, do this. Lyubov, do that. Now I am free, and I can do what I want."

"Bastard man," Viktor enthuses. "Did not like him." He grabs my shoulder and shakes it. "So happy you are hopping here from the world outside; we are deep-woods friends soon!" Viktor has a degree in English from WTF University. I like him immediately.

She and Viktor order shots. Dan's still nursing his seltzer. I'm done with my beer. Their film equipment crowds the bar space. Dan has been through two expeditions with them, and yet his body language remains that of an acquaintance at best. I know the feeling. I want to record my immediate impressions of Viktor and especially Lyubov into my Dictaphone, but it seems awkward and a bit rude with them drinking right next to me. I order another beer, and Dan gives me a warning look.

"Oh, come on," Lyubov says. "She's a grown-up woman."

"Not quite," Dan counters. "She's seventeen."

"Seventeen is the age when you see the world and it is turned inside out like a . . . like a . . ." Viktor flounders in a mud pit of English grammar and washes himself clean with a stream of effortless Russian.

Lyubov sighs. "I would love to be seventeen again! Before I married the bastard. I wore no bra and didn't listen to shit from anyone."

Dan's not big on swearing. He looks uncomfortable. The bartender comes back with two dark shots for the crew. They look like Jägermeister but smell a bit like cleaning fluid. The odor of a pristine bathroom floor that you're vomiting on because you just drank whatever the hell that is. Dan gives an awkward toast.

"One more time up the mountain, folks!" he exclaims. What a dork.

I clink my empty glass against the others and give Dan a look. Toasting with an empty glass will never be anything but sad. Lyubov throws back her head and downs her shot in one gulp. I watch it move in a lump down her long throat. No doubt the gears of her body now hum smoother. I'm already in love. After this journey is over, after I've published my article, I plan on sending it to her. I have a feeling she won't take offense. She'll see the humor in the whole thing, laughing about it as she wrestles bears for drinking money. I can't wait until I can get her alone and ask her what she really thinks of all this Osinov nonsense. Is she just in it for the money, or has she seen something that keeps her believing in them?

"Where's Yuri?" Viktor asks playfully of Dan's discredited source. "Is he off lying? Yuri the rebel, ha-ha! Not true! Pants on fire, right? They say in America?"

"Maybe he's with bigfoot," I say helpfully, a bit affected by my beer. "I hear they are pals and try to get together in the summers."

The Russians find this amusing, but Dan scowls.

"JK," I add.

"JK?"asks Viktor.

"'Just kidding.' Just a bit of English internet shorthand."

"Having Yuri Androv exposed as liar is definitely a setback," Dan says tensely, and a wet blanket made of anti-humor descends over the group. "And Sydney Declay was obviously out for blood."

Sydney Declay. I've just checked her twitter feed. #traitor.

"But I know the family's out there," Dan continues. His voice has suddenly switched to the same tone as the preachers on TV who say, *I know Jesus is alive because He is here in my heart.* "We just didn't go far enough north. That was our mistake. We'll find them this time, I'm sure of it!"

The bartender has already slid Lyubov another shot, and she makes quick work of this, then tells Dan what they really need to find is some *travka.*

"Travka?" Dan asks quizzically, then speaks to them in Russian. "Ya ne znayu slovo." I think that means, "I am a dork."

Lyubov rubs the tips of her fingers together. "Weed," she says.

This is getting interesting. I start typing into the notes app of my iPhone. *Lyubov wants weed.*

Dan sets down his drink. "Weed?" Heartbreakingly, my stepfather from Colorado is momentarily confused by the term.

"Marikhuana," Viktor says. He mimics the gesture of

31

taking a hit off a joint, and Dan's eyes go flat.

"Or mushrooms," Lyubov chimes in. "Someone told me last week there are magic mushrooms in that forest."

"Imagine the colors to see!" Viktor exclaims. "Explosions! Boom! Blue! Maybe even purple! Like fireworks or Lady Gaga!!" His English reminds me of the music a cat makes while running across a piano.

My thumbs are busy. *Russians guides are partyers. Dan unamused.*

Dan looks at his watch. "Let's head to the gate." He pauses over the bill, trying to figure out the tip. Finally writes down a number in his strict, tiny handwriting.

Lyubov and Viktor trail us on the way to our gate. Dan sidles up next to me, touches my arm, and murmurs in a low voice: "Lyubov seems to have gone a bit wild since her divorce, and she's influencing Viktor. They'd drink on the expeditions, sure, they're *Russians*, but they've never talked about drugs before." He sounds worried.

"It's okay, Dan," I tell him. "I've seen their film. They're great at what they do." I have, in fact, seen a lot of footage of their Siberian outings. The beautiful river, the stunning pine forests, the foreboding and beautiful cliffs, evidence of a crude tool at the ruins of a campsite, the sole of the shoe, the charred remains of the Linnaeus biography—everything you'd want from such a film except for what Dan's looking for: a shot, even from far away, of the family itself.

We pass a clothing store whose front window display features a blond, no-nonsense Russian mannequin with a leather skirt up to her thigh. Viktor throws himself against the storefront, kissing the glass.

"I love you, beautiful lady!" Viktor moans. "Beat me up!"

"Come here, Viktor! Save your kisses for the bears," Lyubov calls.

She sits next to me on the flight to Abakan. She's reading a book intently. I glance at it. "You are kidding me," I tell her. "You're reading *Fifty Shades of Grey*?"

"Yes, it is very— What do you say? *Hot.*"

"I've read a few pages," I admit. I've read the whole thing. I might be a studious girl who's never had a boyfriend, but I'm not made of stone.

"These handcuffs," Lyubov says. "I have not tried them. I just pin them down with my knee."

"That works, too, I guess." I try to imagine the man who could take on Lyubov. I picture him in a bar, proudly lifting his shirt to show off the kneecap-size bruise on his chest that proves they had sex. I can already tell Lyubov will figure heavily in my article.

She snickers. "I'm learning some interesting American phrases." She leans over to me and whispers, "'My inner goddess is prostrate,'" and we burst into laughter. Dan whips his head around from the seat across the aisle. There's kind of a haunted look on his face, like maybe we're laughing at him. I'm sure that will come later.

"I had to look up 'prostrate,'" she confides. "It's a gland in your ass."

"No, that's 'prostate.'" I have to admit parts of that book are pretty hot. And I already love Lyubov, and if she wasn't sitting right next to me, I would whisper my girl crush into the recorder. I have a feeling this is a new Lyubov, a liberated Lyubov, because a Lyubov this fun would have never been invited back. Viktor's fun, too. Good, good times in Russia.

I glance at Dan. *For the most part.*

We land in Abakan, where an SUV has been arranged to take us to the hotel. In the hotel bar we meet up with Sergei, the guide who is supposed to take us four hundred fifty kilometers up the river, which, given the recent flooding, is a three- or four-day journey. Sergei doesn't look like much of a guide. He is young, and his high, sharp cheeks are clean-shaven. He could be a student or the kind of frat boy they decide should be treasurer. His muscles, though, are hard as a rock. I know because he immediately invites me to feel his bicep when I tell him he doesn't look how I expected him to.

"Impressive," I say, not mentioning that Lyubov could probably break him in half and eat him on a large sandwich made with dark Russian bread.

He shakes hands with the others. Dan has already explained that Sergei's father was his first choice. But the man didn't want to go a third time, said he was getting too old to go up the river. Dan starts speaking intently to Lyubov and Viktor about exactly what he wants filmed for the next day. He's so absorbed in his conversation that he doesn't notice me ordering another beer. I don't really want one, but I'm a reporter, after all. Reporters drink. At least the ones in movies.

I sit on the end of the bar, next to Sergei. I ask him about his father. Sergei shakes his head. "He's an old man, very stubborn. Doesn't like to guide as much anymore. Likes to hunt."

"And you?"

"Not so much. I like to fish. I caught a salmon this big last week." He spreads his hands wide. It's nice, here on the other side of the world, to have a guy try to impress you with a fishing story instead of a dick pic.

I nod approvingly and sip at the beer, which is darker than the one at the airport. I change the subject and ask him what the beer is called.

"Bochkarev Svetloye."

"Wow, that's about as Russian-sounding as you can get."

"Tell me something that sounds American," he says.

"Taylor Swift."

Dan is showing the crew an old surveyor's map and it looks quaint, like a newspaper or a lava lamp. Lyubov is already done with her drink and interrupts Dan to order another round. Sergei orders another one for me, even though I'm only halfway through my first.

"Are you trying to get me drunk?" I ask.

He smiles. "Maybe."

"I have a boyfriend."

"Where?"

"In America."

"That is very far from here."

I pull out my phone. "I can text him right now." I hope he doesn't call me on the dare. Most boyfriends aren't named Margot or Mom.

"Text him, then," Sergei says, and then stares at the bottles of vodka that line the back of the bar as though he's bored with me. I finish my beer and then slide it away and move the second one toward me, quickly, so that when Dan looks up he'll think I'm still on my first. The truth is, I'm dying to talk to Sergei. Someone like him will be essential to my article. He knows things about the river and its legends that the others do not. Dan says he grew up around and apprenticed under his dad, learning all his secrets. And I want his angle. I want to know if he's a believer in the Osinovs, an agnostic, or a plain atheist, and why.

I can't mumble into my recorder, not while he's sitting there, so I type: *Russian guide is boyish and flirtatious*, then lean in to him and say the word I've been hearing about for the last seven years, ever since a younger, fresher-faced Dan appeared at our dinner table one night, courting my mother with the story of the family and his fascination with its mystery.

"Osinov."

Sergei's still looking at the row of vodka bottles, but he nods.

"Do you believe in them?" I ask.

He shrugs. "Do I believe in God? No, I've never seen God; yes, I think maybe He exists. Same with this family."

"I brought extra salt for them." I reach into my knapsack and pull out a handful of little Morton packets. "I stole these from the school cafeteria."

The truth is, I brought the salt packets along because I like salt on everything. Sure, it's a bad habit. Sure, it will make my ankles swell in old age But whatever. Gotta live now. "You've heard about the word on the jar, haven't you?"

"Of course I have. Ever since I was a boy. But there are rumors that the word was something else."

"And what was that?" The beer seems familiar somehow. Like I had drunk it all my life, since I was a little blond toddler stumbling through the streets.

He leans closer.

"Blood."

The word shocks me, and he smiles, evidently enjoying the effect on me.

"Bullshit," I say. Just on the outside of my hearing, I hear Dan continue to detail the journey. I take a gulp of beer. I'm drinking it faster now. It feels warm and makes Russia seem as familiar as my family's basement. "If you ask me, it wasn't blood or salt. I don't believe in rumors and superstitions. Magic stories. I used to, but I don't anymore."

"I'm just telling you what the people who live on the river say," Sergei tells me. "Down by the farthest settlement, where they found the jar." He shrugs. "Of course, who knows? But what if we find the family, and they are dangerous? They are murderers? Cannibals? Then what? You are going to need a strong man."

"Save me. I'm terrified."

He ignores my sarcasm. "Also, there are bears. If the Osinovs don't get you, maybe the bears will."

I imagine Lyubov jumping in the air, kicking the bear in the throat, then sitting down under a tree with her copy of *Fifty Shades of Grey* to read about spanking.

"You're trying to scare me." I'm surprised when I giggle. My head feels light. It's fun, this flirting thing. My speech is slurred a bit. "Tell me something in Russian."

"You've heard Russian. Your stepfather speaks it fluently."

"I don't mean nerd Russian." I say this a bit too loudly, then correct myself. "I mean real Russian. From a real Russian man, like yourself." My idol always says to find a common ground with your interview subject. I think my interview subject is cute. And he evidently thinks I am cute.

38

My phone dings. It's a text from Mom. Are you at the hotel?

I turn it to "vibrate." Sergei sets down his empty beer and wipes his mouth on a napkin. He takes my hand.

"Ya khochu tebya trukhnut," he purrs. Okay, well, I don't know exactly what he said, but I know from the slang section of my English/Russian travel guide that one of those words isn't so nice to say to a girl.

Suddenly Lyubov, sitting on the other side of him, grabs him by the arm. The knuckles stand out on her hand, she's gripping him so hard. A grimace of pain spreads over his face.

"Zatknis,'" she snarls at him. "Ei semnadstat' let!"

"Ya poshutil!" he protests.

I have no idea what they just said. Maybe Lyubov said: "Leave the girl for me! I'm divorced! I want to try a three-way!" And Sergei said, "I will join you!"

I might be a little drunk.

I glance over at Dan and Viktor, who seem so deep in conversation they haven't noticed the scuffle. Finally Lyubov removes her death grip, and Sergei rubs his arm ruefully.

"Byd' dzhentl'menom," she warns, then calmly signals the bartender for another shot.

"Damn it," Sergei mutters.

"What happened?" I ask. "What did you say to me that made Lyubov so mad?"

He looks annoyed and flushes red. "Never mind. I was

39

joking. I will not joke with you anymore."

"Oh, come on." I bat my eyes. "You can joke with me a little." I'm done with my beer now. I feel my own face flush. My liver is no doubt working overtime, wondering what the hell is going on.

Flrting wth sergee, I type into my phone. Spelling is the first to go, right before judgment, caution, and ability to apply mascara.

Sergei's good mood seems to have faded. He might have a bruise on that arm tomorrow. "You seem like a nice American girl, so I will tell you the truth. My father didn't refuse the job because he thinks the whole thing is bullshit. My father is afraid. And he's not afraid of anything."

"What is he afraid of?"

"You shouldn't be here," he says, not quite answering me. He pushes a thumb toward Lyubov, who is now engaged in the conversation between Dan and Viktor. "Maybe *she* doesn't believe I'm a gentleman, but I am, and I want you to be safe. If I told your stepfather what I know, he would not allow you to come with us. Maybe I should tell him. I do not want to be responsible if something happens to you."

I am not sure whether to believe him or not, about anything: whether the bear warning is true or the family is true. But even in my drunken state, I'm afraid that he'll tell my stepfather not to take me, and I'll be left behind at the hotel. Maybe Sergei's kidding or just playing on my naïveté; maybe Dan would take me anyway. But I can't afford the chance. I haven't done anything special in my whole life except grow up and try to say the right things and do the right things and make good grades and get into the right college.

I want to tell this story of a professor who will go to any lengths to find his imaginary family.

I want to make my father proud, wherever he is.

My lids feel heavy. I sway a bit on the chair. I move closer to Sergei. He says nothing. I close the distance, kissing him on the mouth.

"Don't tell him," I say.

Are the Osinovs monsters? Are they cannibals? Witches? Or are they simply something much more common: the wishful thinking of humans who sit in groups and dream of stories that scare and intrigue them?

Sydney Declay
Washington Post article

four

I wake up in my hotel room, the light all wrong for my body clock. I don't remember much of last night, except that I kissed Sergei. What else did I do? Ah, now I remember Dan's hand on my arm, his voice angry in my ear. "Adrienne, are you drunk?" Two beers don't seem like a lot, but I'm not a big girl, and these beers must have had evil and magic ingredients. Toadstools, hemlock, wolfsbane. Crushed Vicodin. Here I was trying to show Dan I was old enough to go on this trip, and the first thing I do when I reach foreign soil is get wasted and make out with the guide.

Great, Adrienne. Way to win a Pulitzer.

My head is pounding. The room turns very slowly.

I blink and concentrate until it stops, then glance at the clock.

It's six fifteen. We are all supposed to be packed and ready to go and down at the restaurant at six thirty. Time to jump up and take a shower in a stall that is cramped and a brick-red color that doesn't help or hurt my hangover. The shower head comes up to my chin. The water is only warm, not hot, and smells faintly like spoiled wine.

I throw up in my first Russian shower. *Maybe easy on the beer from now on,* I think, on my hands and knees. I've never really been big on beer or any other liquor, considering what it took away from me. So why start now? I'll be more careful.

Everyone is eating when I arrive. The crew stops talking when they see me. Sergei plays it cool. My stepfather looks furious. I'm guessing from his expression that he knows I had too much to drink last night, but I wonder if he knows I kissed his guide.

"You're late" is the first thing he tells me.

I slide into my seat. "Sorry," I mumble.

Dan signals the waitress over. "She'll have scrambled eggs and toast," he says in a tight voice. "And please give me the check."

She pours coffee in my cup and takes off. The others at the table sense the drama and quiet down. I don't usually drink coffee, but I'll try anything. I pour in some cream and sugar and stir.

Dan gets up suddenly. "Come here," he says, gesturing to me, and takes me to a corner of the room. I've seen him mad only a few times, and this is one of them. "You want to be a serious journalist," he begins.

I nod miserably. Out of the corner of my eye, I see the group at the table looking over at me, and I feel my face flush.

His hand is angry, chopping the air. "You wouldn't believe how many strings I had to pull to get you on this trip. With your mother, with everyone."

"I know."

"You were drunk last night, and all over the Russian."

"I'm sorry."

I notice he hasn't shaved. Dan always shaves. There's an edge to his voice that I haven't heard before, and I remember how much this trip means to him. I throw a glance at him. He's staring back at me. I quickly look away. "It's just that I'm not used to Russian beer. I just had two beers, Dan."

"You shouldn't be drinking at all."

"I'm sorry," I say again. And then, "I know you worked really hard to get me here."

His expression softens. A little bit of permafrost leaves his face. "Just stay out of trouble. Can you do that?"

"Yes."

I go back to the table and eat fast, my head throbbing dully from the hangover, avoiding Sergei's eyes. Then it's time to pack up the gear. Sergei's rented an SUV and has a friend meet us at the hotel with an old truck to haul the rest of our gear. Dan estimates our river trip will take about two weeks: four days by boat to the remote area where the Osinovs might live, a week to explore and film, four days back.

We all get to work putting gear and supplies in little piles and go through the inventory to make sure everything is accounted for. Beef Stroganoff, vegetable stew, scrambled eggs, spaghetti, salami, cheese, green peas, canned salmon and beef, and rice. All in foil packages. I actually like eating camping food. It reminds me of all the nights my father and I spent in the mountains around Boulder.

I'm thinking of him now as we pack. We used to do this before our camping trips in the mountains. Mom didn't like to go. Camping was ours alone. I hadn't camped a single time after he died.

Until now.

We have a Coleman stove, Gore-Tex rain slickers, compressor jackets, hip boots, mountaineering boots, purifiers, insulated socks, hand warmers, plastic fuel canisters for the boat, sun hats, glacier glasses, strike-anywhere matches dipped in wax. . . . The list goes on and on. Also: machetes to hack through the forest and God knows what else. A chainsaw for the fallen trees that, according to Sergei, are sure to block our passage through the river.

We have bear spray. Sergei has a rifle. It signals that this trip really could be dangerous, which gives me a small shiver. And yet, it will be good for the article.

"Can I take a photo of you and your rifle?" I ask.

"Of course." Sergei immediately strikes a pose, getting on one knee with the rifle over his head.

"Maybe one where you don't look ridiculous," I add crossly. "Just stand up and hold the damn thing."

He gets up, shrugs, and cradles the rifle in his arms. I snap away with my Nikon, crouching and shooting up so that both Sergei and his weapon seem larger, more intimidating.

We also have video and still cameras, recording equipment, and two satellite phones. And, of course, my trusty language guide in case I need to speak Russian.

Hello, how are you?
I'm an American.
Your country is very beautiful.
Are you monsters?
Please don't kill me.
May I offer you some salt, or blood?

I shiver despite the fleece I'm wearing as we head outside. A June morning is still cold in Siberia. Sergei reports it's been raining off and on for the past month. The river will be up. A little more dangerous. Dan takes in this information, glances at me, and looks away. I know he's worried and having second thoughts about bringing me.

"I'm a good swimmer," I say. "And I've got a life jacket."

"The river is nine degrees below zero Celsius," Sergei says with a sneer that manages, at the same time, to be flirtatious. "You would freeze to death in the river in ten minutes."

I use my Nikon to take some pictures of the passing cars, the green pastures in the distance, the wet roads, the reeds in the ditches, then the sky, at the blanket of dark clouds that looms overhead, sprinkling icy rain. There is no trace of sun. My lips are cold.

I take the very back seat in the SUV, and Dan piles in next to me, probably to keep any other male from taking that position. I curse myself for invoking his protective instincts when I should have lain low. But hey, it was my first night in Russia, and I was drunk. What's a girl to do?

Viktor's driving. We race down the highway. The words on the signs are so strange. The letters are in unfamiliar shapes, turned the wrong way. There's some kind of Russian ska music on the radio that Viktor turns way up. I can tell it annoys Dan, and it pounds against my hangover, but Sergei sings along in Russian and the crew joins in.

We pass miles and miles of wet green fields bordered by fence line. Here and there, groups of cattle graze. It could be a rainy day on the plains of Colorado, except for the unfamiliar signs. I'm a bit disappointed by how ordinary it looks. But I've seen the films. I know that once we get into Siberia, everything will change. I can't wait to see the forests, the ghostly bluffs. Ride that seemingly endless river. I want things to be foreign, exotic. I want to lose my bearings. I want to be shaken out of something, what I don't know.

I turn on my phone and immediately it begins to vibrate with texts. One from my mother: Are you okay?

Yes! We're headed to Siberia! I answer. Everything is great. Don't rent out my room.

Margo: Did you make it?

Yes! Leaving cell reception shortly. I'll bring you back a human skull.

Sergei has heard the pings. He glances at me.

"All from your boyfriend?" he asks.

"Yes, he is already desperate without me. He might even commit suicide."

Sergei laughs. "Any man who would kill himself over a woman is no man at all."

"I think it's sweet."

Another text from Margot. A group of zombies photoshopped on top of a mountain. She's thoughtfully put them all in Uggs.

"How many men have you destroyed?" Sergei asks me.

"Thirteen," I reply. "Except for one who could not kill himself because he was a vampire. His name was Edward."

"What?"

"Never mind."

The bars on my phone have dwindled down to one. I make the call and listen.

You've reached William Cahill. Please leave your message at the sound of the beep.

My throat closes up. My eyes water. He actually sounds closer, here on the other side of the world. He's the one who once called me his "little reporter" because of my habit of asking questions about everything. Now that my phone's about to go out, his voice will be lost for eight days, and somehow that's worse than my mom's voice being unavailable for the same length of time. I put my phone away, then take out my camera and shoot some photos through the passenger window. If I'm to document this trip, not the trip Dan is taking but the trip that will get me into Emerson College, I need some kind of context. The story before the story starts. Wet fields before treacherous river. Grazing cattle before menacing bears. A paved road before a spooky, atmospheric path in the forest. I'm not sure where it will all fit into the final article, but Sydney Declay said this: "Document everything. Listen and look. You never know when the story comes alive."

The ska music station, mercifully, has also faded away, and Sergei twists the dials until he lands on a clear song, which happens to be "Ruby Tuesday" by the Stones. Sergei and the crew immediately begin singing along. To my surprise, Dan joins them. I stare at him. I've never heard him sing, let alone a cool, classic rock song. "Ruby Tuesday" was my dad's favorite song, and though I can't expect the group in the car to know this, I honor him by my silence.

Goodbye, Ruby Tuesday

Who could hang a name on you?

There's a truck up ahead pulled to the side of the road. A man changes the rear tire. A black bird sits on a post, flying off as we pass, and I turn and watch Dan sing. I'm kind of surprised he knows the words, but he does. It's the closest I've seen him to really being part of the group, and I feel a sudden pang for him. There's something so awkward about him, and I wonder if that's why he's so obsessed with the Osinovs. They are the ultimate outsiders.

The song ends and "Gimme Shelter" comes on, and I join in on this one, until the next song comes on, which nobody knows. Viktor turns off the radio, and he and Lyubov and my stepdad start talking about how far they're going to get upriver today. It gives me a chance to talk to Sergei. There's something on my mind.

"Can I ask you something?"

"About my first time to make love?"

"Yes, that's exactly the question I was going to ask. No, I'm kidding. I wanted to ask you about your father."

"What about him?"

I keep my voice low. "You said he was afraid."

"Yes."

"Of what?"

Sergei doesn't smile. "If I tell you, you have to promise not to laugh. Because it's not funny."

"I promise."

"Well, on the last trip with your father, the weather turned bad, remember? Cold, rains came. My father woke up in his tent. A little girl was sitting there. She said to my father, 'Leave and never come back, or you will all die.'"

"Little girl?" I ask. I have a sudden flash of Dan leaning on the wheel. *There was a little girl standing in the road.* "Who was she?" I ask Sergei.

He shakes his head. "I don't know. My father said he blinked and she disappeared."

Finally we reach the little village that borders the river. I've been feeling uneasy ever since Sergei told me the story of his father and the little girl. Not that I believe it—it's probably bullshit—but nevertheless it has stayed on my mind. It's kind of like when you watch a horror movie. You know it's not real, but it still creeps you out a little. The sight of the river, calm and blue, makes me feel less anxious. Maybe Sergei's just messing with me. He seems like that type.

We get out of the SUV. Small wooden houses huddle around the shore. A dog bounds out of one, sees us, and

52

slinks back. The air has warmed up; my breath no longer makes mist in the air. The mountains are smooth and bald. Raindrops dimple the surface of the water. Some power lines have fallen down in the road. Trees spread out in the distance. From my reading, I know that these are larch and pine.

I say into my Dictaphone: *Smooth mountains, larch and pine.*

No one's around, except for an old man walking down the street. Water from the gutter splashes on his shoes and the cuffs of his pants, but he doesn't seem to notice. He's got a knit cap on and wears a long beard and looks very Russian. I take out my camera and snap a photo of him. This seems to make him angry. He comes toward me, shouting in Russian, and I lower my camera, confused. Now he's just a few feet from me, still screaming, and I stumble backward, afraid. His frosty-blue eyes blaze, and the Russian that pours out of him never pauses for a response.

Sergei rushes up and steps between us. They speak back and forth, rapid fire, then Sergei turns to me. "He doesn't want his photo taken. He wants you to take out the film and burn it."

"Burn the film?" I ask, bewildered. "This is a digital camera!"

"Give it to me," Sergei orders. He holds it up to the old man, showing the image in the screen while I look on from a few feet away. The old man peers at it a moment and then snarls something in Russian. Sergei responds—something gentle and calm—and presses the Delete button, and the old man's photo disappears. The old man looks confused for a moment, then throws up his hands, shoots me a final look of disgust, and ambles away, his back stooped and the cuffs of his pants wet.

Sergei hands back the camera to me and gives me a wink. "Lucky I came along and am young and brave, or that old man would have beaten you to a pulp."

Dan rushes up. "What's going on here?"

"Old man got mad at me for taking his photo," I explain.

Dan looks annoyed. "Stop taking everyone's picture. Not everybody likes it. Put the camera away." He walks back to the others. I shoot him a resentful look and take out my recorder.

Just met an old man who didn't want his picture taken. The Sean Penn of Siberia.

Sergei stands with his arms crossed, smiling at me. "You are a *rebel*." He leans on the word. "Just like James Dean."

"James Dean?"

"Yes. I like his movies."

"I remind you of James Dean?" I ask. My voice sounds irritated and clear in the mountain air. Already I feel like the one making all the mistakes, and I renew my determination not to be the weak, dumb, drunken, flirting, camera-happy link. I put the Nikon in my knapsack and throw myself into the task of helping to load the boat, although I can't even pretend to lift the heavy fuel tanks that go in the back.

"These have got to last for eight days," Dan says. "Four days down, four days back."

"That's if there are no unexpected problems," Sergei says. I don't know why Sergei keeps bringing up the dangers—whether he's trying to be a good guide or just has a flair for the dramatic or for making himself sound important. "You just never know which way the river will turn, and with the rains—"

"We've been up this river twice before," Dan interrupts.

"How many years has it been?" Sergei asks.

"Four."

"Well, it's different now. Stronger. Last month, we lost two fishermen on this river. Their boat hit a fallen tree branch and overturned. They drowned."

Dan makes a face. Sergei is just a wealth of good news, and this is good news for my story. The more drama, the better. Sergei is a gold mine.

A family comes out of their house and silently watches us pack the boat. A little boy runs past his father's grasping arms toward us.

"He wants to go with us!" Sergei announces.

"Come with us!" Viktor shouts. "We need strong men like you! Come help us find the Osinovs!"

The boy stops dead, staring at Viktor. His eyes widen. He turns and runs back to his father to loud laughter from the Russians.

"Ha! That stopped him!" Lyubov whoops.

Sergei nods and says to me, "When I was a little boy, my relatives used to scare me, too, with stories of the Osinovs."

Sergei watches as the father picks up the little boy and says something in Russian that makes the crew break into loud, quick laughter. Dan's fellow travelers seem to be getting along well. I guess Sergei has forgiven Lyubov for grabbing his arm in her meaty paw the night before.

I have to admit, Sergei is an attractive man, with that smooth-skinned face and blue eyes and high cheekbones, and after all, a boy's swagger has a way of attracting a girl in the hallways of a high school or among the mountains of a savage land. I smile at Sergei. He smiles at me. It feels like just the right amount of danger.

Five hours in the boat. Water swifter here but fine. The rain has stopped and the sun is shining. I've got my camera and my Dictaphone out, mumbling my observances into it.

Siberia. It's still unbelievable that I am here. It's an intimidating place. I've been on rivers, and I've camped

in forests. The elements are the same: a river of water,
mountains of rock, clouds in the sky, trees, a gravel bank. But
it's all arranged in a way that I can only call bigger than life.
Among the bird cries there is one that sounds so much like a
baby I want to put my hands over my ears. I don't know if
the cry is for hunger or companionship or just to hear its own
echo among the craggy mountains. . . .

I am the one closest to Sergei, so I riddle him with questions.

"What else have you heard about the Osinovs?"

"What kind of fish are in the river?"

"That bird? What is that?"

I ask about the flowers growing from the edge of the forest in beautiful pink clumps. "They are called zontiki," he says authoritatively.

Lyubov laughs and tells me, "He's lying. Zontiki means *umbrellas.*"

"Don't tell her," Sergei warns her. "Or she will not be impressed with me."

"Oh, I am impressed with you." I pipe down until we pass a larch forest where the trees don't grow straight but sway together crazily. "What's that?"

Sergei follows my pointing finger. "That's a drunken forest."

"A drunken forest?" I snap some photos.

With one hand, Sergei guides the tiller. With his other

he gestures. "The ground was hard, and the roots grew shallow. Now the ground is melting, and the roots have nothing to hang on to. So the trees fall."

"What will happen to them?"

He shrugs. "The same that will happen to us all, one day."

"Global warming," I say.

"Yes, global warming," he says. "Siberia is part of the globe, and the globe is melting, yes."

"Are you worried?"

His eyes are heavy lidded, his lips closed. His gaze scans the shore, then the water ahead.

"I have other things to worry about."

Yes, it invites skepticism and outright disbelief:

How could a family keep themselves alive in winters that plunge to -30 degrees Fahrenheit?

How could they eat, farm, clothe themselves?

How could they navigate a wild river, with a small child, in a dugout canoe to begin with?

And yet, I am convinced that this family not only made it to this remote wilderness in Northern Siberia. I believe that their relatives are telling the truth when they describe the route the parents took up the river. I believe that the artifacts we uncovered— tools, rotted shoes, belts, and dishes—belonged to the Osinovs.

And I believe Yuri Androv.

Dr. Daniel Westin
New York Times article

five

Lyubov and Viktor set up to do some filming of my stepfather. Viktor wipes the lens. Dan speaks into the camera. He's got his professor's hat on, so his gestures are more contained, his voice less excitable.

"This is our third river trip in eight years on the trail of the Osinovs. We plan to go farther into Siberia than we ever have before. We know that they can't live far from the river or its tributaries, as it would be difficult to have to hike to a water source every day for their vital needs. . . ."

I am trying to get down as many details about the magical landscape as I can to add color to my article. *Gray and towering cliffs. The trees are enormous, reaching the sky, where their spreading foliage darkens my face. An eagle soars out of the clouds and swoops down low above us.* I speak softly into my recorder: *This place is like the Boulder mountains on steroids. Even in the summer, there's a certain ominous—*

"Adrienne!" Dan's voice cuts through me, and I look over, startled. The crew has stopped filming. Dan looks impatient. "Adrienne, can you please not speak when I am speaking? We're trying to film a documentary here."

"Sorry," I say, embarrassed. I put away my recorder. Sergei shoots me a glance, puts a finger to his lips, and smiles.

"Oh, shut up." I hit him in the arm.

Dan begins again. "The river is stronger this time. The currents more unpredictable. It amazes me, every time I travel this river, to think of the Osinovs negotiating it up here, so long ago, in what their cousin has claimed was a dugout canoe. Of course, that was thirty years ago, and a river changes over time. . . ."

I gaze out into the trees. Dan is so boring. I thought he was going to mention the good stuff: how rumors have circulated that the Osinovs are cannibals, sorcerers, murderers. My article needs some danger. A little atmosphere and tension so I can get the reader to actually think maybe the family exists before, like Dan, they find it was all an illusion.

"Sergei." I say his name softly, so that I won't disturb Dan's fascinating commentary. "Did you ever hear of anyone eaten by bears out here?"

"Of course," Sergei says. "Bears eat meat, and humans are meat."

"Stop coming on to me and answer the question."

He looks at me quizzically.

"That was a joke," I say.

"Ah."

"The bears," I prompt, holding out my Dictaphone.

"Yes. Well, there was a moose hunter from the settlement of Qualiq whose wife ran away with another man. He said he no longer wanted to live. He was going to offer himself to the bears. He walked into the forest and never came out again. They found only his shoes with his feet still in them."

"That showed her," I said.

"Bears are no laughing matter. They are terrifying."

"I saw a black bear once. I was camping with my father."

At the word *father*, Sergei glances at Dan.

"No," I say. "My real father."

"Oh," he says. "Where does he live?"

"He doesn't," I say.

"Doesn't?"

"Doesn't live."

Sergei smiles. "The bear ate him?"

I look at him evenly. "Some things," I tell him, "just aren't funny." Sergei's smile fades. I turn off my Dictaphone and look upriver. It's not like my father has ever really left my mind these past seven years. But the farther we journey up the river, the more I think of him. Maybe it's because this trip—not the crazy quest but the scenery and the adventure—would have been right up his alley. Maybe because this is the first step to becoming something he'd be proud of. Maybe because he was taken from me so quickly and so young. I don't know the reasons, but I feel his presence here, somehow. Maybe when you die you get frequent flier miles everywhere the universe goes.

In the late afternoon, we pass the last remnants of civilization: the settlement of Qualiq. About a dozen small wood-frame houses and what looks to be a central lodge are gathered by the river. As we pass, we hear the howling of dogs. It's different from the dog howls I've heard before. It's clear and unearthly, some kind of warning or regret.

"The old people believe a dog's howl means death," Sergei says.

"In my world," I counter, "it means someone needs to shut up their fucking dog before the angry neighbors call the police." It's gotten colder as the sun moves lower in the sky, and I put my fleece jacket back on. I mumble into my phone: *dogs, death, omen.*

We have lunch at fifteen knots. No slowing down. I eat cold Stroganoff out of a pouch and wash it down with water from a canteen. Sergei steals my recorder and speaks into it in a high sweet voice that I guess is supposed to be mine.

"We are not yet a full day on the river, but already I am falling for the Russian. As he guides the boat, I see his muscles ripple, and my heart beats faster. How can I speak of my feelings? I am burning with des—"

I grab the recorder away from him and speak into it quickly. "The weakling Russian is quickly proving himself the least popular member of the crew. There is talk of throwing him overboard. Tensions are rising—"

"Hey," Dan interrupts. "We're talking over here."

As we go deeper into the wilderness, the cliffs loom higher around us, sometimes blocking out the sun and immersing us in shadows. I watch Lyubov and Viktor filming. Dan's right. They are total pros when it's time to work. They don't joke around. They speak in low voices. Whenever a rapid approaches, Sergei squints his eyes and looks intense, the crew members hold on to their cameras, and all conversation dies until the rapid releases us and the water smooths.

I realize that my article so far is kind of all over the place. Notes on everything from how bright the flowers look to how crystal-blue the sky, to my flirtation with Sergei to Lyubov's *Fifty Shades of Grey* obsession. It's all very interesting, but Sydney Declay would ask, *What is the backbone?*

I glance over at Dan. He's talking about the first encampment they found, about the sole of the men's New-field shoe found there. "Size ten," he says meaningfully. "Grigoriy Osinov's size." (Or, as Sydney Declay pointed out, the size of twenty million other Russian men.) The water is gentle in this stretch—so Dan's not interrupted by the sudden roil of current. He's gotten so excited, he's ditched the serious professor demeanor and is talking faster and faster. Gesturing with his hands. He'd be rising up on his Birkenstocks if he weren't in a boat. His eyes have that strange sort of light in them I've seen before when he goes off at the dinner table.

Dan believes. Dan has taken a few artifacts, some rumors, and some interviews and diary entries and made them into a certainty. Maybe I'm jealous of him. I remember the last time I truly believed I could make contact with my father.

After he died, my mother found two grief support groups, one for adults and one for kids, that met at the YMCA. I didn't have much to say in my group. Everyone had lost a brother or a sibling or a mother or a father. One small girl with wild red hair was there because she'd lost her grandmother, which I didn't think really measured up. Everyone loses their grandparents. She made up for her low Grief Quotient by having more memories and details of her dead relative than anyone else: the incredibly fluffy biscuits she'd made before she took the recipe to her grave,

65

the flowered dresses she'd wear, the scent of lavender, her habit of giving Christmas gifts in cold-cream boxes, her country expressions like "long in the tooth" and "going to hell in a handbasket," the old untuned piano in the house she kept spotless, her specific prayer for good fishing weather . . . and on and on and on. Dumb Red-Haired Girl and her grief dominated the group through sheer volume, taking up so much time, the group leader had to continually warn her to wrap it up.

The only interesting thing about the endless grandmother tale was that the old lady had died from a fall down the stairs, not pneumonia or cancer or other old lady things. She'd slipped one day, and they found her at the bottom of the staircase, although Red-Haired Girl dragged out the fall itself with her imagined play-by-play, every flail and cartwheel, even mentioning the shattered ceramic coffee mug found beneath her body.

I said as little as possible. My grief was my own, and I would strictly guard it. The world had fumbled away my father and punished the wrong people for it and buried his story and put a new one in its place: the story of a blond girl who really didn't mean to hurt anyone.

My father couldn't be nowhere. He had to be somewhere. He had to be. Maybe he was in the wilderness, living wild; in a cloud, weightless and transparent; or hovering nearby, moving closer when I spoke to him.

One day I had a brainstorm.

Once, while exploring our attic, I came upon a treasure trove of old board games that had apparently belonged to one of my parents as a kid: Operation, Mouse Trap, Battleship, Domino Rally . . . and a Ouija board.

I made a secret pact with Red-Haired Girl that during the break in the next grief support meeting, where normally we attacked the jelly donuts, we'd sneak away and try to contact my father and (I added this incentive) her beloved grandmother.

That day, I brought in the Ouija board in a colorful red Macy's Christmas bag I found in my mother's closet. During the first half of the session, a shy boy with dark, expressive eyebrows finally spoke up about his baby brother, who had come into the world stillborn, and Red-Haired Girl interrupted him with a tale of the cat finding her grandmother's wig on a counter and dragging it into the garden. By break time I was annoyed with her even more than I usually was, but I needed her, although I made a mental note to replace her with Shy Boy if the attempt to contact the Great Beyond was unsuccessful.

We found an empty room with a conference table and plastic chairs, cracked out the board and a candle I had thoughtfully included, and got straight to work.

"I'll light the candle," said pushy, grandma-dominant Red-Haired Girl, and I indulged her, handing her the strike-anywhere matches and enduring a quick though terribly dull tale about how the girl always lit her own birthday candles, as though that was something very special.

After the flame got going, we set up the game and turned off the lights, and positioned our fingers lightly on the planchette. Red-Haired Girl's face was cloaked in shadow, only the tip of her upturned nose in light. Our knuckles glowed a faint orange.

"Speakkkkkk to meeee, Grammyyyyyyyy," she said, bullying right in with her spooky voice before I could say anything.

"Speak to me, Daddy," I shot back.

"No," she said, looking at me with irritation. "You have to say it in a special voice, like *Speakkkkk to me, Daddyyyyyyy.*"

I'd had just about enough of Red-Haired Girl. "Listen," I snapped, "I think I know how to talk to my own —"

Just then the planchette started moving.

"Oh my God," Red-Haired Girl breathed. "There it goes!"

The planchette moved right over to "Good Bye."

I glared at her. "Look what you did. You annoyed everyone into going away."

"I did not! They left because you weren't following the rules!"

"Just shut up and let's try again. We're running out of time." I really felt like punching Red-Haired Girl. I was beginning to suspect her grandmother threw herself down the stairs to get away from her.

68

We moved the planchette back to the center.

"Grammmmmmyyy—" she began.

"Shut up."

The planchette began to move.

E—M—I . . .

"It's spelling out my name!" Red-Haired Girl insisted.

"No it isn't. You're moving it yourself."

"Am not!"

Forcibly, I pulled it back the other way as it headed to the *L*. She clamped down with her fingertips and pulled back.

"Stop it!" she shrieked.

"You stop it!"

"Grammy! She's being unfair!"

Just then the door flew open, spilling light, and our group leader stood in the doorway.

"What are you two doing in here?" she demanded.

"Nothing," we said, the Ouija board right there in front of us, cold and shocked into ghostlessness by the sudden light.

After that I gave up believing my father could be found again. At least Dan can imagine his family is still in this world.

We stop for the night to camp on the gray gravel banks of the river. There's a great flurry of activity as we unload our supplies and pitch the tents. Overall, it's been a pretty easy day: calm water and manageable rapids. Sergei says it will get progressively more dangerous as we go farther up the river.

"How did this family possibly make it out there?" I ask. "I mean, if even guides don't want to go that far?"

"Maybe they didn't make it," Sergei says. "Maybe their boat overturned and they drowned in the river. There are hunters, drillers, guides, fishermen that never come back, every year. Sometimes their bodies are found. Sometimes, not."

"Circle of life, I guess." My voice quavers a little as I look out in the dark.

"You look scared," he teases. "Are you sure you want to sleep alone in your tent?"

"Yes. Right after I leave a trail of marshmallows leading up to your tent, just to be neighborly."

I decide it's time to figure out whether Viktor and Lyubov believe in the Osinovs or if they're just here for the money or the adventure. He's busy cleaning his camera equipment when I mosey up to him with my Dictaphone.

"Can I interview you, Viktor?" I ask.

He looks up at me and smiles. "You want to talk to me? I think you only like Sergei." I'm not sure if he's flirting with me or not. It's hard to tell with Viktor.

"What do you think of the Osinovs?"

He laughs. "Think? I don't know, nice family?"

"No, I mean, do you believe in them?"

"Believe? No, I mean yes. Maybe. I don't know. You

see? How do you say it? It is not my job to believe. Dan doesn't say, 'Viktor you believe. Here is more money.' Or 'Viktor you don't believe. You're fired.' My job lives in here. . . ." He taps his camera. "It does not live in here." He taps his head. "That is not my job's address. You see?"

"Right," I say. Trying to talk to Viktor is giving me a migraine, so I move on.

Lyubov has her tent up before I can get mine unpacked. She's pounding in a stake with a rock when I approach her.

"Is there nothing you can't do?" I ask her.

She pauses, ponders this. "I can't dance worth a shit," she says.

"I don't think it's that important out here. Unless the Osinovs communicate only through the art of dance."

She laughs. "You're funny."

"Thanks. I've been trying out my humor all day on Sergei."

She scowls. "You be careful with him."

"Why?" I ask.

"You know why. He's thinks a lot of himself. And he's a stranger to you. You're still very young."

"I can take care of myself," I assure her.

"This is Siberia. Be more careful of everything than you think you should be." She finishes pounding the stake and grabs another one, moving toward the next corner of the tent. I crouch down next to her with my Dictaphone.

"Do you believe in the Osinovs?" I ask.

She scowls a bit. "You mean, that there is a family called the Osinovs and they live up the river? Yes, of course I do. Why would I be on this trip if I didn't believe?"

I admit I'm a bit disappointed. I thought Lyubov was on my side and that we could make fun of Dan together, once I knew her a little better. She reads my look, reaches over, and takes my Dictaphone. She switches it off, then grabs the collar of my shirt and pulls me close to her.

"It's bullshit," she whispers in my ear. "I've always thought it was. But your stepfather is very nice to us, and he pays very well. If he was looking for Jesus, I'd go with him to find Jesus. That doesn't mean I think Jesus will be waiting for us."

She releases my collar.

"I guess I can't put that in my story?" I ask.

She shakes her head. "That is off the record."

Well, at least I have my answer. Lyubov is in it for the money. No disrespect for that.

Time to build the fire next.

"I'll do it," I say. "I've built a fire before, many times."

"Let Sergei do it," Dan says.

"I know how to build a fire," I insist. "I used to go camping with my dad in Colorado all the time."

"I can build a fire with a flint and a rock and a cotton ball," Sergei said.

"Well, I can build one with a strike-anywhere match."

"Will someone please just build the damn fire?" Dan asks wearily. "I've got to go over the schedule."

Of course. Always the schedule.

"Okay," I tell Sergei. "Build the fire. Just know I can do it too."

I kind of like this little flirtation we have going. Margot would love to know every detail. Now I find myself grabbing for my phone before realizing it's not a phone anymore. It's nothing. It's a shell with the internet inside, sleeping like a vampire.

Dinner that night: canned beef with rice for us, and macaroni and cheese for Dan, who doesn't eat meat. The Russians are all washing their food down with something from a bottle they're passing around, but I'm done with that. I'm here to work.

"You need meat," Viktor says to Dan, flexing his bicep. "Meat keeps you strong."

"Elephants are strong," Dan replies, "and they don't eat meat." I can tell by his tone that he means it in a jokey way, but as usual his rhythm is off and they start talking among themselves. I want to apologize for him and tell them that I once had a father who would have fit right in with this crew but that he was taken out and this new man was dropped into his place. But since they've worked with him before, they know his joke-telling skills are nonexistent.

The canned beef doesn't taste too bad. It has enough

salt, that's for sure. The Osinov family would love this food.

It's now dark, and the stars across the sky burn down on us. I thought I knew stars in the mountains of Colorado, but they seem a world away from these stars, this clear sky. It's so dazzling that I have to close my eyes every once in a while. When I do, the patterns of the stars stay there, and I stare at a more immediate sky, right beneath my lids.

"What are you doing?" Sergei asks. He's managed to maneuver closer to me as Dan stares into Viktor's camera, watching a playback of some of his commentary on the Osinovs from earlier in the day.

"I'm looking at the sky," I say. "I want to take a photo, but it won't matter. A photo will never do this sky justice."

"I grew up with this sky. I don't notice it much."

"Well," I say, "maybe you'd notice it if you were taken away from it."

"I have no reason to leave."

I'm looking at his face, studying it.

"What are you looking at?" he asks.

"I'm picturing you with an unfortunate face tattoo," I say. "Like a jellyfish or a Nike logo."

"'Just do it,'" he says.

I'm shocked that advertising has come all the way out here. I picture the Osinovs wearing cross-trainers.

Dan watches playbacks. He twirls his finger and nods in a gesture that means, "Let's see some more." The Russian crew murmurs to each other, deep in conversation. The river rumbles in the dark.

The bottle they were passing around earlier is empty now. Sergei offers me his flask. I shake my head.

"Why not?" he asks.

"I don't want to."

He gives me a look and turns up the corners of his mouth. By firelight I can just see the razor stubble on his cheeks.

"Why?" he asks. "Because drinking makes you want to kiss me?"

"I told you, I have a boyfriend."

"If he loves you so much, why is he not here with you?"

"Only essential personnel were allowed on this trip."

"And you consider yourself essential? Or did your stepfather just let you come to shut you up?"

I can't tell if he's making fun of me or not. I glare at him.

"I'm joking," he says. "I'm happy you are here. If not, it would just be one woman—and she's more like a man." He grabs another piece of wood and throws it on the fire. I wonder how much we have in common, like basic things. Whether he owns a dog or ever threw a chain on his bike or carved a pumpkin or split a wishbone with someone, or fished out a strand of spaghetti from a boiling pot and threw it against a wall.

"What do you want?" he says.

"Want?"

"Yes, want. From life."

"I want to tell stories. True stories. There are enough made-up stories in the world."

"There are stories in America, in your town. Why come all the way to Siberia?"

"Because this is a big story."

"You mean, this family?"

I only shrug in response. I'm not sure I know Sergei enough to trust him with the truth: that my story will be the lack of this family. It will be the lack of my own, after my father was killed. It will be about living with a man too busy chasing legends around to be a second father to me. It will be about the price of an insane and fruitless quest. And I'll throw in some jokes. Readers like jokes.

Sergei takes a drink from his flask. "You've never told me whether you believe in them."

"I don't not believe in them," I lie. "My mind is open. But I do wonder how a family can survive thirty winters in a place like this, at thirty below zero."

"Then why are you here if you're not certain they even exist?" he asks.

"I want my version of this story to be heard."

He sets down his bowl and swigs from his flask. "That's the thing about Americans. I have taken them down this river before, into the woods, hunting, exploring. They always want a story. They want to see something dangerous, uncivilized. They want a little change, a little danger. Then they want to run back to civilization, part changed but mostly the same. The trouble is, you can't control Siberia. It might give you a little danger, or none, or a lot."

"My father's dead." I don't know why I said it. It just came out.

Sergei raises his eyebrows, glances over at Dan.

"How many times do I have to say it?" My voice has an edge to it. "He's my stepfather. *He's not my father.*"

Dan looks my way, then back into the camera. He's heard me. The tone in my voice could not have been kind.

"My father," I say in a lower voice, "was running near our home and was killed by a drunk driver. So don't talk to me about how dangerous Siberia is. Guess what? Colorado is dangerous. The corner of Harper Street and Green Street is dangerous. A fucking Ford Escape is dangerous. A twenty-two-year-old idiot coming back home from a sorority party when you're taking a run around the neighborhood is dangerous."

Sergei looks a bit taken aback. "I'm sorry about your father."

"I think it was quick. I don't think he even saw it coming."

If true, the tale Yuri told me in his cramped and cluttered apartment is a spectacular one indeed. Kidnapped and bound by a menacing hermit with wild eyes and disheveled hair. The hut in the woods. The young sisters who spoke in not only Russian but also in their own language that sounded like the cooing of doves. The severe older woman and her dreamy, gentle husband, who only asked, with sadness in his voice, "Did the Devil send you?" And the boy, who stood very close and demanded if he had any books, then stole his pen and journal like a monkey stealing food.

Dr. Daniel Westin
New York Times article

Why did an esteemed professor fall for the tale of Yuri Androv? Why do any of us fall for tales, legends, rumors? Because part of us is still a child. Part of us wants to believe.

Sydney Declay
Washington Post article

six

The firelight glows through the fabric of my tent. I've always liked tents, the way they separate you from everything, creating a world inside a world. Sometimes I imagine lying inside a series of tents like a Russian nesting doll, going on forever, so that it would take someone years to cut through to get to me.

The warmth of the fire still can't push away the chill in the air. I have on insulated socks and long johns, and my sleeping bag is thick with goose down. But my face feels cold to my fingertips. If Siberian nights are this frigid in June, what are they like in December?

I stare at the ceiling of the tent, my breath making mist in the air as I listen to the voices outside grow louder.

Dan has gone to bed, and the crew is probably partying. Breaking out more bottles. I sniff. The aroma of marijuana smoke drifts into the tent. I'm not sure if one of the crew managed to smuggle it into Moscow or if Sergei did the honors. I do know that my stepdad is not down with marijuana, or any other drug for that matter, and if he wakes up and notices it, there's going to be hell to pay.

I drift off to sleep, and when I wake up, there's a girl in my tent, sitting in the broad stripe of moonlight that comes though the plastic window.

I gasp.

She's small and thin and looks about twelve. Barefoot, a sackcloth dress. Unkempt brown hair and delicate features. Pale skin, almost purplish lips. Something warm and playful in her smile makes me more mystified than afraid.

I raise myself to look at her. She speaks to me in a sweet, soft language that sounds a bit like Russian and yet is something much stranger. In those words I understand nothing but moods and tones. It's like listening to the rain in the woods; whatever meaning lives in the sounds is lost to me, but like the rain, the effect is calming. I can hear curiosity, though, and delight, and wonder. She seems to understand my confusion. She stops and slowly, deliberately says something that sounds much more like the Russian I've heard from my companions.

"Ya tebya vizhu."

She disappears.

My heart is beating wildly. I wave my hand in the space where the girl disappeared. I'm wide awake, skin prickling on my arms. *What in the hell was that?* Slowly, I force my breathing to steady. I can't get back to sleep. I stare at the top of the tent, at the steel bar that holds every-thing up, sounding out the words again and again, afraid I'll forget them.

"YEAH tee BAH VISH U.

"YEAH tee BAH VISH U.

"YEAH tee BAH VISH U."

At first light I'm out at the campsite, where the crew moves slowly, Dan studies the route, and Sergei boils water for coffee.

"YEAH tee BAH VISH U," I tell Sergei.

He raises his eyebrows and smiles.

"I see you, too."

The day is brutal. It's raining. We have to keep stopping to chainsaw trees that are blocking our path, and the river has grown swifter, more dangerous. The boat lurches from side to side. Sometimes it's so shallow that rocks scrape the bottom, and all of us except Sergei have to get out and walk along the river to take the weight off the boat so it can pass through the shallows. My face is sweating and I can barely breathe.

"You okay?" Dan asks me.

"I'm fine," I say huffily. I don't want to be the weak link, that's for sure.

I've decided to say nothing of what I saw—or thought I saw—in my tent the night before, although this theme of a little girl appearing—first in the road on the way to the airport, then in Sergei's father's dream, then in mine—is starting to spook me. Could my mind just be playing tricks on me? At any rate, I keep it to myself. Sydney Declay once said: *A great reporter knows how to pull things out of others—idle gossip, rumors, facts—but one of her best weapons is her own careful silence.*

The river is starting to scare me, too. I know my way around the rapids of Colorado, but these are different. As though they're waiting for me, luring me in, and then pouncing. My nerves rattle every time the boat lurches and the sides scrape the rocks. We have to keep on guard, duck under the fallen trees where there's space so we won't be knocked out of the boat.

Okay, seriously, how could the Osinovs have made it up this crazy river in a dugout canoe? Now that I'm here, living it, feeling it, that notion seems impossible. I glance at Dan. Is that what true belief is, a rejection of all evidence and experience that contradicts what you are already sure exists?

We haven't seen a single soul on the river since we passed the last settlement, and it's a strange feeling to see some part of the world that hasn't been put to use. I think of the people crowding the farmers' market in Boulder, the traffic jams in Denver, the photos I've seen of the swimming pools in China thick with people end to end. The earth is a fat, patient horse being ridden by a hoard of tourists, and yet this river has managed to say, "Leave me alone," and get away with it.

We eat lunch on the boat, passing roasted sunflower seeds and jerky around. Dan eats some kind of plant protein mixture. I speak very softly into my recorder so no one will hear.

I can't stop thinking about the girl. She was so real. Like I could have put my hand out and touched her. And the tone of her voice. It was like she knew a secret about me. Something she was just about to reveal before she faded away. Could this be one of the girls that Yuri described? He mentioned the light brown hair—

"What are you mumbling about?" Sergei asks.

"Just a dream I had."

"Was it about me?"

"Not so much."

Later in the afternoon, the channel gets narrow and canyons close in steep and craggy, denying us sunlight and sky, and the trees withdraw, leaving exposed black granite. The rain slows, then stops.

We round a corner and I suck in a hard whistle of air.

I am the first to see the enormous beast, and my gasp directs the others' attention to the shore ahead, where a bear stands on the bank next to the rushing river. We come right for it, a hard current carrying us toward it as Sergei shoves the tiller hard to the side, trying to guide the boat away.

"Oh my God," Lyubov breathes.

Sergei reaches for his rifle as the bear rears up on its hind legs. A cry escapes Dan's throat, and the sound of it—so tiny, so helpless—freezes me to my place. Time slows down to a crawl so that each moment seems like a frame in a terrible dream about a bear. The motor strains against the rushing current. The bear stares right at me. Its head is enormous.

The urge to scream rises up in me, but my throat closes. No sound comes out.

Sergei is struggling with his rifle and the tiller. Viktor, the closest man to him, tries to rise in slow motion.

I think I hear my name again. I don't even know who's saying it. Maybe I'm saying it to myself.

The bear opens its mouth and lets out a roar. It's not so much a sound as an intent to kill. To destroy, annihilate. The anger is so primitive and ferocious. Lips curled back and teeth enormous. The boat is drawing closer, and Sergei can't hold the rifle straight, and Viktor can't reach him in time, won't reach him in time. I know all these things—I'm not like my father on the night he died, minding his own business—I see death coming. I hear and smell and feel it, it's crazy and stupid and right on top of me, I close my eyes, my heart isn't beating, I'm not breathing, I'm almost dead right now, and all it will take is a swipe of the great paw to scalp me clean, and the roar continues, it forces itself through my body, and there's nothing that can be done anymore. . . .

Daddy, I think, and then something changes. Time is speeding up again. Senses rushing back to me. Suddenly shades of excited and breathless voices rise around me, and I open my eyes to my survival . . . the boat a few yards upriver, the bear behind us, the roar fading but the beast remaining on its hind legs as we chug onward between the sharp bluffs.

"Adrienne!"

I blink, shake my head. It's Dan's voice.

"Answer me!"

"I'm okay," I gasp. I'm still trying to catch my breath, taking great heaves of the warm, clean air.

"Jesus," Sergei whispers.

"Holy shit!" Lyubov declares.

Dan asks Viktor, "Did you get any film?"

"Film? Are you fucking with me?" Viktor answers. "I was busy shooting piss out of my pants!"

There is no fire when we camp that night on the riverbank. No one even bothers with dinner. Sergei seems too exhausted to flirt with me, which is fine, because I lack the energy to flirt back. Dan is not happy with our progress. We're behind schedule by several hours.

"Fuck the schedule," Viktor says.

"No," Dan answers. "We have only so much time to find the Osinovs before we run out of supplies and money. The schedule means everything."

"Tell that to the river," Viktor answers.

Sleep comes to me quickly, despite the sounds of crickets and an owl that calls from nearby. I'm thinking about crickets and owls, how they sound the same in Boulder and Siberia, no change in tone and tempo, that universal cricket-owl symphony that travels the globe. I'm thinking about the bear again, how it stood up by the river and stared at us, just before the roar, that expression on its face that said, *Ya tebya vizhu*, but far less playfully than the girl from the dream. This is danger. This is what I thought I wanted.

I think my story has enough danger now.

The third day on the river is the worst. The rapids are even stronger here. The cliffs so steep that sometimes just a tiny sliver of narrow sky shows above us, the rocks too big and smooth for anything but sunlight and moss to live there. We use poles to help Sergei keep us off the rocks. The motion of the boat makes me want to throw up.

By midafternoon the water has calmed just a little bit,

and maybe that's what takes us off guard. The river turns sharply, and we all see the fallen tree in front of us and all duck, except Viktor, who is loading his camera. There is a sickening crack of his head hitting the tree, and he falls forward into the bottom of the boat. His video camera falls the other way, making a loud clanking sound.

"Viktor!" Lyubov screams. She and Dan lean over him as Sergei looks for a place to stop the boat. But there is no bank in this stretch, just jagged rocks.

"Get the medic bag!" Dan barks at me, and I start pawing through his backpack. Out of the corner of my eye, I see Lyubov, who has been stroking Viktor's head, pull her hand away. It's sticky with blood.

Finally I find the bag and toss it to Dan. He pulls out some compresses and puts them against the side of Viktor's head. Viktor's lids are half-closed. His body is limp. That face, always animated and full of good humor, is still now. A terrible feeling grows in the pit of my stomach.

The boat hits a current and the tip of it bucks. Dan and Lyubov have to hold on to the side with one hand and tend to Viktor with the other. Sergei mumbles something in Russian that sounds too pleading to be a series of curse words. I feel helpless. I would wish and hope and pray, but in my heart I don't believe it would do any good. Instead I stare at Viktor. The shaking and pitching of the boat have no effect on him. He looks as peaceful as a man gently swaying in a hammock, and that's what worries me the most. Once I saw a man who wore that same perfectly serene expression. He wasn't on a hammock. He was in an ICU bed, and he wasn't okay at all.

"Viktor? Can you hear me?" Lyubov pleads.

Dan cranes his neck around to Sergei. "Can't you stop the boat?"

"I'm trying!" Even Sergei sounds scared.

After what seems like forever, the river widens and Sergei finds some calm shallows, and we pole to the shore, tie the boat, lift out Viktor, and set him on the ground. We gather around him. The cloth on his head is darkened with scarlet blotches.

"Get me my flashlight," Dan orders. I find it and hand it to him. Gently he opens one of Viktor's eyes with his fingertips and shines the light on his pupil, which contracts down to a pinprick.

"Well, he's alive, at least," he mutters. Lyubov fetches a blanket roll and puts it under Viktor's head. Dan switches out the bloody compresses for a clean one.

"He's going to be all right, isn't he?" I ask.

Dan doesn't answer. There is no answer. I have the sudden feeling that this is what Siberia is all about. It's trees and water and birdsong and sudden disaster. It will strike you when you least suspect it, when you're feeling safe and calm. I'm not sure I want to be here anymore. As much as I want this article and understand what it could mean to my future career as a journalist, I'm beginning to think the risk just isn't worth it. Dan believes in the Osinovs enough to be here, but I do not disbelieve in them enough to be here. My disbelief is not as ferocious and sudden and strong as the world around me. I want to go home.

We kneel around Viktor. His bleeding has slowed. His chest rises and falls. Lyubov strokes his face as the river rumbles behind us and the birds call. The wind blows a faint licorice scent. My knees hold down crushed ferns. Dan bows his head.

"Come on, please, come on," he murmurs.

An eternity passes before Viktor stirs and moans.

Lyubov leans down to him. "Viktor?"

His eyelids flutter.

"Chyort," he whispers, which I know is a mild Russian curse word. It is good the curse words are coming back. Where curse words are, the rest of Viktor is sure to be found.

His eyes open. He studies us as though we are part of a landscape that is camouflaged, like lizards on trees, and we must be inspected closely to be identified. A wave of relief sweeps through our group. Our collective breath escapes.

"Are you okay?" Dan asks.

Viktor says, "My head is motherfucking hurt."

Dan holds up three fingers. "How many fingers am I holding up?"

"Three."

"Who is the president?"

Viktor blinks slowly. "Kermit the Frog."

Lyubov snorts in relief.

We help Viktor sit up.

"Oh my God," Lyubov says, kissing the side of his face. "Never scare me like that again."

"Are you saying you love me?" he asks. "Because I love you too and I will be your husband except you scare me."

"Oh, shut up."

Dan eyes his satellite radio.

Viktor reads his thoughts. "No," he says. "No emergency calling. My head is good."

"Just stay here and rest for a while," Dan says.

"The schedule . . ."

"Eff the schedule." Dan can't bring himself to say the full curse word, but we're all shocked that he's even tried, and we laugh. We have a late lunch on the riverbank. Viktor has a headache but is speaking rationally and is even using better diction. I'm starting to wonder if Lyubov has a crush on Viktor, the way she's so tenderly looking after him.

Sergei goes off to pee behind a tree and then comes back, standing by himself, looking out at the river. I come up next to him.

"I should have been more careful," he murmurs. "My father says never let your guard down. I let my guard down."

"You can't see everything coming."

He doesn't respond. I've never seen him so intense and troubled. He has a slight red streak on his face and I realize it's a bit of Viktor's blood.

"There's blood on your face," I tell him, pointing it out.

He moves to the edge of the river and leans down to gather water and splash it on his cheek. He rubs vigorously. Red tinged water rolls down his neck.

"It's gone," I say.

He puts his hands in his pockets and looks up at a squirrel chattering away like it couldn't care less who gets bear-eaten or conked on the head or God knows what else. The river will keep on flowing; the squirrel will keep on chattering; Siberia will remain Siberia.

"About your dad," I say.

"What about him?"

"The girl in the tent."

"Yes."

"I saw her too."

He looks at me sideways as if to see if I'm joking.

"Did she say anything?" he asks.

"She said, 'I see you.'"

"That's all?"

"Yes."

He shakes his head. "I don't know what to think of that."

I don't know what to think of it either. "Can I ask you

something, Sergei? If your father was so afraid of going on this trip, why did you take the job?"

"Because I needed the money. And I am not superstitious, usually. But with that bear waiting for us by the water and this, I'm not sure what to believe."

"What are you going to do?"

He wipes his face with the palm of his hand. "Keep going," he says at last. "I don't want to quit. It would ruin your father's trip. And besides, I gave my word." We stand facing the river together, listening to the water. He takes my hand and I shoot a look back at the others, who are still gathered around Viktor, talking to him. I'm not sure what the hand-holding means, if it's attraction or just one new friend holding on to another, but I like it, so much that if I could, I'd take out my recorder and say:

The macho Russian has revealed a new and vulnerable side, and I find that somewhat hot. He might have to accidentally kill someone before he lets me see him cry.

I've been up that river. And the thought of two people traveling that far in a simple canoe—it does boggle the rational mind. Of all the arguments against the existence of the Osinovs, the navigation of the river gave me the most pause.

Dr. Daniel Westin
New York Times article.

seven

The dangers have passed—for now, at least—and we are finally making good time. The rapids finally fade into gentler currents, and Dan decides to stop for the night and make camp. Almost unconsciously I reach toward my knapsack for my iPhone. I have to laugh at myself. Old habits die hard. The world that I know—my mother, Margot, my other friends—had seemed to exist with me in a bubble made of air, magic in the way they could be invoked with a tap of my thumb, and their faces and their thoughts and their voices and their dumb jokes could instantly appear. Now they are inaccessible, as though they are the lights whose cable the power company just cut. We are alone out here as the sun goes down.

The mood seems lighter now that we're on the bank and setting up for the night. Of course anything, including near death, is an excuse to drag out the whiskey bottle. Lyubov takes a couple of healthy gulps and passes it around.

"To life," she says.

Viktor smiles. "To life." He drinks and hands the bottle to Sergei, who throws his head back and really goes for it, a lump in his throat moving up and down as Lyubov and Viktor cheer him on and Dan looks on stone-faced. Sergei finally lowers the bottle. "I needed that," he says.

"You did a good job today," Lyubov assures him.

Sergei holds the bottle out to me, but I hold up a hand. "I'm good," I say. I've learned my lesson. Besides, I have quite a tale to share with my recorder tonight and I want to be clearheaded.

Dan gathers some kindling and starts building the fire. We open our rations as the Russians trade the bottle back and forth.

"How will we know whether you're getting drunk or a concussion is kicking in?" I ask Viktor.

He considers this as he drinks. "Well," he says, "if I die, branch is problem. If I make love to Lyubov, whiskey is problem."

She says something under her breath in Russian and smiles at him. I think she might be saying the whiskey is no problem, then. Or *fuck me, Christian*, or some other sinful phrase. Ah yes, Siberia. Tinder of the tundra.

The Russians laugh and argue over the quality of the whiskey. Dan moves over to me. "How are you doing?" he asks. His voice is gentle, attentive. It's nice to hear him concerned about his own family rather than the one he's been chasing around.

"I'm good," I say. But I wonder if it's true.

"Our last two expeditions were fairly uneventful," he continues. "I got some kind of hives, and Lyubov jammed her thumb trying to set up a tripod, but other than that, there were no surprises."

I realize, suddenly, that he's apologizing.

"Are you sorry you came?" he asks.

"Of course not. This is the trip of a lifetime." I'm not sure if I mean it anymore. Because, truth be told, I'm not sure I don't believe, just a little bit, in the Osinovs. Back in America, on local and solid earth, I would never have thought that. But the things that have happened, mystical and otherwise, are starting to make me wonder just what's possible out here in this wilderness.

"Maybe I underestimated the dangers. The current is much stronger this time, and I'm not sure"—he glances at the Russians and lowers his voice—"if Sergei is the guide his father was."

"But it wasn't his fault that—"

"I *know*, Adrienne." His voice has an edge to it. "His father was just steadier, that's all. And he didn't drink. And you know what? Lyubov barely drank on the last two trips. Now she's drinking like a fish, and so's Viktor."

"They're just blowing off steam."

"You don't blow off steam in Siberia. You stay alert." He finishes his freeze-dried meal and goes to check the footage from the cameras. I get up and wander down the bank to find a place to pee. I walk into the trees but don't go too far; I still remember the bear. And the girl. The shadows fall over me; I finish quickly. *Nothing is going on out here,* I tell myself. *This is just like any woods. It feels dark and spooky, but it's a bunch of trees with all the lights out. A few birds calling here and there. And crickets. Russian crickets.*

I'm about to head back to the campsite, but then I change my mind. I'm safe here. A few steps and I'll be back in the circle of light. But for now, I have a little privacy, and I'm dying to report on the day's events. I rest my back against a tree, pull out my recorder, and switch it on. I'm down to one device: the dream of every parent of a teenager.

Today was insane. The rapids were worse than anyone thought. Sergei was going too fast, and Viktor got smacked by a tree. And I thought he was dead for a minute. That life could be running through you one second and then just stop. I know I should have known this before, but this time it was right in front of—

A rustling in the brush. Footsteps moving toward me. I catch my breath, then release it in relief.

"Sergei, don't scare me like that!"

His face is dark in the shadows. "A man has to pee, too."

"Well, pee somewhere else. I have marked this territory and I declare it Adrienne Land."

He laughs. "You are funny. I need funny tonight. I need to forget things. What's in your hand?" he asks, nodding at my recorder. Before I can answer he adds, "Ah, the reporter is at it again," and grabs the device from me.

"Hey! That's private. Give it back." I swoop for the recorder, but he giggles and holds it away from me, batting away my attempts to recover it.

"Let's see what you've been saying." He presses some buttons, and my voice fills our tiny perimeter.

"The rapids were worse than anyone thought. Sergei was going too fast and Viktor got smacked by a tree. . . ."

Sergei's smile fades. "So that's what you really think. That I was going too fast."

"No, that's not what I meant."

"Well, that's what you said." He hands the recorder back to me, and I stuff it in my pocket. I don't really like the direction this is going. Something about his tone warns me.

"You know what else you said?" he adds. "You said you had a boyfriend. But you kissed me. You held my hand today. You flirted with me. Can you explain that?"

He leans in close, his breath smelling of whiskey and

chili, a combination that should be banned in all parts of the world.

"I gotta go back to camp."

I duck my head, trying to move past him, but he blocks my way and pushes me backward against a tree.

I try to keep my voice calm. "Sergei." He's holding me by the arms and his grip is hard.

"Come on," he says. "Stop going back and forth. You like me, you don't like me. You talk to me, you ignore me."

"I'm not ignoring you."

"Kiss me."

His hands are strong and insistent. He kisses me, hard, and I jerk my head away, thumping it painfully against the back of the tree.

"Stop it!" I manage, but he holds me tighter, pressing himself against me.

He's still kissing me. The weeds we're standing in thrash as we struggle. My arms hurt where he holds me. A feeling of panic is beginning to take over. My thoughts are jumbled up, and I have the sensation of being held underwater.

I twist and writhe, managing to free an arm long enough to reach up and rake my nails down his face. He gasps and lets go of me. I try to run past him, but he catches me again and slams me against the tree. It's so dark that I can barely see his face.

"You *bitch*," he whispers.

Suddenly he wrenches away from me, and I can't understand what just happened until I see that Dan has arrived on the scene.

"You get your goddamn hands off my daughter!" he shouts.

"It's nothing, really," Sergei is trying to say. "It's a joke, that's all. . . ."

My body floods with relief and embarrassment and the shock of hearing Dan swear for the first time ever. I reach down and fumble for the flashlight as Dan marches Sergei back to the campground. Sergei's in much better shape, but Dan has sobriety and rage on his side.

I follow them back to camp, my heart still thudding wildly. My mouth hurts from the angry, mean kiss. Dan pushes Sergei down in front of the fire, where Lyubov and Viktor look up dazed and drunk, trying to follow the action but confused by the scene. Somehow a branch came up and whacked their good time while they were looking the other way. Viktor sets down the bottle and tries to stand.

"Come on," he says. He staggers forward, falls to his knees. His arms are spread wide. "We are all friends! All cut from the same blanket!"

"Shut up," Dan tells him. "And stay out of this."

Sergei picks himself up. By the firelight I can see the red scrapes my nails left on his face. I feel sick. "She teased me!" he tells Dan. "All she wants is information for her stupid story!"

Dan gets in his face, his fist clenched. "There's no

excuse! My daughter told you no. Did you hear her say no? I heard her from ten yards away!"

"You're blaming me. You're blaming me for everything."

Sergei is angry now, pushing Dan.

Dan pushes him back.

I jump between them.

"Stop it. This isn't helping anything!" My voice sounds high and shrill in the cooling night air. Lyubov and Viktor have their heads bowed, saying nothing. They might be drunk, but they still know how to stay out of a fight.

"Go to your tent," Dan tells me quietly.

I obey him, shocked and humiliated about the way the night has turned on me. I sit alone, my recorder hovering close to my lips, but I can't speak into it without crying. I turn it off and pull my knees to my chest, hugging them close, listening to the argument outside turn to Russian, the language of strong opinions. Of all the things I thought I'd run into here in Siberia, a situation like this would be dead last. Not threatened by a grizzly or the weather or a wolf or a family of monsters but some drama with a guy. Maybe Sergei was right. Maybe I did lead him on.

It was shocking how much more you were punished in Siberia. Try to take a photo, you get screamed at. Look down, and a branch hits you. Flirt with someone, and an expedition falls apart.

Not like in Boulder, where you can kill someone and get off scot-free.

I wait as the argument finally fades. The flap of my tent opens. Dan's red face appears. He's breathing heavily. I'm not sure whether he's mad at me or Sergei or both of us.

"Adrienne?" I'm surprised at the way he says my name. Not angry after all but gentle. Concerned.

"Yeah?" I try to keep my voice flat, but I'm still shaking.

"You okay?"

"Yeah."

"Can I come in?"

"Sure."

He crawls in and crouches beside me. He smells sweaty from our day on the river, or maybe from his fight with Sergei.

"I'm sorry," I tell him.

"It's okay."

"He was right. I flirted with him. I kissed him at the bar at the hotel."

He shakes his head slowly. "That doesn't give him the right to insist you kiss him again. You know that, don't you?"

"Yes."

He sighs. The tent is silent. I remember how strong and ferocious his voice sounded. *You get your goddamn hands off my daughter!*

Daughter. No "step" before that word. No distancing himself from me the way I do with him.

"What's going on out there?" I ask.

102

"Believe it or not, they're all drinking again."

"Russians," I say.

"That's a cultural stereotype," he warns me. Then adds, "But in this case, I kind of see it."

We both snicker together, a rare moment indeed.

"I'm sorry," I say again.

"Don't be. The truth is, I shouldn't have taken you here."

"But . . ."

"No." He holds up his hand. "This isn't about anything you did. It's on me. First of all, I underestimated how wild that river would be this time around. And you're not a little girl. You're seventeen, and I was an idiot to take you out here around young guys in the middle of nowhere. An absolute fool."

"No you weren't, Dan."

"You were your dad's little girl, and you'll always be that. But you're my girl too, and I'm in charge of you." He keeps his voice low. His hands aren't moving around crazily. All the exuberance of his quest has been drained out of him, and it hurts me to see him like this. "I think we should call this off."

"No, no, please don't do that," I stammer, my heart sinking. "I'll be perfect from now on, I promise."

"But will our guide? Will the river? Those are my questions."

"But we've waited so long to go on this trip. What

about the Osinovs? We'll never know the truth." I feel terribly guilty as I say these words, remembering the intent of the article I've been writing in my head, the disbelieving one. And at this moment, I honestly don't know what I believe.

"I have a family, too," he says. "And you're in it. My first job is to make sure you're safe."

He's got me cornered. And he's right: How can I say it's safe out here? But I have to try one more time.

"Just sleep on it," I tell him. "Decide in the morning."

Silence. He's thinking, and I don't want to interrupt him. Finally he says, "Okay, I'll decide in the morning. But I've pretty much decided."

"All right," I say at last. "That's fair."

"I'm gonna turn in. I'm beat." He presses something into my hand. I look down. It's the bear spray.

"Bear spray?" I ask.

He nods grimly. "For Sergei."

I almost laugh. "I don't think Sergei's gonna come back and get me or anything. He's basically a cool guy. And besides, are you sure bear spray works on drunken Russians?"

"Says here right on the side," says Dan. I'm confused for a heartbeat, then I realize that Dan has actually told a joke, and it's actually funny.

"That's a good one," I tell him.

He nods, smiles tightly, and crawls out. All is quiet for

a while. But strangely, the sound of voices outside grows louder, less angry.

They are laughing. Playing music.

One of them has an iPod turned way up, and the sound of the Doors fills up the clean mountain air.

When you're strange,

Faces come out of the rain.

I listen as Jim Morrison sends his warning out to bears and wolves and owls and crickets and wild people, and us.

eight

I'm having that dream again. The dream I've been having for seven years, where I'm in the back seat of the sorority girl's car, watching her run down my father. The girl is going fast, the headlights pick him up, he doesn't see her, I scream, and suddenly the tiny smiling girl from the tent is standing in the road.

"Ya tebya vizhu," she says, holding out her hand, and the car collides with her in a burst of white light as I bolt from my sleep, sides heaving. I don't know what time it is. The camp is dead quiet.

I flop back on my sleeping bag and fall back to sleep.

Dan wakes me up.

"Almost dawn," he whispers, lifting the flap of my

tent. I crawl out to greet him. He's slept in his clothes, is rumpled and ready for action.

"Well?" I say.

He looks truly crushed.

"We're going back, kid."

I don't try to argue with him. I know it's over. And to be honest, I feel relieved. I no longer have the heart for this. And the article I was going to write doesn't feel nearly as important. Dan had a dream and I ruined it. Even if there is no family, I didn't want his great expedition to end this way.

"I understand," I tell him.

He nods and then smiles ruefully. "Guess what?"

"What?"

"The Russians are passed out on the ground. Right there where they were partying. They didn't even make it to their tents."

We walk over to the dead campfire, where they lie facing the morning sky. They actually look pretty content, considering the hangovers that will greet them once they awaken. Lyubov has a faint smile on her face. Her arm is stretched out, her fingers curved and touching Viktor's face. Sergei lies nearby, peaceful as a boy.

Dan taps Viktor's boot with the tip of his own. "Hey! Time to get up."

Viktor doesn't move.

Dan leans down and shakes him. "Viktor!"

Nothing happens. And I realize that Viktor's eyes aren't quite closed. Dan touches the side of his face and pulls back in shock.

"My God," he says.

"What's wrong with him?" I ask frantically. I bend over Lyubov, grab her arm and let it go immediately. It's stiff and cold.

She is dead.

I look at Sergei and I realize his eyes are open.

Sergei is dead.

Viktor is dead.

They are all dead.

I myself thought I knew death, until I saw death. Death was not the way I imagined it to be.

Sydney Declay

nine

I can only stare at them as a wave of pure horror takes over my body. Sergei's lips are half parted. His skin is light blue. The mountains close in. The low sun burns. I fall to my hands and knees and vomit.

"I don't believe this." Dan moans. He's running his hands over Sergei's face and throat. Prying his eyelids apart. He moves over to the others, shakes Viktor.

"Viktor! Please! *Come on*, Viktor. . . ."

I vomit again.

"Okay, okay, okay." Dan is on his feet, rubbing his eyes with the flats of his hands, his movements jerky. "We have got to stay calm!" He looks down, notices me. "Adrienne, get up."

He pulls me to my feet and gives me a hard, desperate hug, then wrenches away and looks around wildly.

"Help me find Sergei's gun, Adrienne!" Blindly we both rush into Sergei's tent, clawing through his belongings.

His gun is gone and so is his satellite radio. We rush from tent to tent now, throwing clothes and shoes and dried food around. All our cameras, iPods, the other satellite radio, GPS devices, laptops, tablets, phones, even the flashlights—are gone.

"Oh no." The moan comes out of my throat as the realization sinks in—we have no weapons and no way to call for help. And we are the only ones left alive.

We stumble out of the last tent, enter the clearing again with the dead. Dan is wild-eyed, sweaty. The sight of my stepfather coming unglued makes my heart pound in my chest. My body feels like it wants to explode into a million tiny camouflaged pieces that can be hidden among the rocks and trees.

"Stay calm!" he shouts.

I don't know if Dan is talking to himself or me. A cold rush of pure fear starts in my stomach and goes in all directions. I had this same terrible feeling when I was ten years old and my mother came through the door and I saw the look on her face and knew it meant my father's machine had been turned off. I stare down at the bodies as if they're going to blink, smile, move, sit up. Congratulate themselves on the prank they just pulled. And yet they do not. Viktor has a little smile. Lyubov's head is turned. Sergei's hands are crossed over his chest. His feet are bare and his boots are nowhere in sight.

"Why are they dead?" I ask. "I don't understand. Who took the radios? Who took the gun?" The words tumble out and my own voice hangs in the air, high-pitched and quivering.

Dan closes his eyes briefly. "This is not happening." He puts his hands to his head and screams at the mountains, "This is not happening!" His armpits are soaked in sweat.

I have a sudden thought. I run back to my tent, reach into the inner pocket of my backpack, and feel around.

A chill runs through me.

The salt packets are gone.

Osinovs. The name enters my body as though a gash in my skin. Have they done this? Stolen our weapons, our communications, our salt? Who else could it be but them? I always wanted the truth, but now I just want lies: that there is no family, and they have not been here, and they did not kill the Russians. When I crawl out of the tent and try to stand, my legs are shaky. I walk unsteadily over to Dan, who's wildly stuffing his clothes into a bag.

"Get your things, Adrienne," he orders without looking at me. "We've got to leave *right now*, do you hear?"

"They took the salt." My voice shakes. It sounds so small and fragile in this wilderness, under those tall trees, near those dead people.

112

He glances at me; his eyes are red and watery, his expression wild. He looks utterly lost. "What are you talking about?"

I take a few deep breaths, try to steady my voice. "I brought a bunch of salt packets. They're gone."

His eyes go dark. "They found us," he whispers.

He rises slowly to his feet. "It's true. It's true." I can't tell whether it's terror at the thought or some kind of wild, instinctual pride in himself that his theory was right.

Maybe both.

He suddenly grabs my shoulders and then pulls me close in a frantic embrace. I can feel the sweat dripping through his clothes and the pounding of his heart. I don't know what to do. I can't draw comfort from such a frightened human being and yet I am too terrified to comfort him.

"All right, then," he says suddenly, wrenching himself away. "We're going to get back in the boat and go down the river. That's all we can do right now. We'll be safe on the river." As though anticipating my response, he adds, "Safe from *them*, at least."

We pack the motorboat quickly. We don't take the time to bury the bodies or even pull branches over them. We are too busy trying to save ourselves. For all we know, the family—if indeed it is the family—could be watching us right now from high in the trees. Eyes peering through bushes. Lurking in the morning mist. Is there a rifle pointing at my back at this very moment? My muscles twitch and tighten at the thought.

My breath comes fast. My stomach clenches in fear.

We take only the necessary supplies. We pack the boat like crazy people, grabbing, snatching, throwing.

When we finish, I can't help myself. I try to go back to the dead. I want to touch them, say a prayer. But Dan stops me.

"No." He's calm again. He's pulled himself together. "We can't help them. Now help me launch the boat."

I untie the boat and we both jump in. Dan starts up the motor and we're off, backtracking downstream. I think about the rapids and the rocks and the branches. I think about the Osinovs. And I realize that we are trading one kind of danger for another. The river is calmer here, but rocks lurk below the surface. I know Dan's not a river guide. He doesn't understand its twists and turns and secrets. But what choice do we have? We'd never make it back on foot—even if the Osinovs left us alone.

Dan keeps glancing over his shoulder and peering out into the trees that line the river on either side. "I'm sorry, Adrienne," he tells me over the sound of the motor.

"For what?"

"What do you mean, 'for what'? For bringing you!"

"It's not your fault. I wanted to come." I did, but not for the reasons he thought. I was going to join the rest of the world in making a fool of him. He was going to be the

114

collateral damage of my ambitions as a journalist. I never thought the family was real, or real in such a terrifying and deadly way.

I know the Osinovs exist. The proof lies back at camp in the form of dead bodies and missing gadgets and the absence of salt. I think about a story I'd heard from Sergei and dismissed as pure rumor, of the hunter found upriver sitting cross-legged by a dead fire, a hatchet wound in his head. They had never found the killer. Had their years in the wilderness turned this family savage, made them see every outsider as prey?

I wonder how they killed the Russians, so silently, so bloodlessly, and I shiver as our boat races down the river, in between canyons where the shadows dominate and the light barely comes through. I don't know why my step-father and I were left alive. Had they watched me sleeping? Touched my face? And how did they take my things with-out waking me? Each time we take a turn around a bend, I wonder if I'm going to see a bear or an entire family five feet away. The way Dan's source Yuri described them, so long dismissed by me, comes back to me now: the long-haired, glowering sons; the dreamy father whose beard had streaks of white and gray; the stern and quiet mother; the two little girls who look alike and chattered like doves. Will I have time to scream if the river suddenly rushes me to them?

I don't know how long a person can exist in this state

of fear, the throat tight and the palms wet and the heart pounding. I feel like a belt has been tightened around my chest. I struggle to breathe.

Stay calm. That's what my father always told me, whether it was about danger in the woods or a speech you're about to give or a big test coming up, a million dangers tiny and huge, near and far, things you can do something about, things you can do nothing about: Dad always told me, You must start calm and go from there.

My father was a calm man.

My father is dead.

"Adrienne!" Dan shouts. "You okay?"

I turn and look at him.

"I'm okay," I manage. I meet his eyes. Even in the midst of my terror, I'm impressed by Dan, the way he's taken charge and gotten us out of there. I remember how ferocious he was the night before—*You keep your goddamn hands off my daughter!*—and I realize I've underestimated him. I thought of him as a fool and a joke. But he was right about the Osinovs. And he's the only person keeping me alive.

The canyon through which the river runs has begun to fill with sunlight, showing the red in the short stubble on his face. His hair is uncombed, revealing a bald spot he usually manages to cover. He has the look of a man who just woke up and hasn't had coffee yet, that period where night and day are still sifting into their separate shakers, salt and pepper, and everything is still half a dream.

"Are we going to make it?" I ask.

"Yes," he answers, his voice insisting on that fact. "I'm gonna get you home safe and sound."

"I know you will." I don't know that. I look behind me, at the dark shadows that still hang in the canyons before they fill with morning light. "Why did they have to kill them? Why didn't they just steal our stuff and leave?"

"I don't know. They may have felt threatened."

"Or hated Doors music." My humor sounds hollow, goes nowhere, dies. The faces of the dead come back to me in waves. Every burst of birdsong or tweeting insect makes me jump. Every crack in the forest. Every scrape of the boat against a stone. But nature talking and the hum of the engine are the only things that break the silence, and silence would be even more horrible to bear.

Time is crawling. The seconds and minutes and hours that take us away from camp. I remember Sergei holding my hand, looking out into the water. Sergei was a living, breathing human being with all the good and bad traits humans have. Now everything is gone but his stare and his smile and the way his head was turned.

I shake the thought away. I can't think like this. I have to look ahead and concentrate. The river is up and swift again. Some rapids. I remember this as the last bit of excitement yesterday before we made camp. A couple of bumps and a steep drop in my stomach, but it was okay, not nearly as bad as anything the day before.

I'm not looking at the trees, marveling at flowers or studying the sky and the clouds overhead. I'm not whispering into my recorder. I am no longer an aspiring journalist. I'm a fugitive, and the only story I want to write is one that heavily features rescue.

I'm shivering. It's brings to mind an old feeling . . . one I had during that ride to the emergency room after my father was hit by the girl. My mother was driving. She turned on the radio so there wouldn't be dead silence in the car. My father had used the car last, and it was tuned to sports radio. Neither one of us would turn off my father's station. She had not adjusted his seat, and she was leaning forward to reach the wheel. I think she was afraid if she brought it forward, she wouldn't ever be able to push it back again.

There were scuffs on the dashboard I'd never noticed before and I studied them, their size and shape, because they were the most ordinary things I could think of. Every nerve in my body was tense. I could barely breathe. Every time a traffic light turned yellow and we slowed down a cramp would run through my body.

"Adrienne." The way Dan says my name sounds like he's been trying for a while.

I turn around. "Yes?"

"I asked you how you are doing."

"Sorry, I couldn't hear you over the motor." I don't like

the sound of my own voice in the quiet air. I feel like I might draw attention. *Here we are, cannibals. Bring your salt shaker.*

"I'm doing okay, I guess."

"Just watch for rocks. River's getting stronger here."

"I'm trying," I say. "There's one up ahead. Do you think—"

A sudden loud bang and a shudder, and the boat flips over. The shock of the cold water hits me as I go under.

The water is swift and dark as night. I'm blind and helpless.

Dan. Where is Dan?

Panic and confusion. There is a sky somewhere, but I'm not sure if it's above or below. This suddenly new and violent world, full of sharp things and hard currents. Something scrapes my face, and when I jerk away, I notice a dim glow overhead, the surface calling. My body and brain struggle toward oxygen and sunlight, my arms and legs flailing wildly, the river so strong, holding me under, slamming me into rocks and skidding me along. I know a place where I can breathe, gulp the morning light, but it's just out of my reach. My fingers dig up toward it, I beg silently for it to come to me, but the water is too strong, holding me back.

My head hits a rock, hard. The rest of my breath sprays out of me, leaving a hurting place in my chest. The pain of not breathing is like someone's foot kicking into my sternum.

Daddy.

He'd tell me to keep trying, but it hurts so much. That light above me is so real and so close I give it one last shot, lunging for the surface, but my hand claws nothing but black water. I claw and claw again but I'm weak now, slow. I'm nothing but leaves and tiny sticks, a package of nothing smothered by the same river that carries me along. . . .

Something strange is happening. The dull roar of the river is fading. I hit rocks but don't feel them. And the water is warm. There is not just light above me but around me, orange and yellow. It's like the sun fell into the river and melted and I don't have to reach for it anymore. It feels golden and light. It's summer down here. Summer inside me.

My body lets go. My lungs give up. They don't work anymore. I don't have to try to live, and I'm filled with a great peace. This is what my father felt when his heart line went flat and they turned off his—

A hand grabs my arm and pulls me out of the water and into an expanse of strange swift blankness, like sleep but less gentle, without color or sound. I wake up on the gray bank, soaking wet, my clothes heavy and cold, my body aching as though I've been beaten. At first I'm totally motionless and then I'm seizing and bucking as I cough up river water and take a goldfish bowl–sized inhalation of pure Siberian air, then another, then another, until the seesaw of life and death slowly levels.

Dan saved me. I don't know how he did it, but he managed to swim to the bank and pull me out of the water. I turn my head and see footprints in the mud of the bank, trailing off into the woods. "Dan!" I call weakly, my voice echoing in the silence. "Dan!"

I manage to sit up. I taste blood in my mouth, and my tongue finds a space where a tooth used to be. I slide my hands over my body, up and down each arm, my legs, my neck, my face, bewildered at my wholeness, my breathing, my warmth and movement and thought. This miracle called living that just a few hours ago I was taking for granted.

Dan is nowhere to be seen. Where did he go? Slowly I stand, testing out my legs. The small of my back hurts. My knuckles are scraped. My face feels raw and my head swims.

I look down the river. The boat has flipped and is on its side, held between a rock and a fallen tree about a hundred yards away. I turn and follow the footsteps that lead into the steep woods, calling Dan's name. I don't understand why he'd pull me out of the river and then just take off. Maybe he's injured or stunned or not in his right mind.

"Dan!" I scream. I'm shivering from the cold and limping. The ground slopes upward, and I struggle through the brush, stopping every few feet to call for my stepfather. I step on something and a vine swings out, lashing razor-sharp thorns across my face. I gasp and touch my cheek.

My hand comes away streaked with blood. I give up and make my way back to the riverbank, moving slowly toward the boat.

"Dan!"

Nothing but the rush of water and the echo of his name. Up ahead, a tree has fallen across the river, between two boulders near the bank. I stop. I see something.

I see Dan's red jacket.

I scramble toward the color, holding on to exposed tree roots and low-hanging branches to steady myself until I am parallel to it.

Dan's body is pinned between rocks. His arms float. His face is underwater.

For a moment, I freeze. My cold hand grips a wet root. This can't be. His eyes are open. The current lifts his hair from his head.

Enough breath gathers in me to scream his name. My shrill, broken voice echoes through the canyon. His arms don't move. I can't reach him. The water is too swift to wade in. Frantic now, I scramble around the bank, looking for a fallen branch to use as a lever to free him. Finally I find one, strip off the foliage to form a pole, and dip the pole into the water, trying to push it between Dan and the rocks that hold him down. The rocks don't budge. The branch breaks in half. I find another branch, try again, keep trying long after it's too late to help him.

I fall on my knees on the bank, crying. Dan is gone.

There is only me, and somewhere, them. The sun is hot on the back of my neck. My clothes are drying.

I no longer doubt the danger. I no longer doubt my stepfather. I no longer doubt the family.

I am a believer.

part two

In my study of the Osinovs, I found myself. I found the part of me that wanted to run away, to seek shelter in the wilderness, to leave everything behind me. Just leave.

Dr. Daniel Westin
New York Times article

ten

I look at my stepfather submerged under the water and begin to scream. Somewhere in the back of my mind I know that screaming is the worst thing I can do, that I need to be as silent and invisible as the beasts and the humans in the woods or they will follow my voice as well as my scent and find me here, defenseless.

I don't care. I scream until I am hoarse, and then I finally stop, exhausted.

It's warmed up a little, although my clothes haven't fully dried. I stand up slowly. The boat is still resting down the river on some rocks. Even from here I can see the engine has been ripped off, leaving a gaping hole. All the contents of the boat spilled out when it flipped. I have no food or supplies, and the only clothes I have I am wearing.

I have no knife or weapon. No way to get food. No way to keep warm when night falls. And somewhere in the woods, the family lurks. The strange and dreamy father, the quiet mother, the wild children. The girls who coo like doves. I brace for the sound of that cooing, listen for it in the wind. Is one of them the ghostly little girl who appeared in my tent? And will she appear again, less friendly? Is she behind a tree right now? Is her breath on my neck? I raise my hand to it as though shielding it from the sting of a wasp. I force air into my lungs, count, hold it, willing my body to calm itself. This is no time to give in to horror. I have to get back to civilization. Back to where I belong.

Cold, fresh water flows a few feet away. A small group of silvery fish swims in the shallows. Maybe when I get hungry enough, I can catch one and eat it raw.

In the meantime, I have to walk. I know the impossibility of walking alone through the strange and mountainous wilderness for four hundred kilometers. Possibly I won't make it. But if I die, I'll die walking. My father would have expected that for me. My stepfather too. I almost glance back over at the place in the water where he lies just beneath the surface, but I stop myself.

It's strange to me, this sudden feeling of wanting to live, having that be my only goal. I always took it for granted, this life thing. Even after my father died, I still just assumed my own life would be there, all broken up and full of anger and grief but *there*. And now, it's dangling like a carrot at the far end of the river. Well, fine, carrot. Here I come. I'm going to do what Dan did: defy the odds. Believe in something despite the chorus of voices, real or imagined, that tries to interfere. I'm going to live. And I'm going to write that article. Not the one about Dan, my stepfather the idiot. But Dan, my stepfather the professor, the scholar, the hero. The one who never gave up. The believer who traced his belief to the source of it and found proof at last.

I never could do anything about my father's story. How unfairly it ended. And the press made it less about him and more about the drunk sorority girl who killed him, whose name I won't say because she doesn't deserve to have it said out loud. But I can do something about Dan's story. If I can only survive it.

The sun shows through a blanket of clouds and then disappears, leaving a chill on my face. My heart is still pounding and I know I will never stop being afraid until I am back in the civilized world, but I'm going to be afraid while moving, not standing still like a target or an animal of prey. My shoes are waterlogged and heavy, but I elect to keep them on to protect my feet. I start walking down the bank, putting distance between myself and the dead, my body tense against some kind of attack that might come at any moment from the trees around me, or for that matter, from the river or sky. Everything is so foreign to me that I don't even know the rules of nature anymore. A bird flies over the river, captures a fish, and is gone. I'm still shivering from cold and fear, and by noon a knot of hunger has formed in me.

As the afternoon wears on, rain lightly sprinkles, and the chasm of the river darkens. I hear the drops splatter against the broad birch leaves. When I reach the next turn in the river, I see that the bank is gone, and the forest grows right to the edge of the river. I will have to force my way through the trees and try to follow the river by sound.

"Great," I mumble, trying to take comfort in how casual that word sounds when I say it out loud. *Great.* Like I'm talking about traffic on Route 36 or having to scrape a layer of snow off my car windshield. *Great. How inconvenient.*

"Stupid Siberia," I say aloud, and listen to my voice. I feel a tiny bit calmer. Encouraged, I keep going.

"Stupid boat."

"Stupid Osinovs."

"Stupid life or death."

I shiver and shut up. I've gone too far. That word, *death*, is now outlawed in any tone of voice.

I push inward through the forest. The roar of the river is still audible, but it's exhausting to try to make progress through the thick foliage and uneven terrain. If I think about it, I'll be too scared to go on, so I try to think of something else, anything else, other than what might be waiting for me in the gloom. I'm making a racket, stepping on old branches and blundering through brush, with not much ground covered to show for it. Finally I collapse under a tree. My legs hurt and so do my feet. I feel a ravenous hunger now, and remember that in my pocket I carry a square of wrapped chocolate I'd found in my room at the hotel in Abakan. Miraculously, it's still intact after my swim in the river. I fish it out, unpeel the shiny golden wrapper and eat it. It's bitter and gone too soon.

I lean back against the tree and close my eyes. I'm not sure what time it is. Noon? Three o'clock? I can't tell. The tops of the trees block the sun. It's not only hard but borderline ridiculous to imagine that, this time yesterday, the biggest problem was navigating the river and trying to find a good place to camp.

The rain patters against the leaves but barely touches me. Exhaustion blunts my fear. Frogs around me begin to croak and I make note of one other class of familiar things that I join to the others: Frogs, trees, rain, chocolate . . .

I sleep. Or I must be sleeping, because the same little girl from my dream comes to me again, moving barefoot through the forest. She is easier to see now, wearing a dress of plain muslin, her shoes of the pelt of some wild animal, showing crude stitching. She is beautiful, with large green eyes and a perfect nose and a bewitching smile. A strawberry-shaped birthmark on one cheek. Still smiling,

133

she kneels in front of me, although her dress doesn't get damp in the rain.

Privyet, she says, and I answer her back without understanding what the word means.

"Privyet."

Ty boish'sya? she asks, and I don't understand, so I shake my head. This seems to perplex her. She bows low, tilting her head to look up at me, raindrops on her face and lashes and yet her clothing and hair completely dry. She seems friendly, curious, as though she had no desire to harm me. But what is she telling me? My Russian-English travel guide was in my backpack and, with the rest of my earthly possessions, has found some wild and useless resting place, pages pulled apart and caught on branches, there to dry and be taken by birds and tucked into their nests.

Ty boish'sya? She emphasizes the phrase, then repeats it again slower, louder, as though that will make me understand. *Ty boish'sya?*

"I don't know!" My voice is a shriek now.

She shakes her head sorrowfully, her smile slipping a little. She leans in close, her face inches away. *On idyot!* she whispers. And the words suddenly come to me. They leap off the page of the travel guide.

He is coming!

I jerk awake, finding myself in a cross-legged position under a tree and the rain now stopped, the entire forest dripping and fresh, as though summer itself was a stalk freshly cut and leaking sap. Fatigue courses through every bone in my body, but I scramble to my feet and begin to run.

On idyot! Branches scrape my face. My heavy legs bog down and fight their way out of mud, my lungs heaving for breath. I finally have to stop, bracing myself against a tree, panting hard. Then suddenly, it comes to me, distinct and certain.

A footstep.

I freeze and listen.

Another.

I move back against the tree, fighting the urge to scream, my heart racing again. I can't decide whether to bolt or stay still. I elect to stay still, and keep my breathing shallow, although every nerve in my body feels ready to explode.

Another footstep. Another. Slow and methodical. Closing fast.

I can't stay. I have to run. He is coming, he is coming, and I plunge through the trees and the vines, branches scraping me, briars tearing at my clothes and face. Behind me, a crashing sound as the stranger pursues me. This is no animal. This is a human being. No bear or wolf or mountain lion runs that way. I'm shouting for my father, *"Daddy, Daddy, Daddy!"* He needs to come back and help me, or I'll be lost in these woods forever, pieces of me carried away by animals and birds.

I turn around and see him. I take in his features with a shock: young, bearded, hair around his shoulders, pale skin, eyes blazing, coming at me. I scream and turn back around, desperately trying to outrun him, but he's gaining on me. He's going to catch me.

"Daddy, Daddy, Dad—"

I fall off the edge of the world.

eleven

Slowly I open my eyes.

I'm lying inside a hut. A rough blanket covers me. My right arm hurts terribly, and I pull it out from under the blanket.

I gasp.

My sleeve has been cut away. There's a purplish hump between my wrist and elbow. The pain subsides, then comes back fiercely, and I draw in my breath, inhaling the scents of mulch, ashes, pine shavings, and something more pungent. The last odor is familiar. Suddenly I place it. Hemp. Strands of it are mixed in with the shavings on the spongy floor beneath me. Gritting my teeth, I manage to put my injured arm back under the blanket. My eyes adjust to the light coming through the windows, which are just holes cut into the walls. I look around the hut.

A table made of halved logs. Long, straw-covered benches on either side of the table and more benches lining the walls. Rolled animal pelts and spears stacked neatly in a corner. A crucifix on the far wall, next to a cold stone fireplace.

I try to rise, but the pain in my arm turns sharp and I cry out. The sound I made must have stirred someone, because I hear quick footsteps entering the hut and I hold my breath, terrified and helpless.

A girl stands over me. She's older than the girl who appeared in my dream, probably at least sixteen. She is small boned and tiny and shares the girl's delicate features and shy smile. Her hair is the color of sand and long around her shoulders. Her dress is made of sacking material, covered with patches of different colors, and reaches her feet.

She says something to me, in a language I immediately recognize as that of the little girl in my dreams: that strange, lilting collection of sounds, so much like the cooing of a dove.

"What?" I ask.

She giggles. Shakes her fingers in front of her in some kind of fit of delight, and motions to me with a tiny hand, then back to herself.

"I don't understand," I say, and again the giggles, the

delighted squeal, the shaking of her fingers. Like a child playing in a sprinkler made out of language. She gestures, her hands motioning back to herself. She wants more words, and so I give them to her in a voice I hope sounds harmless and reasonable.

"My name is Adrienne Cahill. I come from America. We were looking for your family. Everyone's dead."

It must be my expression and my flat tone and the way my voice throttles on that word *dead* that makes her throw her hand over her mouth and look at me with wide eyes.

"Day." She says, and I realize she's trying to repeat it.

"Dead." I say.

"Day."

"Never mind." I pull my good arm out from under the covers and point to myself.

"Adrienne," I say. It's strange how utterly calm I feel in her presence. She and her family might eat me for dinner, but right now, in this sliver of a moment, in this soft flood of window light, I feel welcomed and consoled. She radiates goodwill and seems just seems too friendly, too sweet, to have been a party to the murders at the camp. She might've helped carry off some of our supplies, but she seems incapable of harming anyone.

I say it again. "Adrienne." I then point to her. "Kak tebya zavut?" *What is your name?*

She suddenly turns shy, sweeping up her arm to cover

139

her face. Only a red-lipped smile is visible. Her lips move but no sound comes out. She takes her arm away and shrieks, "Clara!"

"Clara," I repeat. She whoops, delighted, and points at me. "A-drum!"

"Right," I say. "A-drum."

She comes closer to study me, eyebrows arched. She touches the silver strand of the necklace Margot gave me, holds it between her fingers, and lets it trail until she finds the pendant. She touches the smooth jade with the first letter of my name inlaid in silver. There is nothing to compare it to in her world, perhaps, besides a stone polished by the river or the smooth shell of a fallen egg or the fangs of some dead beast her family cut up for dinner.

"My friend gave me that," I tell her in English, and she laughs. I keep talking, trying to calm myself. "She said you didn't exist. She's going to feel pretty bad when I send her a selfie."

A selfie, I think. *A selfie in this world is something drawn with a stick on the forest floor.*

She gently places the pendant of my necklace just over my breastbone, and releases a string of syllables in dove language that is so soothing my lids start to feel heavy. If I drifted off to sleep, would I ever wake up again? She touches a fingertip to my face, then leans forward bit by bit until she rests her nose on my neck. She takes a deep

140

sniff and giggles. In the process, she touches my hurt arm and pain shoots off in ferocious sparks.

I shriek.

She jerks back, eyes wide. Slowly she peels back my coverings to reveal my injured arm. The sight of it seems to concern her. She strokes the air above my arm and coos to it. Finally she rises to her feet and leaves me alone. I hear her calling outside in what sounds like normal Russian, and I begin to feel afraid again. My body begins to tremble. I wonder if, even in my state of pain and exhaustion and fear, I should get up and try to run. Then the voices, growing louder, come toward the door.

One of the voices is deep and harsh.

My heart rises into my throat as the family rushes in, surrounding me. I shiver under the blankets as fear rushes through my body. And yet the reporter in me can't help but take in every detail as I stare up at the faces.

An old lady. The mother? Her eyebrows are bushy, nose sharp, mouth slightly twisted. Her gray hair is pulled back and covered by a simple kerchief. Her eyes contain not a drop of warmth. This must be the mother—although *mother* is way too soft a word to describe any part of her.

I drag my eyes away from her to a man who looks angry enough to own the angry voice. His glowering stare and crazy locks remind me of a possessed Maine coon. His beard is so thick that it's almost impossible to tell his age. But his expression tells me his mood and he's not in a good one.

Beside him stands a younger guy, the one who chased me until I fell into something—a pit? I can't be sure. He has more of a curious expression—something approaching awe, as though I am a great mystery, a meteorite, or a wounded unicorn. I can see more of his face. His skin is paler than the others. His eyes, a lighter color. The young guy doesn't look quite as wild as his older brother. Stripped down to a pair of board shorts, he could be a vagabond in Venice, California, who dropped out of college to surf. It's hard to say what he looks like under his beard, but I suspect he would be considered what one calls *handsome* in a land that puts a value on such things.

He's dressed head to toe in burlap like the rest of his family. They all smell vaguely of pine.

I decide right then not to move a muscle or say a word. Perhaps my stepfather and I were spared because we were quiet and sleeping, and not loud and insulting the gods with rock 'n' roll. I feel the urge to break into tears, I'm so frightened, but I'm afraid tears will anger them somehow.

Clara points to me and coos, "A-drum." And I have a sudden memory of my father, who grew up on a farm, once telling me he named the chickens in the hope they wouldn't be slaughtered.

"A-drum," the younger man repeats as his brother glares at him and barks out an admonition in Russian, gravelly and rough. The whole family begins arguing, except the mother, who stares coldly down at me, and I can't take this anymore.

I shut my eyes tight and wait for them to decide what to do with me. The words bounce into my ears, growing louder. I don't understand any of the words; they're running together so fast. I just know that I should make myself as small and still as possible, to let them know I am not a threat. I'm just a girl who means no harm, a girl who's stumbled into the wrong place, in the wrong century, a girl who just wants to go home.

The older brother's voice dominates now, making some kind of case against me, by the tone of it. I don't know what manner of death he is suggesting, but I hope it is merciful and leaves no marks, like whatever they did to the others. A heart-stopping poison or quick strangulation or merely some muttered curse.

Two tears escape and run down each side of my face. I'm not going to just lie here in terror and have my fate decided. I have to speak for myself.

I open my eyes and utter a single word. "Osinov."

The family stops arguing. They look down at me, astonished, and I feel a very tiny spark of satisfaction through the fear, wishing that Dan was here to see them in person, even though I have no idea what's in store for me.

I keep talking. I speak their language, everything I remember from the guidebooks, leaning on the wrong syllables, consonants crashing into vowels, verbs instead of nouns, the grammar of a rabid parrot. I make no sense at all. I don't care.

"*Do you think it will rain¿ How old are you¿ I'm from America. Can you please speak more slowly¿ I am looking for a restaurant. How old is your dog¿ Here is my passport. Which way is the hotel¿*"

They listen. They have no choice. I won't stop talking. People are strange when you're a stranger, and my goal is to be less strange. More like them. Because maybe they could sneak up and kill a bunch of obnoxious Russians encroaching on their territory, but they will not be able to harm this quiet, hurt girl who looks up at them and asks them to please bring the check. It's a one-way conversation that means nothing and everything; I want to survive. I want to live to tell the tale, and by the time I finally run out of Russian, I'm really crying. Tears pour down the sides of my face as I ask them if they take credit cards.

Clara reaches out to me, gathers a tear on a fingertip, and holds it up to the light from the tiny window. I imagine she doesn't have many distractions here or sources of entertainment. A stranger's tear will have to do. The angry brother mumbles darkly but seems confused. The others simply stare.

The woman finally speaks, which draws the respectful attention of the rest of the family. I have no idea what she's saying, but the tone sounds reasonable. She could be telling them to have mercy on me because I am so young and so harmless, or she could be giving them instructions on how to tenderize my meat. Whatever it is, the family seems to be in agreement, nodding along, except for the older brother, who gestures at me and snarls out something that sounds distinctly hateful.

Someone must have taken his iPhone away.

The mother gives him a stern order. She's a head shorter than her son, but that tone is clearly law, in civilized Boulder and wild Siberia, and the son seems suddenly cowed. He asks her something in a pleading voice. The woman shakes her head; he gives up and huffs out of the hut. Clara claps her hands together. She seems delighted, and the pounding of my heart settles a bit. I don't know what's happened, only that I've bought myself some time. Something Sergei didn't have, or Viktor, or Lyubov, or Dan.

For now, I can do nothing but try to stay alive until I can form some kind of wild, hopeless plan to leave this place and find my way back down the river. The fact that I have a broken arm and no food and no boat are problems I will have to think about later. In the meantime, I need hope. I have to believe that I will survive this ordeal and have a story to tell. And so I resolve to soak up as much detail as I can. Yuri Androv—Dan's main source—was an unreliable narrator. But Adrienne Cahill is not. Adrienne Cahill will leave this forest carrying proof that the Osinovs exist.

I will avenge the crew. I will avenge my stepfather. I vow these things as I lie quietly, my broken arm throbbing.

In a few minutes, the younger brother comes back into the hut and hands his mother a length of leather cord and an armful of tiny, uneven boards, about the size you'd use to build a sturdy birdhouse. The old woman and Clara kneel around me. With surprising gentleness, the mother takes my broken arm, holding it on either side of the fracture. Clara coos out some kind of encouragement, and the mother suddenly tightens her grip and leans on my arm with all her force.

I scream as the lump disappears from under the skin.

Darkness.

When I come to, I'm propped in a wooden chair. A blanket covers my knees. I look at my arm. Those tiny boards are arranged around it from wrist to elbow, and the leather cord has been wrapped tight, securing the boards into a kind of crude splint. My arm still hurts, but I can move it without the searing pain I had before. More than that, I feel a surge of hope. After all, if they were going to have me for dinner, would they really have tried to fix me up like this beforehand?

A fire has been lit in the stove, and the mother and Clara are cutting potatoes with folding knives that look brand-new. They seem so excited about the knives that they don't pay me any mind, and I realize, with a sinking feeling, that I saw Lyubov and Viktor whittling with knives that had those same red handles.

I drag my eyes away from them and study the hut. Everything is as Yuri Androv described it, down to the giant book on the mantel, the framed oil painting of a saintly-faced woman wearing scarlet robes, the spinning wheel, the enormous open Bible, and the stove made entirely of stone.

Yuri was telling the truth. And Dan's article was telling the truth. And my hero, Sydney Declay, was entirely wrong. New tears form as I think of how thrilled Dan would be to know this. Except he would not be thrilled to know I am their prisoner, just as Yuri once was.

The article I write, once I'm safely out of this predicament, won't be called "Wild-Goose Chase." Not anymore, now that the geese have caught me.

Two people, though, are missing. Yuri said that Clara had a sister with whom she shared the secret language, and yet she is nowhere to be seen. Neither is the father, a man Yuri described as having "a thin, gentle face, tangled eyebrows, and a square beard that is dark on the sides and gray around the mouth." No one here matches that description.

The older brother comes in with an armload of wood, and his mother gives him an order, calmly and casually, her hands never leaving the chore of cutting the potatoes. I imagine mothers everywhere in the world, of all different races and religions, ordering their sons around while cutting up potatoes, and this has just given me the slightest bit of comfort, when he turns back around and I see it.

He's removed his woven smock, and in its place he wears a black, short-sleeved Mighty Mouse T-shirt, stretched tight over his large frame.

Sergei's shirt.

I cry out, trying to struggle to my feet. The brother's eyes widen in surprise and then turn angry, and he says something in harsh Russian. Clara comes running, kneeling before me, petting my face, trying to calm me in the language of doves.

"Yes, they gave me a balm for infected bites on my arms," Androv told me. "But they were planning to kill me. I heard the older brother tell the younger one that before night fell: he was going to cut my throat."

Dr. Daniel Westin
New York Times article

twelve

My eyes open. The details of the cabin come into focus. My rapid heartbeat and dry throat return. I must have dozed off despite my pain and fear. I'm still propped up in a wooden chair. Rough blanket still across my knees. The homemade cast feels heavy on my arm. My feet are bare. I see my shoes and socks drying by the fire.

The brothers are nowhere to be seen, but I hear them working outside digging something, from the sounds that drift in through the window. Clara and her mother sit at the table, a pile of clothing between them—more of their booty from our campsite. They have two pairs of ancient scissors. I watch as they sharpen them on the whetstone; the sound goes through me, feeling ominous, like the harshest tones of their language. They start cutting the clothes up into squares the size of playing cards. When they have collected enough scraps, they pull some tattered dresses from a woven basket and begin to sew the patches over the tears in the fabric. I recognize a patch of Lyubov's plaid shirt and another from Viktor's canvas pants. I picture their bodies lying together on the bank, and I bite my lip to keep from crying again.

Something tells me crying is both a nonessential and potentially annoying activity this far out in the wild. I imagine that a family who has lived through thirty Siberian winters on the brink of starvation, surrounded by wild animals, has long ago dried their tears.

I guess my role is to sit here and be glad to be alive, and that is a role I'm fine with, for now. My arm has stopped throbbing, but the homemade cast feels tight and uncomfortable.

The sunlight grows less intense. The shadows move across the wood shavings on the floor and an open sack of seeds. My bladder has begun to ache and I have ignored it up until now.

I speak haltingly, apologetically. "Tualyet." It's one of the first words I learned in Russian, and I used it to great effect at the airport.

The women look over at me.

"Tualyeeeet," I say, drawing the word out slowly until Clara jumps up and releases a song of comprehension. She calls to her mother in something that sounds much more like Russian, and I realize this girl has two languages. One she uses with the family, and one she apparently shared with her sister. She uses that "special" language to talk to me alone. I am the replacement for a dead girl? And is that a good or a bad thing? The mother answers her in words I can't understand. She sounds reluctant. Are they afraid I'll run? My bladder's about to explode, and while the odor of urine in this shack would not be as unfamiliar as in, say, Martha Stewart's kitchen, it would still be noticed.

Some kind of agreement has been reached, because Clara leaps up and holds out her hand to me. Ah, so even out here in remote Siberia, girls go to the bathroom in pairs. I take her hand with my good hand, and she draws me out from the chair, across the spongy floor of the hut, and out into the light.

I blink. I'm in the middle of a meadow. I see the brothers about twenty yards away, digging in the dirt with axes. The older, mean one has on Viktor's cap that spells out something in Russian. And he's giving his brother orders.

The way he's already decorated himself with the booty of our camp and the way he orders everyone around point to him as at least the ringleader of the murders. Maybe the others weren't even there. Maybe he did it all by himself, lurking quietly in the dark and then striking while the others slept innocently at home. That's my hope at least.

They look over at me and I quickly glance away,

looking back at the hut and its surroundings as Clara stands patiently holding my hand. The hut is blackened at the front, possibly an effect from the fire pit, which has been dug perhaps fifteen feet away. Around the fire, six large stones have been placed. From the looks of them, they have been there a long time, and I guess they must have at one point held the complete family. Now, two of those members are missing.

I look around, determined to remember every detail. I'm still a reporter. I still have eyes and ears. I'm still alive.

Around the hut, birch bark containers are piled, as well as bones, pieces of wood, carved troughs, and broken spears. The trash a family makes even out of the wilderness. A hundred yards up the slope from the hut is a garden, filled with crops and surrounded by a sea of tall sunflowers. I am so happy to see anything familiar. The basics. The things that make up an hour or a day, all around the world, even here. Trash, gardens, sunflowers. A girl and her brother. Weave those together with electric lights and indoor plumbing and the internet and a little Rihanna music, and I'm home.

Clara leads me past the fire pit, where strange things lie in the ashes. Misshapen lumps and wires and blackened glass. I look closer.

Technology.

Satellite radios, iPhones, laptops. All crushed and burned. This is what's left of the society I can no longer reach for. It looks like someone has literally beat them to pieces, although the laptops are still vaguely recognizable. It disturbs me, like these are evil spirits cast away by a church, and I want to speak for my century. Explain that there are both good and bad within those wires and circuits, and that they communicated the voices of the people I loved. These things used to talk to me, like Clara's missing sister.

My eyes fill with tears. Clara is upset to notice this. She pulls on my hand, tries to urge me away.

"Pochemu?" I ask her, pointing down.

Why?

She begins to explain in her own language, waving her hands and knitting her brows, occasionally gesturing to the sky, and I can only interpret that their god is displeased by such gadgets.

As she speaks, I look down the mountain, searching for a pathway. There's nothing that appears the least bit navigable. Just a seemingly impenetrable mass of trees and briars. I could never force my way through these woods. But how does the family get to the river? I'm still thinking about it when Clara tugs on my good arm to get me moving again.

I notice butterflies rising blue-winged into the sky as Clara leads me into the meadow and we wade through sunflowers together, hand in hand. Something seems so weird about my predicament—wading through sunflowers on the way to a Siberian outhouse—I can't help but laugh.

The sound delights Clara, who releases a few peals of her own to the wind. I wonder if she's mystified by the moods of the captured stranger, tears and laughter in quick succession.

We stop to look at the garden. Plants grow in neat rows, and I point at them. Clara immediately understands my question, and she kneels and burrows in the dirt until she takes out the prize: a small potato. I nod. Of course. I'm very hungry, and I don't mind potatoes at all. Of course I usually like them cut into fries and covered with chili, but something tells me the mother is not much of a short-order cook. Crops of other kinds grow along the edges of the garden, and in the center is an unmistakable patch of hemp. Now I understand how they make their clothing.

Farther up the hill is another crop, covering a square space about the size of the average kitchen. I can't tell what it is, although it looks like some kind of flowering grain. Clara looks at me as though to see if the garden gets my approval. I look at her and smile, giving her a thumbs-up. She carefully puts her thumb up, mimicking me. I wonder if she knows what that means. I'll save teaching her emojis for later.

"Good!" I say in English, and she whoops with joy. She takes my hand again, and we head to a stream that serves as the border between the meadow and the woods. It's clear and shallow, tumbling down the mountain out of sight. Clara leads me across a rickety wooden bridge.

On the other side of the stream and in among a sparse grove of pine trees is, finally, the family outhouse. And then I see something else. A narrow path that leads back down the mountain.

This is the way home.

Clara doesn't seem to notice what's caught my eye. She gives me a handful of leaves.

I look down at them. "I prefer Charmin, thank you," I tell her.

I smile, and she smiles at my expression. My mind is whirling with the new information. Clara is small, a tiny slip of a girl. She couldn't hold me back if I bolted into the woods. But first things first. I take the open outhouse door, prepared for the horrors within.

I'm pleasantly surprised that, though it consists of a low bench with a hole cut in it, I can actually detect nothing but a brisk pine odor. I've encountered far grosser bathrooms in my high school.

It's awkward to go through this process with a broken arm. It makes everything more difficult. The leaves are not terribly absorbent. But I do the best I can. It takes me quite a while to get my pants up. I crouch by the door in the dimness, gathering the courage for my escape attempt.

Clara calls to me. "A-drum? A-drum?"

"Coming!" I call in English. I grab the rope that opens the door, take a deep breath, and burst out into the light.

I pull up fast, stopping in my tracks.

The younger brother stands next to his sister. He's holding Sergei's gun in his hands. He's not pointing it at me, but the meaning is clear. I'm not going anywhere.

"A-drum!" Clara cries, seizing my hand in delight, but the brother does not look so delighted. Maybe he read my guilty expression, I don't know.

We troop back together across the stream, into the clearing, and past the garden. I keep glancing at the younger brother. Under that beard, he really has a pleasant and even handsome face. Although he is carrying a weapon, his body language is rather shy.

He needs a name. I can't keep calling him "the younger brother" or "the possibly non-murderous one."

I'm going to name him Woody. It just feels right, something homemade and at home in the wilderness.

As we are walking toward the hut, we pass the older brother, busy at work with his pickax, and I glance down at the hole the men have been digging.

I gasp. My empty stomach clenches.

It's not a hole. It's a grave.

Yuri told me that the family was clearly starving, the father thinnest of all. Yuri could see his veins through his skin.

Dr. Daniel Westin
New York Times article

thirteen

I'm back in my chair. Every nerve in my body on edge. Thoughts racing. Mouth dry.

It's true, what Yuri said. They are planning to kill me, just as they were planning to kill him before he escaped. They are simply taking their time.

I watch the women prepare dinner. The fire inside the stove warms the boards of my homemade cast, but I take no comfort in the sensation. They've made a stew with some kind of meat I can't identify and potatoes and onions, as well as some herbs and a few sliced carrots. The aroma of blood is strong. I wonder if whatever animal they are cooking died in fear.

Clara and her mother talk among themselves,

occasionally throwing glances at me as though to make sure I'm still there. Each time they glance at me, I look away, afraid I will somehow antagonize them. Part of me wants to jump up at that very moment and run for it, but I can hear the voices of the brothers outside over the chopping of wood.

They are strong men. With sharp utensils. I don't stand a chance. All I can do is wait for a chance to beg for my life, although even the Russian word for *life* escapes me. Tears and a pleading tone and a few words are all I have. Very primitive tools for such an urgent task.

Just as the hut begins to darken, the men come in, and I stiffen. Woody throws me an unreadable glance. The older one scowls, sets a torch in the middle of the hut, and lights it. The hut fills with an orange glow. I'm amazed to see the mother start ladling soup into small white bowls. It's hard to imagine a family who looks and sounds this strange to be eating out of bowls that look very much like the ones in our house.

I watch the bowls. I haven't eaten in twenty-four hours. And yet, I count four bowls, and the amount of soup the mother ladles in hardly fills any of them more than half before the ladle makes a scraping sound against the bottom of the kettle. I notice, for the first time, how thin the mother's arms are. I imagine that, like all mothers, she takes the smallest amount for herself.

The family gathers at the table. The mother sets down

their bowls and then sits down herself. They bow their heads as the older brother leads what must be a prayer in a grim and gravelly voice.

I've heard prayers before. There seems to be no love in this prayer. Instead I hear a tone of grudging obedience, as though God were a father that the son secretly hates. I bow my head too, in case someone might glance over at me and take offense if I did not.

Thou shalt not kill.

As I listen to the grating Russian prayer, I whisper prayers of my own. I have to admit that my belief in God took a giant hit when my father died, but now I send out a prayer to that vague being out there to please let me live until the morning. When I finish, the brother is still praying, his voice full of resentment. I imagine his god getting tired of the prayer, rolling his eyes.

At last the older brother falls silent. His mother passes a tiny plate over to him with a tiny white packet on it. He breaks a small white packet over the plate as the family murmurs. I realize it's one of the salt packets from my backpack. They are using this to flavor their meat. Will they use it to flavor my meat? I shudder. Whatever hunger I had earlier is gone now. I wouldn't be able to take a single bite, even if they offered it to me.

They pass the tiny plate around, each of them gathering the smallest amount of salt with their fingers and sprinkling it on their stew, the rest of the family watching.

I never thought much about salt or going through a lifetime deprived of it, but it seems to fascinate them.

Finally they are ready to eat. My hands unclench a little. Their focus is on the food for now at least. Clara, though, is not eating. She stares at her bowl. Suddenly she rises from the table with the bowl. The family stops eating. Her big brother calls to her sharply, but she ignores him.

To my horror, I realize that she is walking over to me to offer me her bowl of soup. A kind and honorable gesture, except when directed at someone who wants desperately to keep a low profile and not make a fuss. And apparently, this is making a fuss, because the entire family now is arguing some point I can't understand. The older brother is especially angry. He jumps to his feet.

"Clara!" he calls sharply.

But she doesn't pay him any mind. She's reaching over to me now, handing me her bowl of soup, although I am shaking my head. "No, no, no, no!"

But she's insisting with dove talk, pushing it on me so that finally I reach to take it, an action that so outrages the older brother that he barks out something suddenly just as my fingers touch the warm bowl.

My hand shakes. The bowl tips and falls to the floor. China shatters. Hot soup flies onto my bare feet and I shriek and jump out of my chair.

Silence falls for a second. Clara's mouth hangs open. The family's eyes are wide.

"I'm sorry!" I cry. "I'm sorry, I'm sorry!"

I turn around and run out the door. My body's gone rogue on me; it's running away before I can stop it. I slam the door behind me. I know I have only a few seconds before that door flies open and I'm caught. In my desperation, I hurl myself at the nearest hiding place: the grave.

I lie, there, face to the night sky, the stars very sharp above me, as the door opens and the shouting family pours out. I hold my breath and curl my hands into fists, waiting and praying. Sweat pours down my face despite the chill in the air. Up in the sky, the same Big Dipper looks down on me as it did during my nights camping in Colorado.

The older brother's voice gets louder as he comes closer to me. I shiver, every muscle in my body tense, willing myself to put off no heat or sound. I want to be an object, a mold of something plastic, a baseball bat—anything but a living human being.

His voice gets louder. He's almost here. He calls out something to his brother, then moves on. Their voices fade into the night.

"A-drum! A-drum!"

It's Clara's voice, calling to me from near the open door. She sounds wistful at first, then concerned, then sad. Her voice breaks. She sniffles. Then I hear the voice of her mother. Soft, reassuring. As though consoling her over some kind of dead or missing pet. I haven't yet heard a sound this maternal coming from this woman, and it intrigues me even as I remain frozen, letting my breath out through my nose and then drawing back in so as not to draw attention.

Finally the voices cease. The door opens and closes. I wait another few moments. This grave fits me perfectly. An inch of room at my head and my feet. It fits me at the shoulders and the hips. It fits me so well that it could fit me forever.

I definitely need to go.

Cautiously, I raise my head out of the grave and look around. I gulp. Clara is nowhere to be seen, but her mother is still standing outside, her back to me. She's taken off her kerchief and let down her long gray hair. A cool wind moves it as she stands there in her burlap dress, looking up at something in the trees.

I'm not sure whether I should wait or make a dash for the stream and the path beyond it. I decide to wait. I watch her as she raises an arm.

A sudden fluttering of wings. A winged creature dives from a branch and alights on her arm. I stare at it in wonder. It's an owl.

She begins to murmur to the owl, something calm and friendly, a string of Russian words that have the cadence of a chant. The owl watches her and I lean forward, fascinated.

Just then the owl swivels its head and stares directly at me.

The mother swivels her head too. They both stare at me as I half crouch in the moonlight.

"Podozhdite!" she shouts.

I bolt out of the grave and run as fast as I can past the circle of stones, plunging into the field of sunflowers.

"Podozhite!" Again she screams the unfamiliar word. Far away past the stream, the older brother's voice answers in the darkness.

"Mama?"

I turn and head toward the woods to my right, reversing course. I stumble, fall, get up, fight the darkness that prickles and dips and buzzes and shrieks and tears at my clothes, trampling the stalks of the sunflowers.

The mother cries out one more time, and then I hear a fluttering of wings as the owl swoops for me. I cover my head and charge straight into the thick forest, tearing through the brush as I struggle to get away. I battle things I can't see, tangles of vines and branches and sticks and webs, all kinds of textures that rattle and break, pushing where the owl can't follow me, squeezing between trees and crawling on rotted leaves, the stars blocked out by the dense treetops overhead. I'm the wildest thing out here, the most out of place, the least evolved. My arms and legs are stupid, useless. I need claws and teeth. But I keep lunging forward until there are no voices anymore; the owl is gone and the family is gone and I crouch completely out of breath, alone in the forest.

I lean back against a tree and try to gather myself.

There is no chance of rescue. No one will even know we are missing for another two weeks. And then what? Even if somehow a rescue party did make it this far, where would they look? I'm on my own. I have to use my wits to stay alive.

The woods are recovering from the shock of my intrusion. Night birds begin to call. Crickets start up again. Every now and then something skitters nearby, and I jump. Mosquitos bite my arms and face. I slap them away, making small wet splashes on my face with my own blood as their bodies explode.

The memory of the mother and the wild owl play on my nerves. I don't think the owl can get to me now, or the mother. And the sons must be looking in the wrong direction. Unless the mother is truly a witch and drifting through the trees to me right now, her feet barely touching the ground.

I shake the thought away and decide to stay where I am and wait, and let some time pass by before I attempt to make a move. In the meantime, I think about my father. Think about the outline of the Big Dipper I saw from my own open grave. I look up and can barely make out a patch of night sky between the trees.

"Dad, are you up there?" I whisper.

✦

He didn't die immediately. It took him twelve days. In that time period I invoked my ten-year-old magic, praying to a variety of gods, casting spells, even burying my marble collection in the backyard as a sacrifice. A candle flame burned my nose when I tried to chant into it. I walked around the neighborhood, retracing his last route, stopped in the place where the tire marks still hadn't been scrubbed, and stared beseechingly up at the sky, as though the sight of my sad ten-year-old face would move some celestial court into action. *Look at that kid. Let's wake up her father.*

My mother explained, in that quavery voice that meant she was trying to be strong for me, that they were doing tests on his brain, and that machines were helping him breathe. He was here, and he wasn't here. Dead and alive. Present and absent. Not quite of the earth anymore but hovering somewhere above it, in the part of the atmosphere that is neither cold nor hot, above the treetops, below the weather balloons.

Somehow I was still supposed to go to school and come home to a sitter who would make my dinner and help me with homework while my mother stayed at my father's side in the ICU.

The sitter, whose name was Heather, was an older girl, nineteen or twenty, who lived down the street and moved back in with her parents after flunking out of college. She was large and heavy footed and made a lot of noise on our floors. She'd make the same dinner every night—Hamburger Helper—and we'd eat it while she stared at the Travel Channel.

"I'm going to go there," she'd say to just about everything, in a voice that sounded spacey.

I watched with her: the dreamy islands, the ice-blue sky spilling off glaciers, the rain forests of Ecuador.

I didn't want to go to any of those places. I wanted to go to the hospital.

One night Heather peered at me, studying me. "So your father got run over."

I didn't know how to respond. Having it put that way, so casually, made him sound like a dog or a squirrel. But then again, my mother told me Heather had trouble communicating with people. I didn't really care. I just wanted her to keep her snout in her Hamburger Helper and mind her own business. "He was hit by a car," I said.

"That's tough," she said.

"I'm praying a lot," I said. "To a bunch of different people. Do you want to pray with me?"

"Prayer's bullshit," she said.

That night when Mom got home, I told her what Heather said, and the next night, some girl named Samantha had taken her place.

I kept up the spells, the magic. Samantha helped me light candles and bury toys. I saw my father in a dream one

168

night, and he told me he was going to make it. When I told my mother this the next morning when she was cooking me breakfast, she didn't answer but gave me a pancake that wasn't done in the middle and went to her room.

She let me visit him only once in ICU, on the eighth day. He looked very normal, and the ICU room looked more like a cleared-out storage closet. I expected everything to be dramatic, like the ICUs on TV shows, but everything just seemed very neat and clean and calm, a few tubes running in and out of him, a monitor over his head, and the breathing machine.

I had a gift for him: a pinecone I'd saved from one of our hikes and spray-painted gold in a special healing ceremony I'd thought up myself. I put it on the table next to him as I left and said, "I'll see you, Daddy," starting out very casually but crying by the time I reached the end of the sentence.

It was all over on a Saturday. Samantha and I were watching *River Monsters* when my mother came through the door with a strange expression on her face and handed Samantha her money and said, "That's it for us, dear. You don't need to come back." Samantha's face studied hers, and by the time the meaning sank into her, it had sunk into me and I said, "No, wait," as if Samantha being handed the money was what would actually kill him and I had to stop it.

My dad didn't want to be buried. He wanted to be cremated, and my mother respected his wishes. There was no big funeral, just a ceremony out on the mountain with some of his running buddies and his lawyer friends and our grandparents, who were too old to climb the mountain and so we moved everything to the base, which made sense to me, actually, because that's where every trip begins and ends.

My mother washed and dried his jogging shirt and shorts and ironed them and kept them in his drawer, as if he'd be back some day needing to look really sharp and collected on his next run. There were a lot of things to decide: like, what to do with the half-finished Scotch that he liked and Mom didn't, and where to put his clothes and his rowing machine, and what to do with the failed magic of the pinecone that the nurses thoughtfully wrapped up for us, and how to live without him. The entire event, from the night the door shut when my father went jogging until the day after the funeral, seemed to have taken place in the blink of an eye, just long enough for the house to be lifted up and have its parts twisted around like a Rubik's Cube and set down with none of the colors matching.

For a while, I'd make my mother drive me to the mountains where his ashes were scattered just to see if maybe I could catch a glimpse of him. She took me a half dozen times until her grief counselor, right or wrong, told her to stop. But I never saw even a glimpse of him. I stopped believing then, in magic spells and wishful thinking and dreams that mean something. I didn't even believe in God. I believed in what I saw and what was true. I had no more belief left for anything.

The girl who killed my father went on trial for manslaughter. Mom let me skip school for four days and go to the trial and sit with her and stare at the back of the blond head of the sorority girl who had blown .23 on a Breathalyzer (I was taking notes of the testimony) and had refused the offer of at least two sorority sisters to drive her home. Later, I got to stare at her horrible face and her sob-ruined blue eyeliner as she tearfully stated that she did not recall any events of that night, and her first conscious memory was coming to in the back of a squad car.

I looked straight at her, staring her down like her headlights had stared down my father. Nothing she said moved my heart. My mother sat beside me, never commenting, her expression totally blank, even when they read the verdict: guilty, as of course was the case. Not even when it came time for sentencing and this stupid drunk girl was given ten years' probation plus mandatory alcohol counseling and six months' suspended license for killing my father.

I hated her. I wanted to find her house, throw a rock through the window. Find out her number and call her in the middle of the night shouting things at her. I wanted to see her on the street and run her down with my bicycle. I wanted to send her anonymous letters full of curse words. Wanted to cut her hair off as she slept. Let the air out of her tires. Have a bunch of big kids hold her down while I ask her to her face: *Do you know what it's like to try not to cry when you're doing the dishes? The way the back of your throat hurts and the steam makes your nose run but you don't want your mother to notice that the joke she reminded you of that your father used to tell made you cry instead of laugh? Well, do you?*

My ten-year-old mind teemed with revenge possibilities. I didn't know how to un-hate her or how to turn it down into the low boiling resentment my mother seemed to have—the way her eyes narrowed when people stopped her in the grocery story to say "ridiculous" and "travesty of justice." I couldn't even say her name.

That's when I decided to grow up and be a journalist. Tell the real story. The real truth. So girls like that girl couldn't hide in her story. I'd rip it out page by page.

fourteen

Night birds call. Things buzz and rattle. The forest cracks. My nerves jump. A light rain starts up, wetting my hair and driving away at last the mosquitos that have been pestering me. I scratch at the vicious welts on my face. My stomach, shrunk from fear and lack of food, feels like an overboiled egg. The pain from my broken arm comes in waves.

Somewhere in the dark, a wild family hunts for me as though I'm a wounded animal they need to drag back and salvage part by part.

Siberia means business. I'm still astonished at the speed with which it destroyed my trip, killed everyone I knew there, and left me alone. And yet, I'm proud of myself for getting away. Using my own grave as camouflage. The article I write, defending my stepfather and condemning this murderous family, will also contain this little fact.

That's the hope I cling to now. I have an article to write. I have a story to carry. I stand up on tired and aching legs, using the hand of my good arm to massage each leg in turn, listening to the forest around me for sounds of my captors. They must have given up on me, the way they had to finally give up on the other creatures that outran them or outmaneuvered them and left their stew pot needy.

It's hard to see in the gloom in front of me as I move through the trees. I inhale groups of bugs, exhale mist. Claw vines away from my face. Step on the sponginess of the forest floor, breaking through every few steps and sinking up to my ankles in wet ground. My progress is slow and painful, but finally I reach the edge of the forest and the great dark expanse of the giant sunflowers, their heads lit by the starlight. Half a moon shines nearby. Low-lying dark clouds make monster shapes. I stop, listening for footsteps or voices or breathing. I look up, watching for that deranged owl to swoop my way again on orders of the witch.

The hut is out of sight, farther down the slope. My fervent hope is that the family sleeps inside, surrendered to the possibility that I've escaped forever, content, at least, with their clothing and their salt.

The sunflower heads tickle my fingers. My wooden

cast bumps against my thigh. I feel like a ghost girl, invisible to the naked eye. Every few feet I stop and swivel my head around, listening. But there seems to be no intrigue tonight beyond the swirl of the usual Siberian nightlife: little things being hunted by bigger things, wind in the trees, the clouds releasing rain and the sky waiting for the new light of dawn.

I reach the stream and cross the bridge, my feet silent on the wooden boards. The path is a welcoming rectangle of gloom, and I enter it and begin slowly moving down the mountain. After fifty yards or so, I start to hear the roar of the water. That seemingly endless river that shows the way back.

Just keep breathing. Just keep moving.

Maybe I can catch fish from the river. Unlikely, I know, with a broken arm, but maybe I can trap them. Or eat cattail tubers. People can survive on plants. . . .

Just keep breathing. Just keep—

I freeze.

I jerk each time I hear a gunshot.

It's far away, somewhere in the darkness. I can't tell which direction they are coming from, but the sound is unmistakable.

They've got Sergei's gun. Somewhere, they are using it. On who or what, I don't know.

I fight the temptation to curl into a ball. The rain has stopped. The mosquitoes have found me again, but I don't move. I just let them feed on my face and the backs of my hands as I hold my breath. One more shot—that makes five—and all is silent. At last I slap the mosquitos away, clawing my face until the itch excites itself and then subsides.

Oh, Adrienne, my father used to say. *The things you get into.*

I force myself to smile at the memory, only because I need the smile. I need something, anything, to force myself to keep walking down the path instead of just giving up right now, letting them find me and doing with me what they wish.

I keep moving toward the water, reaching out to touch the tree trunks to help guide my path. Finally I reach the gravel banks of the river; its familiar sound drowning out the birds and the crickets. Even water isn't the same in Siberia. In Colorado, you float down it in the summer and keep your lawn green. Here, it breaks boats and drowns stepfathers. Even water is not a friend here.

And yet I kneel at the bank, the gray stones hurting my knees, and scoop it up in my palms as best I can, as it soaks the cords of my cast and chills my hands. It tastes clean and cold and I don't stop until I've quenched my suddenly rabid thirst.

It's still dark when I begin to make my way down the river again, holding my arms out for balance, stumbling over the rocks, trying to find the stable footholds. I force myself to keep going, counting my steps through chattering teeth. Hundreds of miles down the river, past a few dozen impossibilities, exists the hope of rescue. My arm feels heavy, and my entire body aches. I round a corner and stop.

I gasp.

Woody saunters toward me, rifle cradled in his arms, several dead rabbits slung over his shoulder. I'm so shocked that I just stand there as he catches sight of me, and an expression of anger and surprise crosses his face.

I turn and begin running down the riverbank, feet sliding, trying to get away from him, and he'll be on me before I can try to run uphill into the shelter of the forest. I hear the pounding of his feet closing on me fast. I do the only thing I can do. I flounce into the river like a fish.

The shocking brace of it closes over my face, and the current grabs me and rushes me along as I try to keep my mouth above water. In a matter of seconds I slam into the branches of a fallen tree. They snap in all directions and I am pinned there fast, trying to extract myself one-handed but helplessly trapped by the current. I struggle and kick my feet in the freezing water, my lungs on fire, screaming, *"Go away go away go away!"* as he drops the rabbits, sets down his rifle and picks his way down the bank.

His face has turned beet red; he's shouting back at me in anger something I can't understand.

"Glupaya devchyonka!"

He wades out to me, bracing himself against a boulder until he can reach my foot and pull me toward him. I can't do anything but allow myself to be fished out of the water and thrown like a rag doll over his shoulder where I dangle, the eyes of the rabbits staring at me blankly, as he continues up the bank.

Woody says nothing. I say nothing. What is there left to say?

I ride on his back and try not to feel like one of the dead animals across his shoulder. I smell sweat and blood, hunter and hunted. The arm holding me is shockingly strong. He could have given even Lyubov a run for her money. I have a quick flash of memory about her tossing supplies from the boat to the campsite. If a woman that strong and that capable cannot survive out here, what does that say about me? I decide not to think about it. Instead, I name the dead rabbits. Benjamin, Jared, Gaga, and Kanye. They dangle and turn. Water drips out of my clothes and taps on the rocks.

The woods lighten. The minutes pass. The blood slowly pools in my head as I contemplate plan B, since plan A did not come off as spectacularly well as it does in James Bond movies. Clearly escape is not an option, not when they are so at home in the woods and I am such a hapless, bungling stranger. I decide to beg for my life, to appeal to whatever's left that's human in them. Right now I'm at dead-rabbit status at best. But a status can change.

When he reaches the part of the bank where the stream feeds the river, he turns and hikes straight up the mountain, as effortlessly as though it's flat land, and as he hauls me up toward the hut, my heartbeat speeds up and my skin prickles with sweat. Is this the end of me?

When we arrive, the tiny family is gathered around the stones, eating gruel out of their bowls. Woody says nothing, just drops me to the ground and then dumps the dead rabbits on top of me, and there we are, welcome food and unwelcome girl, staring up at them. Nobody says anything. None of their expressions are particularly friendly, except Clara's; she seems glad to see me back. She gives me a smile and a quick shrug.

I sit up, dead rabbits sliding off me. "Ya ustala," I say in a strong voice as I rise, unsteadily, to my feet.

I'm sorry.

Or maybe that doesn't mean *I'm sorry*. Wait a minute. Now I remember. "Ya ustala" means, *I'm tired*. So now I'm not only not sorry, I'm whiny too.

Clara evidently tries to argue for me, but her mother holds up her hand and Clara falls silent. The mother glares at me. I feel the urge to fill up the world with talking. If I just can keep talking, then maybe I can be spared whatever punishment is in store for me. I abandon their language. English pours out of me in a flood. "I'm sorry, I'm alone and afraid and you people are scary. The truth is, I had no right to interrupt your peace and quiet. I know you want to murder me, but it you spare me, I promise—"

I stop. Out of the corner of my eye I've caught sight of my open grave.

My grave is full of potatoes.

Relief floods my body. I sink to my knees and begin to cry. Tears pour down my cheeks, irritating my mosquito bites. No one says anything. When I get hold of myself and look up at their faces, they seem bewildered, as though I am one of the dead rabbits and I've just recited a verse from Revelation.

The family starts arguing among themselves. I wait, trying to make sense of the blur of words. Then the older brother takes out a knife from his belt and moves toward me. I cringe and cover my head, but he brushes past me. He disappears behind the hut and comes back holding a length of cord. He comes up to me, leans down to me, and ties one leg roughly. I cry out in pain as he pulls too tight, and Clara bursts out with a shriek. He glares at her and adjusts the cord slightly, then ties the other end to my left leg. There's about fifteen inches of cord between them. Enough to waddle but not to run. If I had any thoughts of escaping again on foot, they are gone now.

"So, what's for dinner?" I ask in English. It's my pathetic attempt at a joke. They stare at me.

Still holding his knife, the angry man picks up the rabbits and strolls toward a wooden plank table standing a short distance from the hut. Meanwhile Clara heads toward the garden with her mother. No one pays any attention to me. The message seems clear: I am being deliberately ignored for the breach in courtesy of running for my life. I try to follow the women, but it's super awkward to try to get up and walk with my legs tied this way. So I stay on the ground. They know, and I know, that I can't escape. Wherever I go, they'll come and find me and take me back. I'll have to come up with another plan. In the meantime, I'm just glad to be alive.

When Clara and her mother return a couple of hours later, they carry a bucket of potatoes. I suppose it's peeling time again, and I'm determined to show them I can make a good guest, or at least a good prisoner.

I wait a few moments after they disappear into the hut, then I struggle to my feet and make my way in. It's weird, walking with your legs tied this way. Kind of a shuffling thing I'm doing. There's something about being tied that really confirms one's prisoner status.

They are already spreading out the potatoes on the table. Clara smiles at me, but her mother stares at me, her face as neutral as broom scratchings on a dirt floor.

"Privyet," I say cautiously.

Hello.

"Ya khochu pomoch."

I want to help.

"Da!" Clara affirms, but her mother glares at me, shakes

181

her head, and waves a gnarled hand toward my chair.

"Ya khochu pomoch," I repeat, but the old woman just goes on peeling potatoes and Clara shakes her head sadly. I suppose that peeling potatoes is a sign of status in this house, and I will have to earn my way up.

I surrender and slump in my seat, watching them. It's going on two days since I've eaten, and I'm so hungry I could eat the potatoes raw. I could eat the rabbits raw. Even the boards of my cast look gnawable to me.

I glance at the window and catch my breath. There's a face staring back at me.

It's Woody.

I want to tell him that swinging from his shoulder with a bunch of dead rabbits was the best date I've had in ages, but I don't quite have the words. I wonder if he's still mad at me for running off, but I meet his glance and hold it. He blinks and smiles shyly but doesn't look away.

Maybe he's not dangerous. Maybe he's just a guy who has never seen a girl who is not his sister. His eyes are wide, his mouth slightly agape. I astonish him, and I wonder if he knows that he and his family astonish me. Just then Clara notices him and laughs, says something in a teasing tone of voice. These woods and these primitive conditions haven't buried the duty of little sisters to embarrass their brothers.

He scowls and ducks away. The mother turns to me, her expression severe, as Clara continues patching her dress with the clothing of the dead. I look away. The mother scares me almost as much as the intense, angry older brother, who I've just decided to call Scowly because Killer is probably too on the nose. I wonder if she thinks I'm going to take her boys away. I want to reassure her that I have absolutely no plans to wear a wolfskin wedding dress any time soon.

I picture that scene and almost smile at the thought of standing at an altar made of beaver tusks with Woody by my side.

And then suddenly I have an idea.

I've accepted the fact that I can't escape on my own. I'm weak and woods-dumb, and I have no supplies, no food, no technology, and a broken arm. But I am a girl, last time I checked, and this boy has probably never seen a girl in his life besides his sisters.

I'm going to do what I never bothered to try to do in high school. I'm going to make a boy fall in love with me. And instead of a date to the prom, I'll win my own survival.

Clara and her mother keep cutting potatoes, unaware that I am sitting here with a new, devious strategy in my heart. To get Woody to swipe right, Siberian style. Then convince him to take me back to civilization, all while managing to avoid the attention of Scowly, the older brother, who looks at me like he'd like to bash my brains out against a tree. Not so much the romantic type. Somehow in the past twenty-four hours, I've convinced myself that Scowly acted alone when he killed the crew. Woody and Clara seem too gentle and the mother, too frail.

At least that's what I tell myself. I have no way of really knowing what happened out there, and I'm guessing no one will be holding up a hand to confess.

Just then, Woody's face appears in the window again and he throws me a quick, soulful glance. I wave at him, just the merest turn of my fingers, before he disappears.

This could work.

That night, just before the family sits down to dinner, Clara approaches me with a plate of rabbit stew. They all watch me as I take my first delicate spoonful and then throw caution to the wind, driven mad by the smell and taste of it—the meat rangy, the soup stock watery, but *who cares it's food it's food it's food*. I drop the spoon and attack the stew with my fingers, devouring the rabbit meat until it's gone and then throwing back my head to drink the contents of the bowl. When at last I pause for breath, I look up to see the whole family staring at me with horror.

Apparently I've violated some kind of Siberian Emily Post manners guide.

"Ofitsiant," I say, which I think is the Russian word for *delicious*, then I realize, too late, it's the word for *waiter*.

I have just accused them of cooking and eating a waiter.

I shrug and smile apologetically.

Scowly scowls, and the rest go back to their dinner.

They glance at me once in a while but don't speak to me. I mostly keep my head down. After dinner there is a time where they all go to their own activities: The women sew, Scowly stalks out to hobbies unknown, and Woody reads what must be the giant Bible Yuri Androv reported. Its pages are blackened and torn at the edges. That book would go for seven cents on eBay, tops. I'm wondering where in that Bible it says, "Kidnap and murder." Come to think of it, people in the Bible weren't very nice.

As I watch him, I take the time to mentally go over all the blogs I've read on Tumblr about how to make boys notice you.

Always look your best! Okay, let's see, I'm half-drowned, half-starved, in the same clothes I've worn since two days ago, my hair has dried funny, and I just pulled a tiny leaf out of it. Hmmm, next.

Show an interest in the things he likes! I look over at the Bible. Other hobbies: hunting, gathering, kidnapping. Okay, I'll try.

Don't forget to play a little hard to get! Right. Well, since I'm a prisoner in his hut, I'd say he's got me.

By now the past twenty-four hours have caught up to me. Later, I watch through heavy-lidded eyes as the family prepares to turn in for the night. Scowly and Woody bed down near the front door. The women throw down blankets near the stove. The mother drops something made of animal fur and points to a space on the floor by the wall, no more than two feet wide, where I suppose I am to sleep. I quickly obey.

The candle flickers, putting off a musky, animal scent, and the mother reaches up, takes it off the table, and blows it out, leaving everything dark around me. I hear some prayers, some of them guttural and sullen-sounding— Scowly nagging his god—and then all is quiet except for the breathing around me. Through the paneless windows, I can feel a cool breeze and see the stars in the sky. As my eyes adjust, I can make out shapes in the dark.

I wait, listening to the breathing deepen. Before I know it, I'm asleep.

I awaken with a start, sometime in the night, minutes or hours later. I'm in a hut with the same family who were once part of the darkness around me, tantalizing and frightening. Now they are more real, and I am less. Stripped of my possessions, my family, my friends, and my world. Unable to speak and be heard. Made mostly of shadows and fear. My broken arm heavy in its clumsy cast. I know the dark Siberian woods are full of danger, but dark Siberian huts don't seem like day care centers, either.

I glance over at the sleeping figures. Woody is closest to me. The glow of the moon lights up his face. The light accentuates his high cheekbones, the strong line of his jaw. Give him a haircut and a shave and a week of hot showers, and he might be Instagram-ready.

It's time to put my plan into motion. Very quietly I crawl across the floor toward him, being careful not to rest too much weight on my broken arm. I just need to get him to like me—as a person or an object of intense desire or *whatever*—and then have him get me the hell out of here. I'm amazed at my own courage as I approach him and whisper in his ear.

"Menya zovut Adrienne."

My name is Adrienne.

Yes, I know his little sister already announced my name to the family, but it wouldn't hurt to say it again. I have a name. I am a person. I am an object of desire.

His eyes pop open and I jerk instinctively. He moves his gaze to me, stares at me.

"Menya zovut Adrienne," I say again.

He shakes his head. I've scared him. Maybe I've been too aggressive. Came off like those girls at parties you find draped all over the football players. The ones the other girls talk about. I start to crawl back to my place on the floor, but suddenly he grabs my arm.

I stifle a shriek as he pulls me toward him.

"Menya zovut Vanya," he whispers in my ear.

fifteen

The next few days pass in relative peace. Clara seems delighted to have me around. Vanya is openly curious with short-lived stares and then bursts of shyness, his face flushing red. Scowly grumbles and growls. Silently I experiment with new variations of his nickname. Scowletariat. Scowl Doggy Dog. Oscar Scowlarenta. My presence is clearly not a pleasure to him, and I remember how I once treated my new brother when he appeared in my household so long ago. Fifty Shades of Scowl has the same long-suffering stare. Maybe he liked his family just fine before I came along. And it's hard to know what the mother is thinking. She neither smiles at me nor talks to me directly, although sometimes I do catch her looking at me and then looking away when I notice. It's strange. She seemed so ferocious at first—what with that severe expression and disgruntled owl friend of hers—but from time to time, there's something soft in her gaze. I'm not sure what it means.

In the following days, I watch and learn and try to stay out of the way as I plot my strategy with Vanya. I've got to figure out his movements during the day and night. How I can catch him alone without his scary big brother around.

It is Clara who serves as my tie to this strange family. She is the one who leads me to the outhouse and stands patiently outside. She is the one who pulls green, moist shoots out of the ground, takes a bite first, and then offers to me something that tastes very much like celery, nodding approvingly when I swallow it. She's the one who loves the words from me she doesn't understand. And so I give her words. I'm glad to.

My own voice comforts me as I tell her a story of my father from our camping days, of how he accidentally set the tent on fire, pantomiming the action while I describe it, and she suddenly lets out a peal of laughter and claps her hands together. She shouts out a word that is lost on me. She repeats it in a pleading voice, the same word, over and over, even clasping my hands, and finally it dawns on me that she wants to hear the story again.

So I tell it once more, to her great delight. She makes me tell the story three more times, and then she gets up out of the grass, motioning for me to stay seated while she wades away, first through ferns and then sunflowers, leaving me there with the sun shining bright in a sky that has one drifting cloud.

I wait for her. It's almost pleasant out here, considering the circumstances, the air so warm it could be the same degree of sunshine they're enjoying right now in Boulder. I think about my mom. Dan told her that since we had no cell signal out in the wilderness, not to expect any messages from us for two weeks unless we ran into trouble, so she's going on about her life right now, completely unaware that her husband is dead and her daughter is a captive. In that part of the world, the civilized part, it's a Saturday—if I've counted the days right. I can't imagine it being a Saturday here. It's way too wild and exotic for that.

And yet I can smell honeysuckle. And yet I can see butterflies. And yet the breakfast I was given this morning, something of a cross between Cream of Wheat and mulch, wasn't entirely terrible.

Clara returns, a stack of birch bark in her arms, each piece the size of a postcard. She flops across from me, breathing heavily. She wipes her face and smiles brightly, then hands the top sheet of birch bark to me.

I look at it, shocked. It's a drawing that looks like it was done with a stick dipped in the ashes of a fire, and it is a perfect image of her, down to the eyebrows and the curve of her face.

"Clara," she says, pointing.

I wonder how she did it. I don't recall seeing a mirror around the hut, but maybe the mother has one stashed away that she borrows to study herself. The girl has talent, that's for sure.

I smile big at her. Dig around in my mind for a word I know that will convey how impressed I am.

"Potryasayushche."

Incredible.

And it is. It's her face, her expression, her nose and eyes and mouth. She carefully sets the self-portrait aside and shows me the next one.

Why, if it isn't Luke Scowlwalker.

She's captured her moody older brother exactly: the broad face and the large thick lips. The stern and world-weary expression, the disagreeable brow line. The shading gives dimension to his scruffy beard, the shape of his nose. Once again, it's an amazing reproduction.

"Marat," she says, pointing. I don't understand at first, but she points at herself—"Clara"—then back at him. "Marat."

"Marat." I repeat it several times. It sounds slightly menacing, the name of a killer who hunts by night. I guess I was hoping for *Bobby* or something equally tame.

Then it's Vanya's face I see, perfectly rendered. It's as though he's staring at me from the birch bark canvas, and I stare back at it a long time. Yes, his beard *is* slightly thicker on the jawline. Yes, the front of his hair *does* curl that way.

Yes, his eyebrows have that slant, and yes, that stare is open and that smile is polite and embarrassed. There's a certain hopefulness about his expression that is hard to put into words, but his sister has captured it with ashes and bark. I give it one last look before handing the drawing to her, nodding my approval.

"Vanya," I say before she can speak.

Her eyes widen in wonder. How can she have known he's already introduced himself? She nods. "Vanya."

Then it is time for the drawing of her mother captured in her quiet and mysterious stateliness. It is just as detailed and meticulous but reveals nothing new. Even her mystery is captured by the girl who must know her so well, or maybe her mother confounds her, too. I can't get her actual name; Clara keeps calling her *Mama*, the closest thing to English I've heard since I've been out in the wilderness.

"I can't call her that," I say in English.

"Maaaaa-maaaa." She draws out the word in case I'm not following.

I shake my head, frustrated, then say the Russian word for Madam.

"Gospozha."

Clara stares at me as though she's never heard this term in her life, and that makes sense. It's not like she's probably ever met any woman outside her family. At any rate, I decide that a little formality couldn't hurt around the older woman. Gospozha it will be.

Finally she recovers enough to show me the next drawing. It's of an older man, wearing a tall fur hat. He looks nice. He must be the father that Yuri described, the dreamy and kind one. Unless he lives in a tree, he must be dead or missing.

"Papa," she says sadly. Then she hands me one more drawing.

I gasp.

It's the girl. The one who appeared in my tent and, later, in the woods. That sweet little girl with the tiny body and the knowing smile.

"Zoya."

I look at Clara. "I saw her," I say, too excited to think through translating the words into Russian. "She talked to me."

Clara looks at me intently, then shakes her head. Of course she doesn't understand me.

I point to the pictures of the older man, then the girl.

"Gde?" I ask.

Where are they?

Clara gathers up the drawings in a loose pile, takes me by the hand, and urges me to my feet. She leads me to a place, high in the meadow, that is sheltered by young birch trees growing in a circle, as though planted that way. Inside the circle are two graves. Upon each grave is a six-sided wooden cross, upon which each name has been carved.

Zoya. Grigoriy.

"Chto sluchilos?" I ask.

What happened?

The light leaves Clara's face. She tries to smile, but just as suddenly, the smile crumples and her eyes fill with tears. Suddenly I feel like crying myself. I never had a sister, but I had a dad.

"Prosti," I tell her.

I'm sorry.

Just then Vanya approaches. He doesn't look happy. He and Clara argue for a moment in rapid Russian, his voice getting louder, her voice getting softer until she's quiet. Whatever the argument, Vanya has won.

He glares at me, gestures me away from the grave.

"Idi!" he orders.

I know what that means.

Go.

The tips on seduction I've read on the internet never warned me not to approach the sacred graves of my crush's family. Apparently I've offended Vanya, because he doesn't speak to me or even look at me the rest of the morning. But later in the afternoon, he catches my eye and smiles.

So perhaps I'm forgiven.

I'm still amazed at Clara's drawings.

How could it possibly be that this girl—Zoya—appeared to me in my tent and was as real and alive as any other person I'd ever met but at the same time was dead

194

and in the ground? And had Zoya been the one whose apparition appeared to Sergei's father? It was a wonder, this land where the living and the dead mixed so easily. And yet I was totally, completely unable to share the miracle.

No internet. No phone. No mail. No texts or Twitter or Instagram. Here the air is completely clear of any kind of voice that could add to the discussion of what is real and what is a dream. I have to get out and share this story with the world. Make them believe me. Make them understand that I had met the strangest family in the universe, alive and dead, primitive and polite, considerate and terrifying. Make them understand that my stepfather, Dr. Dan Westin, was not only strong and brave and protective but was right all along, and those who doubted him should be ashamed of themselves.

I should be ashamed of myself.

Later that day, I try out the names. Vanya. Marat. Gospozha.

Vanya smiles, and Marat snarls at me. Saying his name is like stroking a bushy dog's pelt the wrong way, tail to head, and I retreat as fast I can with my legs tied like that.

When I address the older woman simply as Gospozha, she looks at me in surprise and then flashes a grin that fades so fast I think I imagined it, and I can't figure out whether I'd mispronounced the term or she's found it funny in its formality, hearing it for the first time in thirty years or so. At any rate, I am happy that at least I'm serving as some kind of amusement and decide to call her that from now on.

I wait for a chance to be near Vanya, to talk to him, smile at him, flip my hair with my good hand, ask with interest how he skins a deer: do all the things you're supposed to do to make your magic on the opposite sex—though I'll admit to being only an apprentice sorcerer. After all, my mother never took me aside and said, *By the way, you'll have to make a boyfriend really quick before you starve or freeze to death someday when you're being held captive in Siberia.*

Late in the afternoon, I see Vanya and Marat chopping wood on a large stump in the back area of the cabin. Vanya holds the logs while Marat splits them. I hobble closer, watch from a short distance. Try to catch Vanya's eye. Finally he looks at me. I smile my best *I'm-not-interested-in-survival-just-you* kind of smile. He blinks, looks away, then back at me. Just then Marat swings. Vanya's hand jerks and the unchopped wood goes flying.

Marat screams a long string of words at Vanya, so harsh and run together I don't understand a thing. Then he turns on me.

"Ukhodi, ukhodi!"

Go away, go away!

I stumble backward, fall into a nest of thistles. He's still screaming at me so I crawl away through the weeds as fast as I can with my broken arm and hobbled legs.

There is no lovelorn advice Tumblr that I know of on the web that describes what to do when a boy's possibly murderous hermit brother cock-blocks you.

Back to the drawing board, I guess.

Before dinner, when the women are peeling potatoes and chopping onions and green herbs on a plank of wood, I approach them, make gestures that I can chop up things as well. Chopping exists in Boulder, Africa, Thailand, Antarctica, and possibly Mars. Chopping is as universal as smiling.

Clara looks surprised and turns to Gospozha, who regards me skeptically but finally nods.

I'm actually good at chopping potatoes. I mean, not a master of the art like they are, but I can hold my own. Usually. Except when I have a broken arm. I try to hold the potato with one hand and steady the knife with the other. The knife slides off. I try again and gouge the potato in the time it takes Clara to expertly chop a whole one. Gospozha rolls her eyes. I didn't know the eye-roll was the universal sign for *You are lame*, but here it is, in deepest Russia. Clara tries to help me, steadying my hand, but Gospozha interrupts her with a burst of Russian that sounds like, *Indulge the idiot American girl and we won't eat tonight. Just accept that she is utterly useless.* Finally she sends Clara and me outside to the cellar to fetch some kind of strange vegetable I can't identify. The cellar is dark and cold, just basically a hole in the ground we crawl into. I can't wait to get out of there, but I manage to gather some of the strange, twisted shapes and follow Clara to the stream, where she quickly washes hers. I'm washing vegetables one-handed when I sense a presence on the other side of the stream. It's Vanya, spear in hand. I'm not sure whether he's returned from target practice or an unsuccessful hunt, since he doesn't have anything dead draped over his shoulder.

I drop the wet, clean vegetables in the bucket and stand. Vanya and I look at each other across the stream.

Clara pulls on my arm. "Poshli."

Come.

"Podozhdite!" Vanya calls.

Wait.

Clara looks startled, and slightly annoyed. She calls to Vanya in singsong Russian but he ignores her, wading across the stream until he is close to me. He looks into my bucket.

"Ya moyu," I say.

I wash.

He nods. I nod. We both stare at the wet vegetable whose name I don't know. Clara grabs my hand and tugs on it impatiently. Coos something in dove talk, yanks harder. Reluctantly I hobble after her to the hut. I wonder if I made any progress with Vanya. At least he crossed the stream to talk to me. That must mean something.

I'm not invited to the table at dinner, although they do share some precious salt with me. They go outside, leaving the door open so I can see them sitting on the circle of stones under the stars. There are two empty stones. It's not as if there's no room for me. And yet no one calls me over.

It's weird. I'm not sure what I mean to this family. No banishment. No acceptance, either, just some kind of uneasy peace in which I am somewhere between guest and captive, enemy and pet.

Later that night, we bed down on the floor. The breathing steadies around me. The family is asleep. But I am not leaving tonight. I'm biding my time. Becoming familiar to them, harmless, even helpful, all the while seducing their son and brother behind their backs until the hour and the moment come when they turn around and I'm gone, and they will wonder if I ever existed at all.

The next day, I renew my efforts to try and contribute to the family. After all, Vanya is obviously a family man, so getting close to him means getting close to them. I hobble after Clara into the woods and help gather firewood. With my bad arm and tied legs, I'm not as fast as they are, but I do a pretty good job, and Clara rewards me with a smile. I have to admit, this morning is glorious. Butterflies are everywhere, mostly yellow but also orange and blue, different colors and shapes like the patches on the women's dresses. Purple flowers grow from the base of the trees and the air smells of spice. We both collect an armload of wood and start back toward the hut. I stop. In between the garden and the hut, Vanya and Marat are setting up a tent.

I drop my armload of wood. I recognize that tent. It was Lyubov's. The brothers look up and notice me. Clara appears confused.

Lyubov was proud of that tent. It was brand-new. Something to stand up to the weather and the chill of the Siberian mountains. She died before she could spend her third night in that tent.

It's true, I can't prove the Osinovs—or at least Marat—are killers, but the evidence is pretty damning: the missing salt packages from my backpack and all the booty from the campsite are now here, the clothing of the dead cut up and sewn onto the tattered dresses and trousers of the family, technology shattered, tools appropriated, and I am here helping them, and this tent seems obscene to me, and what they did to get it.

"That's not your tent," I say, pointing. "That belonged to Lyubov. She had a name. They all had names."

Marat and Vanya exchange glances.

"Lyubov," I say. "Her tent. Not yours."

I walk away, wading through sunflowers, and keep walking to the place where the birch trees grow in a circle.

I stand a respectful distance from the graves and say their names.

Zoya. Grigoriy.

Whatever killed them is the worst story of this family, and this family, in turn, is my worst story. I will try to keep my wits about me, try not to make waves, but I will never forget who they are.

sixteen

Today marks a week with the Osinovs. I have learned to walk past the tent full of firewood. I have watched Vanya and Marat try on the dead men's boots. I've seen Clara carefully shatter the lenses of Sergei's tinted sunglasses with a rock and then arrange the jagged shapes into the irregular petals of a flower. They have also taken apart the knapsacks, except for the one which they use to gather nuts.

I learn to avert my eyes. Think of other things. Breathe. Smile. Now is no time to avenge their deaths. Now is the time to join. To make myself useful. I've taught myself to put wood in that tent as though it were any other shelter in the world. Wood-gathering is something that I can do to help. So is sweeping the area in the front of the house. So is clearing dishes. So is grinding pine nuts under a stone.

And so is working in the garden.

The garden amazes me. It's about the size of a large dance floor and crawls up the side of the mountain in neat rows. Potatoes, hemp, carrots. Onions and parsley and peas. Every day, the women go into the garden, tilling and turning the soil, fussing over the sickly plants, expressing happiness over the healthy ones, and pulling weeds. Every morning, there are more weeds. Weeds are universal pests.

I have one good hand to pull weeds and I have gotten pretty fast at it, but not even close to how fast and efficient the others are. I really miss my recorder. Now all the notes are in my head and that is not a very reliable machine. I do the best I can to observe and remember. If by chance I survive this ordeal, this is going to make one hell of a story.

Gospozha uses a hoe that consists of a carved wooden stake tipped by a bit of iron. She turns the earth, singing. Clara joins in. I can't understand the words, but the reverence in them leaves me no doubt it's a hymn to their god. I hear the same song so much that I learn the sounds. Finally, on the seventh day, I decide to sing along, joining in lustily.

The women stop singing and stare at me. I never was much of a singer. My off notes may have killed something vital in the garden, or maybe they are just astonished at my attempts at harmonizing. My voice trails off. Now there's just quiet. Birds calling in the distance.

"Sorry," I say. "That's what Auto-Tune is for."

They exchange glances. We all go back to work. They have stopped singing, maybe afraid they'll encourage me.

Early that afternoon, Vanya ambles into the garden. He kneels next to me and silently starts pulling weeds. This seems to be a source of great merriment to his sister, who immediately begins laughing at him and speaking to him in a teasing voice. My guess is that the men never usually work in the garden. At first he ignores her, shaking the dirt off the roots of the weeds before throwing them to the side. Finally the torment becomes too much and he snaps something at her angrily, gets up, and stalks away as Clara laughs merrily.

"Perestan," Gospozha admonishes Clara as Vanya disappears into the sunflowers. *Stop it.* She shakes her head. I see a hint of a smile. Sometimes I think the old lady actually likes me. The way she gently checks my homemade cast and presses upon me some kind of milky substance in a birch bark cup, all the while tapping my broken arm lightly and repeating, "Sil'ny, sil'ny." *Strong, strong.* And yet, other times she gives me a look of sadness and fear. I wish I knew what she is thinking.

When the garden work is done, I go farther into the meadow, following the scraping sound to find Vanya hard at work hollowing out a canoe from a section of thick log.

He's taken his shirt off and I'm amazed at the shape he's in. The chiseled muscles of the chest and arms. I imagined Russian men as hairy all over and am surprised to find he just has a small dark patch on his chest. He looks up at me and drops his tool. He scrambles to put on his shirt.

"Sorry," I mumble in English, and turn to go.

"Nyet, ostan'sya," he says. *No, stay.* He looks at me a moment, picks up his tool, and begins to scrape the wood, hollowing out the log.

I watch as long shavings curl and fall away. He's perspiring, sweat running down his face. His hair is wet. His motions are careful and methodical. I can't help thinking, *This is the boat that will someday bring me home. And here is the man who will take me.*

"Rybachit'?" I say in his language. I make a motion like I'm hauling a fish in.

He lets go a stream of Russian then, at what must be my confused expression. He puts away his tool, takes up a stick, and kneels on the ground. I watch as he draws a line in the dirt, then the figure of a boat on top of it. He points in the direction of the hut and makes a small *x* below the river. He traces his stick down the line drawing of the river, then draws, very carefully, a familiar-looking animal. He's not as good as his sister but better than me.

I plot my next move. We're going to need some kind of way of communicating beyond gestures and smiles.

"Deer," I say.

Hey, you've got to start somewhere with flirtatious banter.

He looks at me, tests out the word. "Dee-uh."

"Deer," I correct him. I hold his stare a little longer.

"Deer," he says.

I smile at him. After a moment, he gives me a slight smile back.

I make the motion of a spear, throw it into the air, then move my fingertip from the drawing of the boat forward a couple of feet. "The deer are farther upriver," I say in English.

He nods, at the motion if not the words.

Our eyes lock again. We've communicated. Part English, part line drawing, part Russian, part goodwill, part pure effort. Now that we're having a conversation, sort of, I decide to keep going. After all, conversations lead to feelings, and feelings lead to Boulder, Colorado. Or so I hope.

I search for the phrase I'm looking for.

"Skol'ko tebe let?"

How old are you?

He smiles. "Dvadtsat."

Twenty years old.

He points at me. "Skol'ko tebe let?"

"Semnadtsat."

Seventeen.

I feel a surge of triumph, as though communication is a fire we've started out of breath and moss in the middle of a snowstorm. We're leaning close over our marks in the dirt. I do feel a certain electricity coming from Vanya. He's interested in me. My plan is working. All I have to do is act interested and be the only captive female in eighteen hundred square miles.

Vanya stands and motions me to come with him. I hobble after him into the woods. After a few feet he stops. An enormous pine log, stripped of bark, lies horizontally across a series of stumps on the forest floor. It is sanded and looks coated with some kind of polish. There are marks on the log that begin at the bottom and extend upward as far as I can see.

Vanya moves his finger up the marks until he finds a name.

Clara.

He looks at me, folds his arms and moves them as though rocking a little baby. I realize that the pine tree is a calendar, counting back the days. And on this day, in a moment of time that is now recollected in wood, was this when Clara was born? I can't be sure.

His finger continues to trace the marks, tiny slivers in the surface, dozens upon dozens of cuts the width of a sewing needle, all of them in neat little groups.

He comes to another name. His own.

Vanya.

He looks at me. He continues down the log until he finds another mark. Next to that mark is written *Zoya*. He looks at me sadly, puts his hands together, resting his head on them, closing his eyes as though he's asleep.

I think I understand. On this day in history, his little sister died.

He moves his finger until he finds his father's name again. Looks at me. Shakes his head. So the sister died and then the father. Children should never die before their parents. Parents should never die before their children.

"Kak?" I ask.

How?

He says something rapidly.

"Ya ne ponimayu," I tell him.

I do not understand.

He tries some more words.

"On bolel," he says.

I nod. *Sick.*

He covers his mouth and begins to cough, demonstrating. In the back of my mind I chalk up one more similarity between his world and mine: in the deep woods of Siberia, in the coffee shops of Boulder, it's polite and medically sound to cover your mouth when you cough.

He keeps coughing. The sound goes deeper. It's a dangerous baritone now. I've heard that sound in sad movies before the nurse comes in and shakes her head. Finally his hand falls away. His eyes water.

We look at each other a long moment. Now my eyes are watering. I forget my plan for a moment. Maybe it's the pure, crisp air, but his grief buzzes out of him, fills me. Another thing we share. I wonder if he wandered the woods, calling for his lost people, trying to bring them back with magic.

Everywhere in the world, magic works and doesn't work and no one's ever figured out how to make it more consistent, not with technology or potions or prayers.

Suddenly a harsh burst of Russian fills the air. Vanya stiffens. Marat comes out of the trees. He's furious, gesturing at me and then the log. I don't have to know Russian to know that this is a sacred place, like the graves, and Vanya has let me intrude.

Unlike Clara, Vanya doesn't back down. He shouts back at his brother. The two of them draw closer together, their voices heated. Marat's fingers curl into fists. The cords stand out in his neck and I don't know what to do: apologize or run or simply stand there.

Finally I hobble back to the meadow. I can still hear them arguing from the edge of the garden.

I open my eyes. The hut is dark. The little girl is back. Moonlight streams through the windows and lights up her hair as she crouches near me, smiling.

"Privyet, Zoya," I whisper. *Hello.* She's familiar to me now, a tiny replica of Clara, but even lighter, more angelic. As though Clara and a rainbow were combined.

"Byd' ostoroznha," she whispers. She reaches out to

touch my face and disappears, leaving just darkness and the breathing of her family.

He is coming.

Long after she has faded into the darkness of the hut, I stay awake, eyes wide in the darkness. Nothing in my life so far has equipped me for a Zen riddle from a ghost while I'm lying captive in a dark hut in Siberia. I missed that lecture. That was never supposed to be on the final. I'm still astonished at her presence, so real and so magical and strange. But now I'm more intrigued by her message. What could it possibly mean?

Who is coming?

I want to sleep, but I'm afraid she'll come back to me, crouch down, and whisper it in my ear again. *He is coming, he is coming, he is coming.*

seventeen

Who is coming?

I don't understand. And I don't understand if it's a warning or the promise of a gift. Alongside all the terror and the discomfort is this wonder, this mystery. This little girl must be the dead sister, Zoya. And, like Clara, she seems to love me. But why?

I have to tell Vanya about this. I have to let him know that his sister is alive. At least alive in the sense that she can speak and appear in a room. I'm not sure how it will be received, or if it will make me something terrible and frightening. Maybe it will even make Vanya not like me. Which means the end.

Because I can see the end coming.

211

The truth is, even with the food from our expedition, there is not enough food for the family. Marat grumbles when he sees me get my share. And my share is very little. They parcel out the potatoes and the root vegetables carefully, and the only animals Vanya has managed to find were the rabbits he killed on the first night. Vanya and his brother go fishing in the river with homemade poles but return with nothing. And this is the summertime. What will winter be like? Yuri Androv told a grim tale of the family half-starved and eating their shoes. And this is a family who grew up in the woods, trained in survival. What will it mean for a girl from Boulder, Colorado, who once came unglued at the age of thirteen when her iPhone was taken away?

What if I start coughing and can't stop? What if my cough deepens and what if one day I'm appearing in a dream to my poor mother?

The next morning, breakfast is a potato gruel that barely covers the bottom of the bowl. Marat growls at me and it startles me. I try to scurry to my seat, get tripped up by my tether, and fall down. The contents of the bowl soak my shirt and I gasp. I sit up, chest on fire, pulling at my shirt as Clara rushes to me.

Vanya's on his feet. He's angry now. I've made him angry. He doesn't want a stupid, clumsy girlfriend who can't carry gruel across the floor. He points at me, shouting something. I pick up "girl" and "stupid" and I cringe.

212

But then his finger swings. He's pointing at Marat. He's yelling at his brother. Marat yells back at him. They stand up and scream at each other face-to-face as Clara waves her arms, shouting encouragement at Vanya:

"Vanya prav! Vanya prav!"

Vanya is right! Vanya is right!

Gospozha sets down her spoon. "Khvatit!"

Be quiet!

But Vanya's all riled up. He grabs a knife from the table and approaches me, his eyes wild. I don't know this Vanya, and I try to move out of the way. He leans down to me.

Before I can react, he grabs my tether and cuts it through. My knees fall to either side. I'm free.

Marat's face is bright red. He releases a stream of Russian words, so hot and angry I'd need a hot, angry dictionary to translate them. He storms past me and out of the hut.

Silence now. Clara picks up my bowl. Vanya unties each tether from my legs, one and then the other. I rub my legs, look up at him.

"Ya ostayus," I tell him.

I stay.

I lack the vocabulary and the stupidity to elaborate: *I stay because I know damn well you'll hunt me down, and what chances do I have in the wilderness anyway? I stay because I have a better plan, one that involves being your friend and becoming your pretend girlfriend so that I can get the hell out of here before winter.*

Vanya looks at me. "Khorosho."

Good.

Gospozha says something quietly, wearily, and her children go back to the table and finish their breakfast. There's nothing for me. That is all the food there was.

It is on the eleventh day that I finally prove my worth.

It's early in the morning, just after a breakfast of gruel. My clothes are loose on me. I dream of turkey sausage and pancakes. And yet I act grateful, humble, like a good guest should. That's what I want to become to them—a guest. Unlike prisoners, guests can leave.

Meanwhile, I'm learning as much Russian as I can from Vanya and Clara. I'm picking up a lot of words. And every once in a while, I manage a passable sentence. When I'm not learning Russian or building my sham relationship with Vanya, I try to mentally take note of everything around me. I'll need details for my article. And the book that follows. I want to remember everything about this little world, even as I plan to leave it behind.

This is the most resourceful family I've ever met. I watch them reuse thread, patch their ragged clothes, make spearheads out of rocks. I watch the canoe take shape as Vanya and Marat work on it every day using old axes, their motions as careful as if they were making a giant watch. Chores seem very parceled out here: the women in charge of gathering firewood, cooking, and sewing, and the men in charge of hunting, fishing, repairing the house, boat-building, and chopping wood. I've tried my best to help out with the chores, and to stay out of Marat's way. Lately he's begun playing horrible tunes on some kind of hand-made wooden flute. I think they're supposed to be hymns or maybe Nine Inch Nails. Whatever they are, they sound like what hell must sound like to a new, disoriented soul. Late one afternoon, when he was playing his flute outside, I came out a polite distance away and sat myself down to listen, swaying to the music as though it actually had a melody. Marat glowered at me for a few moments, then suddenly threw his flute at my head. I ducked just in time, got up, and beat it out of there.

So much for that.

And Vanya. What interests him? Seemingly every-thing. He reads the old books in the cabin voraciously. He makes tools and slingshots. He plays with frogs. He hunts. He fishes. He can even weave baskets out of grass—which is evidently women's work, the way Marat, from his tone, makes fun of him. I suspect Vanya's mind is a teeming place, filled with crazy dreams and wild plans and ghosts and monsters and gods. I want to get to know this mind. I need to get to know it if I ever expect to know him. But that's no easy task. I know only a handful of Russian words, and I need to spend more time with him.

All of a sudden, the chance of that falls in my lap in the most random of ways.

On this day, I've helped clear the dishes, and Gospozha is sitting on a bench attempting to thread a needle under the flood of morning light. I watch as she tries again and again. Finally, Clara takes over. Both women squint and hold the needle and thread right up to their eyes, so close I think they'll puncture themselves. They murmur, as though trying to urge the tip of the thread through the eye. Even Clara gives up in frustration. I'm not sure whether it's through bad diet or bad genes, but the entire family seems to struggle a bit with their vision. Marat holds his whittle stick close to his face to examine his progress; when Vanya reads, his nose practically touches the page.

And I realize that the Osinovs seem to measure the precious salt grains by feeling them between their thumb and finger, not by sight. But how can Clara make those amazingly detailed drawings?

It's yet another mystery. Not surprisingly, I have no answers.

I approach Clara. "Mogu li ya pomoch?"

Can I help?

She relents. In two seconds, I thread the needle and hand it back to Clara. She draws the thread taut to show her mother that victory has been achieved, and the two of them chatter excitedly. Apparently, I've actually done something right. Who would have known that threading a needle would bring you such praise in this corner of the world? If I read the bottom of an eye chart, they would make me a god.

Gospozha gives an order and Clara bolts from the hut and returns with a small sack in one hand. She empties a quantity of grain out on the flat table. It makes a small hill, which she flattens out with the palm of her hand into the shape and level of a sand painting. The women look at me expectantly. I look back at them, not sure what I'm supposed to do.

Clara coos me an explanation. I stare at her blankly. Finally she gets up and returns with one of the flashlights, shining it on the grains. I stare into them, trying to see whatever they're talking about. I narrow my eyes. Some of the grains are black. I begin sorting out the black grains from the light brown ones, putting them into their own neat pile.

Apparently I'm doing something right because a delighted murmur rises from the women. When I am finished, Clara scrapes the black grains off the table with the side of her hand, gathering them in her palm and rushing out the door. After she leaves, Gospozha keeps sending me glances of approval. I suppose, in the Russian outback world, separating bad seed from good is like playing a board game by the rules. Family harmony ensues.

When Clara comes back in, the men troop after her. They lean over, inspecting the grain. There is a general family discussion in which they seem to forget I'm even there, but the tone seems happy, excited. As though they are discussing a warm Christmas. Marat goes over to the hearth and bends down beside it, retrieving a small box made of birch bark. It's grimy and streaked with black from the soot. He carries it to the table and takes out a chunk of flint. Marat looks at me, and it feels strange, watching his rigid face register a glimmer of enthusiastic intensity before it passes and his expression goes blank again. He holds the flint up to the window, turning it so that the stone catches the light in shimmers, studying my face to see if I understand.

I don't.

It's a rock, turned to the light. Glinting. I shake my head and turn my palms upward, feeling helpless and frustrated. Moments ago I was a hero. Now I'm an idiot who can't understand a simple rock language.

Clara has a brainstorm. She takes the flint from Marat, grabs my good hand, and leads me out of the hut, into the clearing by the side of the outside fireplace. She puts the piece of flint down near some stones and then backs up, sweeping her hand over the area and then looking at me expectantly. From a distance, the flint doesn't look much different from the surrounding rock, but when I move my head I catch the glitters of it. I look at Clara. She looks at me. As though she's willed it, I finally understand: the Osinovs want me to find flint for them. Evidently it's a precious resource, the way they keep it in a box and treat it like gold.

I nod, and she whoops and runs back to the hut with the news.

I thought I had trouble understanding my new family in Boulder when Dan and Jason moved in. That family was a walk in the park compared to my new hosts. Still I feel I have achieved some kind of major Viktory.

A few minutes later, Vanya has fetched what looks like a very old pickax, the handle worn and the blade rusty, and the two of us are on a quest. In addition to his other roles, Vanya must be the finder of flint.

I'm overjoyed at my good fortune. In those blogs about how to find a boyfriend, they never say, *Have incredibly sharp eyesight.* But they should have. Now, amazingly, the family is letting me go off alone with Vanya.

I'm determined to make some progress with him. I need to speed things up on this whole romance. Cold weather is coming. And my empty stomach hurts. I want him to believe I'm hungry for love, but the truth is, I'm just hungry.

The air is warm. The mountain is alive with flowers. Birds call, flying low over our heads. I duck when one swoops down especially close, and Vanya laughs. I like hearing his laugh. It's shy and high-pitched, like his younger sister's. I'm happy to get away from the hut and have some time alone out here, where I can pretend I'm out hiking in Boulder and a hot cup of cocoa waits for me an hour away. Vanya, it turns out, can make a sport out of anything. The woods have no internet, no *Grand Theft Auto* or *Minecraft*, so he makes do with whatever he finds. He shows me he can juggle rocks. He paces off and hurls them at saplings, where they hit their mark every time. He swings from branches. He makes a conch shell out of his folded hands and scares a bird off out of a low-growing bush. He is clearly flirting with me.

Maybe.

I point up at the retreating bird.

"Bird," I say.

He seems delighted by the English word. "Burr," he repeats. "Birddddd." His eyebrows furrow as he forms the hard "D."

"Khorosho," I say. "Good."

"Goodddd." He points at another bird. "Ptitsa."

I sound it back at him until it's right, and that's how we spend the next hour, hiking through the mountains and sharpening the languages between us, simple words that one day might join together into sentences, rough and scratchy but usable, like his hemp clothing.

Tree, blue, red, cold, wind, rain. We repeat the words back and forth, Russian and English.

He teaches me some words I already know, but I play along: *mother, father, sister, brother, baby.* When he repeats the last word, slowly for me, he rocks a pretend baby in his arms, and I imagine him performing that very task for his own little sisters, and it is with a sharp stab that I realize that one of those sisters, one that he knew every day of his life, is now gone. He looks up, notices my sad stare, and drops the pretend baby to hold up his hands.

"Chto takoye?" he asks.

What's wrong?

"Nothing," I say in English. "You just dropped the baby."

We're facing each other now. We point to each other as we continue learning: *hair, arm, splint, broken, eyes, knuckles,* and—I stop now; I know what I'm doing; just elect me Permafrost Tease of the Year—and slowly I reach out and touch my fingers to his lips.

"Lips," I say, touching one and then the other. They are remarkably soft after a life spent in such brutal conditions.

He's looking at me. He doesn't say the word back to me in Russian. It's as though he's hypnotized. I must admit the feeling of his lips is rather nice. And we're all alone out here, no Gospozha, no Clara, no Marat and his tragic flute. Gently I stroke his beard.

"Bearddd," I say. "Beard."

Suddenly he grabs my hand and pulls it away from his face. He starts walking again without speaking. I guess I've gone too far. Maybe touching a beard is second base in this country. I'm a Siberian tramp, a wilderness whore. I follow him until finally he slows his steps and I catch up to him. I want to tell him I'm sorry or explain myself or something, but I'm not sure if I should. I am hopeless at seduction. I will die this winter and be buried here and my tombstone with spell out, in Russian words: *Cock-blocked herself, starved, froze.*

Finally he points to a sunflower.

"Podsolnukh," he says, which either means "sunflower" or "a skank like you would blow a Yeti for a boiled potato."

I nod. "Sunflower," I say. I'm going to have to move slowly with Vanya, I can tell. *Tits* and *ass* maybe shouldn't be on the lesson plan for a while.

I go back to pointing at things and saying their English words. A little more friendship building here before I attempt romance again. We reach a stretch of rocky ground where the vegetation is sparse.

He stops, shows me his piece of flint, then sweeps his hand over the area. I scan the rocks, searching for a telltale glimmer as Vanya waits expectantly. I squint. I thought it would be easier, that I would triumphantly bring him to the miracle rock of fire and warmth and I'd be a hero. I look at Vanya.

"Kremen'?" he asks.

I don't know what he's saying, but I imagine it means, "So you are not useful after all?"

I shrug.

We walk another thirty yards and stop. I look again. This process repeats itself over the next hour, and I begin to understand why flint is so precious to this family—it is extremely rare and perhaps even extinct. A dodo bird of a rock. But suddenly I see something: a glimmer up ahead and off to the right. I start toward it, Vanya following me, his steps quickening as he gets close enough to recognize it.

He kneels reverently beside the rock. I sink down next to him.

"Khorosho!" he cries. "Khorosho!"

I raise a hand to high-five him.

He stares at me.

"High-five," I say weakly, then, "Never mind." I lower my hand. "Khorosho. Good."

He smiles. "Good."

He rises and gets to work, bringing his pickax down again and again, the heavy crack of metal against rock ringing through the forest, until he's freed a small chunk of the flint. We look for another hour, but I can't find any more. He says something in Russian that has a forgiving tone and holds up his sack and the heavy bulge the flint makes in it.

"Good," he says. Then he adds in rough but understandable English, "Let's go home."

I stop. I stare at him. I have never taught him those words.

"Hey, what the hell?" I sputter in English. "Where did you learn that?" By what sorcery has a Russian boy learned English in the middle of the Siberian woods?

People ask me what I would say if I met the Osinovs. I'd simply shake hands with each of them and say: Thank you for existing.

Dr. Daniel Westin
New York Times article

eighteen

Another week passes. My homemade cast itches my arm terribly. It's a long way from fiberglass. I find sticks in the woods to scratch under the cast.

I am officially missing now, along with Dan and the crew. We have not arrived back at the mouth of the river; we have not gone back to the hotel; no texts or emails or phone calls have been made. The secrets of our whereabouts lie buried in twisted metal. The signals are like flat lines on a heart monitor.

Yes, my mother—and perhaps Lyubov's mother, Viktor's mother, Sergei's mother, too—has no doubt sounded the alarm. The university has been notified, the US Embassy in Moscow. We're probably on the news. A search party is being organized. But things are not so simple. I am a tiny speck in an almost endless wilderness. The river is nearly unnavigable. And no one knows exactly where Dan was going because he was so paranoid about someone else getting there first, he kept his planned route to himself. The chances of me being found are about as good as those of this family being found—and since 99 percent of the world thinks they're a fairy tale, I have a pretty great chance of staying lost.

And so, the only strategy that makes sense is my own—to continue to make Vanya my friend, then my boyfriend, then my savior. He's obsessed with learning my language, pestering me with questions—*How you say this?*—and I can't help noticing, again, that his English is advancing far faster than my Russian. How is that possible? How does he suddenly come up with words I haven't taught him, then retreat as if he's been caught with his hand in a cookie jar? Has he ever even seen a cookie jar?

Late summer makes the woods beautiful even as it carries the warning, in the early morning frost, of the coming fall and winter. I can't get over how clean everything is, the smell of the plants, the variety of birdsong. The trees tower above me. Even the sky looks different, foreign, like the kind of sky that hangs over some undiscovered planet. I've never seen a plane in this sky, and I think the winters must be terrible indeed to keep humanity from wandering up this far, to see such beauty. I'm afraid of such a winter and if such a winter comes, which it will, and I am still here, I will be toast. A popsicle of a teenage reporter, frozen stiff on the ground.

I've gone a little feral. My hair is tangled. My clothes are filthy. I feel microscopic creatures crawling on my skin at night, and in the morning I scratch new welts. I imagine the critters passing the word down the line, using tiny iPhones: *American flesh, come and get it!* Clara and her mother go to the riverbank to bathe, in a place where the water pools and is warmed by the sun. One day I go with them, and leave my clothes on the riverbank as we wade in together. I feel shy, naked. Mostly because I am naked. The water is freezing. The women wash themselves with some kind of weeds whose roots make a lather. They offer them to me. The lather will never be bottled and sold at Nordstrom. But I feel so clean afterward that it is hard for me to put on my clothes. It turns out, though, that Clara and Gospozha have a surprise for me. After they dress, Clara reaches into a burlap bag and pulls out a set of jeans and a T-shirt, handing them to me. I stare at them, dumbfounded. These were the clothes that were in my knapsack when we overturned in the river. Somehow they have been recovered. I put them on, stretching the sleeve carefully over my cast. The T-shirt has the name of a coffee shop in Boulder.

Tears fill my eyes. I miss that coffee shop. I miss my mother. I miss Dan. I even miss my idiot stepbrother.

Clara and Gospozha seem confused by my reaction. They exchange anxious glances.

"Spasibo, spasibo," I assure them.

Thank you, thank you.

I have to leave. I can't live here with them. Can't die here with them. Don't they notice how thin I am? How thin they are?

I smile at them.

Every day, the family seems a bit more accepting of me, a bit more unguarded.

Except for Marat.

If anything, he seems more agitated around me. Angry. As though I had airlifted myself out here and plunked myself down in his life just to annoy him. One night I wake up from a dead sleep and look straight into his eyes. He's on his side, lying next to me, facing me, his eyes dark and unblinking in the moonlight. There's nothing flirtatious in them, nothing warm or friendly. This is a threat. My throat goes dry, heart starts up. He can't strangle me here, can he, with his family sleeping all around us? I shut my eyes tight, lie there shivering until I finally hear his breathing withdraw, and when I open my eyes again, I'm staring only at a wall.

I'm shaken by the weird encounter, but decide not to tell Clara or Vanya about it. What good would it do me?

Instead I resolve not to get in Marat's way and hope he decides I'm not worth harassing.

Two days later, I've been sent to gather tubers in the woods. They grow under some bushes with red berries on them that, through Gospozha's pantomime, I've been advised are poisonous. But the tubers themselves are harmless, and when added to soup, taste a bit like onions.

I kneel on the ground, still cold in the early morning, and use a small rusted trowel to find the tubers, my good hand moving speedily and efficiently. I've done this a few times now, getting better at gathering them every single time. Dan would have been proud of my trowel-manship.

I try not to think about Dan and where he is now, submerged in freezing water in his red jacket. There's nothing I can do about it.

Not yet.

When the bucket is half-full, I decide that's enough. I can always come back for more later. I rise and brush the dirt off my knees.

I hear footsteps, and look up expecting Vanya or Clara, but it's Marat who emerges from the trees and lumbers toward me. The hand holding my bucket trembles, but I force myself to face him as he approaches me.

My father once told me during a camping trip to put my arms in the air and make myself look big if a mountain lion ever stalked me. I don't think this is going to work for

Marat. Neither will climbing a tree or curling into a ball.

His eyes are staring into mine, and now he's so close that I can sniff the musky odor of his body.

"Privyet, Marat," I say in greeting. My voice sounds weak and scared.

He comes closer.

I take a step backward. The bucket of tubers slides out of my hand and falls to the ground. I keep backing up. Marat keeps moving forward. Finally my back comes to rest against a tree. I can go no farther. I decide to try to reason with him.

"Ty khochesh, chtoby ya ushla?"

You want me to leave?

He doesn't blink. His eyes seem to blacken.

"Ty ne mozhesh uyti," he growls.

You can't leave.

I recognize something in his eyes. It's not anger. It's fear. I realize that he's afraid if I leave, I'll spread the word about the Osinovs, and his family will be discovered. Then what will become of them?

"Ya nikomu ne zkazhu," I offer, trying to stay calm.

I won't tell.

I hold a shaking finger to my lips to show him.

His eyes darken.

"Vy ne mozhete uyti!" he insists.

This isn't working. I have to try something else. "Ya ostanus zdes," I lie.

230

I will stay here.

This seems to piss him off even more.

"Nyet!" he hisses, and shakes his head. "Nyet! Nyet!"

He grabs my shoulder roughly.

I scream. Watch his expression change to something like surprise. I take a deep lungful of air and scream again. It echoes through the trees. He releases my shoulder and I scream again.

This time, I hear answering voices coming from the cabin. Vanya's. Clara's. They sound frightened and uncertain. Marat looks toward the cabin, glowers back at me, turns, and disappears into the trees. I sink to the ground and burst into tears.

Someone's running up to me. I feel another hand on my shoulder. Lighter, kinder. I look up. It's Vanya. His sister hovers nearby, looking worried.

"Chto sluchilos?" Vanya asks.

What happened?

I struggle to stop crying, to catch my breath.

"Tvoy brat . . ."

Your brother . . .

I wipe my eyes.

"Nenavidit menya."

Hates me.

I expect Vanya to jump in, tell me no, of course not. But he exchanges glances with Clara. The two of them help me up, and help me pick up the tubers. Later, Vanya tells me never to collect tubers alone again.

I don't know what they think they would do to protect me. Vanya is strong, and even little Clara has a kind of catlike grace, but the muscle of the whole family together would be nothing against Marat. After all, look what he did to the crew.

I notice Vanya glancing at me more and more. I really do think he's starting to actually like me, and Vanya has the keys to the canoe. We have a broken language all our own, missing key ingredients that make a sentence a healthy, happy thing.

A prepositional phrase is replaced by a motion of the hand. Meaning is often lost. Sometimes we laugh at how ridiculous it is. I try to show him where I am from, a land called Colorado.

"Co-lo-ray-do," he says.

"America," I say, and he nods.

"Way over there," I add.

"Cold?"

I can't think of the Russian, so I say in English, "In the winter, yes."

He cocks his head. He may understand, may not. It would be amusing if the circumstances weren't so dire. Not so long ago, I had the power to say anything that was on my mind to anyone in the world. I had emojis and a screen and a lot of opinions. And now I am back to the basics again.

Pointing and drawing things in the dirt. And yet Vanya seems to listen more intently than the boys back home. And sometimes, I have to admit, when Vanya looks at me a certain way, I get a slight shiver. Like a tiny bit of Boulder snow has just been sprinkled on my head. But this is just the electricity of hope. The chemistry of being rescued, of getting away from this place and never coming back.

He wants to know everything about the world outside this wilderness. I tell him, with pictures drawn in the dirt, gestures, and with whatever words I have, about the twenty-first century. All the things he has never seen or experienced. Refrigerators, cars, spaceships, space heaters, televisions, dishwashers, microwaves. Just the appliances exhaust me. But there's more. So much more. Streets and cities and football stadiums and restaurants and coffee shops and the ocean and doctors and music and video games and voice mail and Christmas trees and alarm clocks and ice cream trucks and fireworks and candles and Band-Aids and M&M's.

In fifty years, I'll get to Spanx.

As I attempt to describe these things, they haunt me. A Kleenex is a tiny miracle ruined by snot. A lightbulb should be worshipped as a god. M&M'S are nature's perfect food. The thought of butter makes me want to cry.

I miss everything.

Vanya's eyes don't blink. He barely breathes. The modern world is a religion—dangerous, beautiful, fantastic—

and he struggles to believe.

He's never seen a dog in his life. He's never had to decide between paper or plastic. He's never been to get his hair cut, or used a crosswalk. He's done the things that boys all over the world do: skip rocks across the water, climb trees, whittle on sticks, learn to swim—but he's never gone on to Algebra or baseball or sexting. He's stuck with what he has, and I don't know if it's helpful or cruel to let him know what he's missing.

Could it be that Vanya wants to escape here just as much as I do? I can't imagine the woods and those few books can keep up with his seemingly endless curiosity.

He gets wildly excited when I tell him about planes. He points at the sky. "Ya vizhu, ya vizhu!"

I see, I see.

"You've seen planes?" I ask in bad Russian.

He nods excitedly, holds up three fingers. I'm hoping that, very soon, he'll also see a helicopter. The one that might come rescue me.

The one that might not.

One afternoon Vanya leads me to a place in the woods I have never been before. I can't really read the look on his face. We stop at a tree, it's half-dead, leaning a little.

"It's a tree," I say. "Apparently not a very healthy tree."

Then I notice that the tree has a hole in it the size of a basketball. Vanya reaches his hand inside the hole, rummaging around.

He pulls out a clothbound notebook and hands it to me carefully. It has Russian letters on the cover. I remember the words of Yuri from Dan's article:

The younger boy in the family stole my notebook. . . .

I open the notebook to the first page and see tiny, strict handwriting on it, margin to margin, careful use made of every bit of the page, in the same way his family consumes a rabbit or bird of prey. I look at the writing wonderingly, then back to Vanya.

"This is your writing?" I ask.

He nods.

I turn the pages. "I guess you stole his pen, too," I said.

"Stole?"

"Never mind."

I can't believe it. Vanya has been keeping a journal. On these pages must be life as he knows it. There must be secrets here. Lore. Amazing stories of survival and hardship. Vanya studies my eyes. I keep turning pages. Weeks, months, years. Then I see my name.

Adrienne. I had once spelled it out for him, with a stick in the dirt, and I can see he has a good memory. It's weird to see my name appear in ink on paper. As though affirming I still exist.

I see my name farther down the page. Then again.

Vanya is writing about me.

I see another word. *Krasivaya.*

Beautiful.

Is that what he thinks of me, or have I misinterpreted?

Quickly he takes the notebook away. He's seen what I saw. He puts the notebook back in the tree and starts walking back to the hut, his body tense, as though he's told me too much.

I follow silently. I wonder what is written about me in that diary. All I know is he's been thinking about me.

But there's something else on my mind today.

"Vanya," I say. "Mne nuzhno chto-to."

I need something.

We stand at the bank of the river. We've been looking for flint most of the day, and we've had little luck. So we've given up, and I've led him here. Downstream, the remains of the boat are still caught on the rocks, the bent frame of the engine visible just above the waterline.

I'm standing near the place on the bank where my body lay after I nearly drowned in the river.

I want to know if Vanya saved me.

I tell him the story of the tragedy in English, hoping he follows some of it.

"We were trying to get away," I say, pointing at the boat. "The boat hit a stone. . . ."

I slap my fist hard against the flat of my hand and Vanya nods, his face serious. I throw my hands in the air, spreading my fingers to indicate our flying bodies.

I don't know how to say *stepfather*, and I don't feel

236

like trying to explain the intricacies to a man for whom a blended family is one who adopts a bear.

"Dan," I say.

I wave my hand to where Dan's body still lingers in the freezing river.

Vanya nods. "Dan," he says. "Dead."

"Yes."

"Father?"

"No," I say. I think a moment. "Friend."

It's true. Dan was always my friend, even when I didn't want to be around him. Even when I made fun of him.

I kneel. With the point of a stick I draw the waterline and a figure of a girl beneath it.

The girl is me.

"Drown," I say, then pant as though I'm gasping for breath.

He looks at the drawing, then at me. "Down."

"No, not down. Drown." As I say it again, water fills my throat, because I remember it. The frantic clawing, the aching of the lungs. And then a hand clasping mine, pulling me out. Then nothing. Just blackness and waking up in the space where now I kneel, drawing another stick figure standing above the waterline, reaching down. With the point of my stick I approximate the two hands clasping, the savior and the saved.

I look up at him.

"Ty," I say.

You.

He shakes his head. "Nyet."

The answer takes me by surprise. "No?"

"Not me."

"Marat?" I ask, barely believing.

He laughs in answer.

"Right," I say. "Who, then?"

Vanya shrugs. "Tebe prisnilos."

"Tebe prisnilos?" I don't know the words.

His eyebrows knit together as he searches his mind for the English equivalent. "Dree-yum," he says at last.

"No, it wasn't a dream. I was really drowning. I didn't imagine this."

"Imagine?" Vanya says.

"Imagine is not real," I say, then give up. Sometimes it's exhausting trying to talk to Vanya. I stand and scuff out the line drawing with the sole of my shoe. The identity of the person who saved me from drowning is just one of the many mysteries piling on top of one another, like why was I born and why did my father die and why am I here in the middle of the forest, and what will become of me? But there's no time to ponder these questions.

The afternoon is passing.

Dan's body lies dripping on the bank. The freezing water has left him remarkably preserved. He looks like he is asleep. His boots and clothes are miraculously intact. His springy hair is drying. He looks peaceful, ordinary. Nothing to indicate terror or fear. For this I'm very grateful. At first, after Vanya had navigated by fallen tree limb and boulder to the place where Dan's body lay submerged and dragged it back to the bank, I'd avoided looking at my stepfather's face. But now I find myself stealing glances at it, curiously reassured, as I kneel on the bank and help Vanya dig his grave.

Vanya's wet with sweat as he swings his pickax into the ground and then tosses it aside, kneeling to help me dig out the loose soil. I have to work one-handed, but I haven't rested since we began, and we have made good progress. The afternoon is waning, the sunlight moving back up toward the low-lying clouds. A sense of sadness emanates from Vanya, although he has spoken very little since we started digging. Maybe Dan reminds him of the death of his sister, or his father, or some unnamed sorrow in his past, something involving a hard winter or a lean spring. Or maybe he simply realizes that if he loses his family, he is alone. I have told him Dan's name and age and that he was a "good man" and, when I didn't know the word for brave, settled for "strong." I lack the vocabulary to tell Vanya all Dan's peculiarities, the kale shakes and the weaving back and forth while in thought, the way he rose on the tips of his toes for emphasis and his habit of saying "you guys" and—my heart hurts—how he'd invite me to work with him in his garden, *Come on, kid*, an offer I never accepted.

The grave is finally deep enough. Vanya and I get to our feet. My legs are cramped from kneeling for hours, but I'm satisfied with our work. Vanya goes to get Dan and I try to follow him, but he waves me away. I turn, grateful not to have to hold my dead stepfather's feet. I have realized I'm stronger than I think, but I'm not that strong. I watch the river continue down its course as though it never killed a man, looking across into a bunch of mushrooms that grows around the base of a tree, imagining faces in those clumps as I try not to hear the sound of Dan's heels scraping the soft earth.

Vanya's heavy breath and then a body-shaped thump.

A few minutes pass as Vanya fills the grave. I hear Vanya stand up and knock the dirt from the knees of his pants. I turn around and there's no Dan anymore, just a patted-down mound approximately as long as Dan was tall.

I kneel and burst into tears. Vanya stands by silently. I take my good time, crying. This is Dan's funeral, and he deserved to have his family there, his friends and the colleagues who stood by him after Sydney Declay's article came out. And the Osinovs, the family that made him famous and then a laughingstock, should be lined up in the first pew. Dan deserves that. Instead, he'll get a few tears now, some grateful thoughts, and a cold riverbank for a grave.

Eventually Vanya wanders off. When he comes back,

he carries two sticks with him. I watch in wonder as he takes out Sergei's pocketknife and whittles down a point on one of the sticks. He trims a length of hemp off the bottom of his shirt, places one stick across the other and winds the strip of cloth around the place they intersect, forming a cross. He puts the pointed stick in the ground, finds a rock, and pounds the cross into the head of the grave.

I find a cluster of purple flowers, pull them up by the roots and lay them at the foot of the cross. I've finally stopped crying. Vanya and I stand looking down at it.

"Spasibo," I tell him.

Thank you.

He nods. He folds his pocketknife and grabs his pickax. Suddenly he stiffens. His eyes go wide. He looks up and so do I.

I see it, small as a bird in the sky, beyond the tree line, downriver but coming closer.

It's a helicopter.

The twenty-first century has finally arrived, looking for its lost comrades. Dan, Lyubov, Sergei, Viktor . . . and me. Vanya freezes for a moment. I do not. I bolt away, running down the bank, stumbling on rocks, my hands in the air, screaming at this tiny metal rescuer.

"Help me!" I scream. "Help me, help me!"

Vanya has recovered from his stupor and is chasing me. I hear the thud of his leather moccasins against the bank, and I stumble faster, arms wide, as the helicopter grows slightly larger in the sky.

"Help me! Help—"

Vanya tackles me. The weight of him cuts off the air in my lungs as we go down together on the bank, my cheek hitting smooth pebbles, my body flopping like a fish, Vanya's heaviness on top of me. His heart beating against my back, his breathing hard.

I can't move. My face hurts from the fall. My home-made cast is trapped beneath me, digging into my ribs. I try to struggle, but Vanya's holding me down. Everything is silent but for the wind and birds and river and Vanya's breath steadying. I have screwed up. Showed my hand. All this time I've pretended that I am totally cool with living off the land as a guarded pet of his wild family and never seeing my own family again. Totally cool with strange rashes and bug bites and bears in the woods and weird ghosts who appear in the darkness of the hut. Cool with the near starvation and the hard work. Cool with the fact that my friends are dead, that Dan is dead. Now he's seen me for what I am. A frightened person who just wants to get away.

His weight is painful. My cast hurts my ribs so much I'm afraid I'll cry out. But I don't. I surrender.

Finally he gets off me and stands. My breath whooshes back into the starving parts of my lungs. I rub my sore rib cage. He doesn't hold down his hand to help me as I stagger to my feet. I don't dare look into the sky, because his eyes will follow me, but I know that modern society is gone. It flew off somewhere to send a text or download a podcast or eat a Cronut, leaving us here several centuries behind, bitter, tired, alone.

Vanya's clearly pissed. If he had the English mastery I'm sure he'd snarl, *This is the thanks I get for digging your stepfather's grave.* He motions me with his hand and starts trudging up the bank in the direction of the hut.

I wonder if I've just completely botched my escape plan, if he no longer likes or trusts me and will no longer wish to save me. On the way back, I try to speak to him in English, then in Russian. He won't answer me. He stays several steps in front of me. He juggles no rocks. He makes no whistling sound at the calling birds. He kicks at no Siberian pinecones. I've taken away his playfulness with my traitorous pursuit of freedom. And I think to myself, how oddly nice it must have been for him to live so long without being suckered by a girl.

"You know what, Vanya?" I say to his back. "Sorry I tried to save myself. But I come from a place where winter means a Rag and Bone sweater, not death. Do you care that there's not enough food? Do you care I'm going to freeze? Or maybe that if somehow I do survive, your crazy brother will finish me off? Yeah, believe it or not, girls in America aren't that easy. You just can't bury their stepfather in a riverbank for them and expect to get in their pants." My voice is angry, my tone defiant. He glances back at me and keeps on walking. "Oh, don't pretend not to understand me. You understand a hell of a lot more English words than you're supposed to. Which makes no sense at all to me."

He walks a few more feet, stops, and turns around. We lock eyes. We are not friends. We are adversaries. Tarzan and Jane will never make Boy.

Vanya enters the hut, where Clara and Gospozha are immersed in their sewing. Clara puts down her fabric, comes and hugs Vanya, then me. It's nice to feel her warmth and joy at the sight of me. Something Vanya evidently doesn't share. Without a word, he empties the sack of flint we've collected. We haven't had a productive day, and disappointment shows on Gospozha's face.

"I eto vse?" she asks.

That is all?

"Prosti, mama."

Sorry.

She frowns, looks at me.

"Prosti," I say.

Vanya suddenly bursts into rapid Russian. His finger twirls in the air like a helicopter blade. Clara and Gospozha look fearful. He must be telling them about what happened earlier this afternoon, how we were almost discovered.

Gospozha shakes her head and says something I don't understand.

They go back and forth. I wait for Vanya to tell on me, let them know I was trying to escape again, express what a traitor I am, but evidently he says nothing, because they don't even glance at me. I can't really blame Vanya for tackling me. He was just protecting his family, trying to keep them a secret from the people who had come looking for me.

Finally Vanya and his mother finish their conversation and she goes back to her sewing. I'm not really sure what just happened. Why didn't he tell on me? Could it be that he might forgive me a little?

"Vanya," I say softly, trying to get his attention. I want to apologize, start over. I don't want to blow all the progress I've been making, earning his trust.

He doesn't look at me. He leaves the flint on the table and takes off out the door, closing it hard.

Gospozha and Clara exchange glances. There is nothing I can do except pretend that all is well. I make a gesture to help them with the sewing. Gospozha shakes her head.

"Nyet, pochisti kartoshku."

No, peel the potatoes.

She hands me a knife and points to a bucket of potatoes next to the stove.

After dinner, by faded light, I slip off into the woods. I

know Marat may be lurking nearby and I'm not supposed to wander off alone, but I'll take my chances. I still have an hour before sundown, and I make my way down the main path past the outhouse and keep going, following smaller paths until finally nothing is left but the floor of the forest. I remember a landmark of a rotted tree stump, find it, and continue on a few hundred paces. Yes, I remember that enormous pea shrub. Yes, that cluster of stones. And then there it is: Vanya's tree. The one that contains his secret writings. A shiver runs up my spine. I feel like some kind of deep-woods detective.

I look behind me and listen hard. No footsteps. I'm alone. And I realize how few times I've really been alone in the past month. Maybe I shouldn't have come here. But I want to see those journals again. Maybe there is some clue to Vanya that I can discover there. I don't even know what I'm looking for. Something that might explain how to get close to him again.

I turn and shove my hand into the hollow of Vanya's tree and feel around. My hand touches his notebook. I take it out and reach back in. I touch two more books, withdraw them. Stare at the covers.

An American in Russia: A Complete Field Guide to Familiar Words, Phrases, and Idioms.

Fifty Shades of Grey.

I don't have time to ponder the irony of a Russian hermit learning English from a field guide and a sex novel. I

realize that Vanya was there for the murders at the camp—
maybe not as a participant, but he didn't stop his brother.
He was too busy grabbing plunder. I reach my hand into
the tree a final time and touch something completely foreign in these woods. My breath catches in my throat as I
draw out the object and stare at it.

It's my recorder. Saved from the fire, intact. I turn it on.
The light glows faintly. I hear my own voice.

> *It's the third day on the river. Viktor's got his shirt off.*
> *He's really pale. Lyubov tells him to put it back on. Dan*
> *adds to the freewheeling sense of fun by staring grimly at a*
> *map.*

The recorder slows and stops. The light goes off. I have
lost myself. Lost who I used to be. I'm just a primitive,
dusty, tangled-haired girl holding a gadget from a distant
world. I stare at it. It's a hunk of metal now. Enough heat
and pounding and maybe you could make a spearhead out
of it.

"Adrienne." I jump at the sound of my name. Vanya is
standing there. I don't know when he slithered up through
the woods. He's caught me with all his possessions. The
ones he stole from other people. I'm suddenly afraid of
him. And yet, I'm angry, too. So angry that he's not what
he seemed to be. I hold out the recorder. "Why, Mr. Tech-
nophobe, would you hold on to this?"

He must understand at least the first word, *why*, because he lowers his eyes. "You," he says. "You speak."

"Uh-huh." My tone is completely lacking in warmth and civility. "And my friends speak. Who are dead. And my stepfather. Who is dead. I guess saving the solar charger was too much trouble for you." I let the recorder fall to the ground and pick up the books. "And these. These explain why you learned English so fast. And you're probably learning how to treat a lady too. What are you going to do, make me a pair of handcuffs out of vines?"

Vanya looks bewildered. I'm talking too fast for him to understand, I'm sure, but my tone is unmistakable.

I throw down the books. "You were there, Vanya. And maybe you could have saved them. But you didn't even try, did you?"

He is shaking his head. I can almost see the stream of language flood his ears and get tangled up inside him like panty hose in the dryer, knotted, useless. I speak slower.

"What happened . . . to . . . my . . . friends?"

His eyes widen as the words register. Then suddenly he lunges forward and grabs my hand, pulling me off balance and into the woods.

The Osinovs invite belief, not idealism. One day when I finally meet them face-to-face, I may find out they are not the family I want them to be, that they are the family they are.

Dr. Daniel Westin
New York Times article

nineteen

The cold water had preserved Dan. Sergei and the crew were not so lucky, as though luck of that sort would matter when you're dead. I smell them before I see them. The odor is terrible. The reek of death, that bracing rot, hits me before I even see the bank.

I stop. "I don't think I want to see them," I tell Vanya in a shaky voice.

"Come," he says sternly. He tugs at my hand. Reluctantly I allow him to lead me down through the brush at the edge of the woods to the bank where the bodies lie. I put my T-shirt over my face and don't care that this exposes quite a bit of my stomach. I thought they'd be naked, in the positions that they died in. Instead, they lie partially covered with branches whose leaves have paled into a sickly yellow. Animals have gotten to them, scattering rotten parts around the bank. I see bones. I see a scalp, a black hand with bones sticking out of the fingers.

I turn away and vomit. When I turn back, I see Vanya approaching the pile. His shirt is also pulled over his face. He reaches his hand beneath the branches, feeling around.

"What?" I shout at him. "Forget something? *Fifty Shades Darker?* Well, it's not there. Why don't you just leave them alone? Haven't you done enough?"

I can't look at what they've become. Instead, I rush back into the woods and lean against a tree, waiting. If I close my eyes, I know they'll be alive again. Lyubov reading her trashy novel; Viktor laughing. Dan gnawing on his pistachio nuts, letting their shells trail down the current. And Sergei. The smile he wore when he was flirting. Even his scowl of drunken intention, frightening as it was at the time, meant he was still warm and breathing. Still making mistakes and living to regret them.

Vanya's footsteps move up behind me. I'm not afraid of him anymore. Why should I be afraid? What is there to worry about now that everyone is gone? Why should I be the one left anyway? I turn around.

"What did Marat do?" I ask. "Smother them? Strangle them?" He squints at me, like my question is the eye of a needle that's too small to see. "Did you just watch him kill my friends?"

Finally he shakes his head. "No."

"YES!" We glare at each other. His face is red. There is no friendship in his eyes. We are enemies.

His breathing slows. A bit of the flush leaves his face. Never taking his eyes from mine, he offers up his closed fist for my inspection.

I look down at it. "Chto eto?"

What is this?

He opens his hand. At first I can't identify the dried-up and blackened objects. Then I see the tiny caps, the pieces of stem.

Mushrooms.

"Bad," he says softly. He thinks hard, struggles with the word. "Pizone," he says.

"Poison," I correct him in a whisper. I shut my eyes tight and see so clearly the four of us in a bar in Moscow, taste of dark beer on my tongue, Dan's unamused stare, and Lyubov and Viktor laughing merrily. *Someone told me there are magic mushrooms in that forest. Imagine the colors to see!*

I sink to my knees. My eyes flood with tears. A rush of pure guilt washes over me. I've misjudged him and Marat and the rest of the family. None of them are murderers. And they are only holding me out of self-preservation. They can't trust me to keep their secret. The people I have found, and who have found me, are not monsters. They are just a family who wants to be alone.

"What is the matter?" Vanya says.

I just shake my head.

On the way back to the hut, I ask Vanya about the story Yuri Androv told my father, how they kidnapped him, how he feared for his life, how he heard Marat telling Vanya he was going to cut his throat.

Vanya smiles. "Pravda," he says.

True.

"Pravda?" I repeat.

Vanya stops, touches my arm, smiles again.

"Marat khochet vsekh ubit."

I still don't understand. So he tells me in English.

"Marat wants to kill everyone."

I'm starting to think that even Marat is all bark and no bite. I ask Vanya more about Yuri's story. Yes, they did capture him. He was drunk. No, he didn't escape. They got tired of him, decided no one would believe his story, took him by canoe halfway down the river, then let him go on a bank.

I want to tell Vanya that I'll get drunk too, if his family will just let me go. But I like my other plan better. The one where I up my game by walking close to him and repeatedly touching his arm.

We're halfway back to the hut. Darkness fell as we walked, and now Vanya has apparently decided that we're going to camp here for tonight, on this riverbank. I wonder how many hermit-family rules we are violating right now, how many pages of the household Bible are curling with indignity.

Thou shalt not go off to clear yourself of murder and not return by nightfall.

Now that I've realized that the Osinovs are not going to harm me, I'm much less afraid of them, although I still have a healthy respect for their wrath, especially Marat's. Vanya sits me down on a large stone, rolls up another one for him, and goes off to scout for firewood as I wait and watch the evening sky. I've finally gotten used to my homemade cast, its bulk and unbending boards, although it itches a little. I find a stick to scratch under the boards and then contribute my homemade tool to the pile of kindling as I think of Vanya, immediate as the river, Vanya digging my stepfather's grave, Vanya innocent of any terrible act that would make him terrifying. Vanya who now returns with wood from the forest, places it down, and begins to arrange it.

I watch him work, the graceful way he moves, as though born to the woods and the harsh tasks within it. And yet, there is nothing primitive about him beyond his beard and clothes and his scraggly hair. I imagine him now holding the strange device to his ear and hearing my voice. That astonished expression at the tiny box with the girl's voice. Had he heard my voice first there, or had he been nearby in the woods, watching me, listening?

Something tells me that he has grown up in these dark woods and can easily lead me back to the hut without a flashlight or torch, by the light of the stars and half-moon, or simply by instinct. Maybe he has seized upon this occasion to be alone with me. I'm thinking tomorrow morning we'll be in trouble, though exactly what trouble means in this instance is unknown and probably unprecedented.

I try to tell him in Russian that I want to learn how to make a fire, give up and say it in English.

Vanya pauses, then nods, looking pleased. "Okay," he says. The night is cool but tolerable. An owl cries out. The leaves flutter in the wind and the river runs past us, calmer in this stretch.

"Vanya," I say.

"Yes?"

"I'm sorry."

"Sorry because why?"

"Because . . ." I wave my hand toward the miles of woods now between us and the bodies. "I was wrong about you. Wrong about your family. They are not monsters. They're a family, just like my family back in America. I should have thought maybe the crew ate something poisonous. I guess I was too busy looking for someone to blame rather than think maybe it was their own fault, that they died because they weren't careful. Maybe it comes from being an American, thinking when something bad happens, there's got to be a bad guy somewhere responsible for it."

His face doesn't change. It's hard to say whether I'm forgiven or that Vanya's concentrating solely on the task at hand. He arranges a few big sticks so they fan out from one another, then places the smaller sticks in the same pattern on top of them, until they form a structure about a foot high. He sprinkles the center of the contraption with a measure of twigs. His movements are easy, effortless. Vanya wears a sack around his waist that seems to function as a mini tool kit. He removes from the sack a tinderbox containing a piece of steel and a shard of flint. He finds a flat, dry leaf and sprinkles some dry moss on top of it, then gently lays it between us.

"Come," he says, holding his hand out. I move over next to him. Sit really close. Lean in. I feel the heat of his body. I smile very close to his face. Look him in the eyes until he lowers his own, embarrassed.

He demonstrates how to strike the flint against the steel until it produces a spark, then shows me how to catch the spark on the moss, stoking it with his breath until a flame rises, tender and fragile like a prayer from an unbeliever. He breathes on it encouragingly until it becomes a busy little flame, then suddenly blows it out, leaving the masterpiece to live on in a puff of smoke. He gathers some more moss, places it on another dry leaf, and then hands the tinderbox to me.

I like the perfection of the story he's telling me, one about the birth of fire that I understand from beginning to end without the use of words. I never knew that in silence, intentions could be made so clearly and simply and eloquently, and it's with this sense of wonder that I take the items from him and try to build a flame with what I've learned.

Clumsily, I take the flint and try to strike it. Nothing happens. I might as well be clicking two marbles together. Vanya laughs, the corners of his mouth turned up flirtingly. Making a fire, like the pottery scene in *Ghost*, must be sexy the world over. He adjusts my fingers and the angle of the strike, nods at me to try again. This time I produce a series of sparks that die in the wind. Vanya mutters something encouraging in Russian and shields the operation from the wind with the shell of his hands. I try again. Finally one catches, and Vanya helps me breathe on it. Gently, the flame so small, spreading, smoking, our faces close, the crosswind of our breaths encouraging the blaze to grow. We feed it slowly and keep breathing. His eyes meet mine. Slowly he leans forward and so do I, feeling the warmth of the tiny fire on my chest and under my chin.

Our lips are moving closer. In a moment they will touch.

"I like to bite those lips," he murmurs.

I pull back, shocked.

"What?"

His eyes fly open wide. He looks confused. He touches his lips. "Bite . . . lips?"

I let out the breath in my lungs. "No," I say pointedly. "You don't *bite* on the lips. You *kiss* on the lips."

"Yes!" he says, his eyes lighting up. *"Kiss."*

But suddenly I feel cold and annoyed. The moment is gone. *Fifty Shades of Grey* reached out its long, long paw and ruined it. When we get back to camp I'm going to burn that novel.

I've never slept in the woods before, not this way, without a tent or even a blanket. After we eat our dinner (some berries that Vanya scavenged), I close my eyes and stretch, the universal signal for *I'm done with this night*. The fire is strong and warm on the front of my body, the woods cold and dark on the back. I gather some ferns and pile them together for a homemade pillow, then lay my head on it, drawing up my knees. Vanya watches me, says nothing. He's seemed hesitant ever since our epic almost bite/kiss. A breeze comes up and I shiver. Vanya adds more kindling to the fire, but it's no use. The back of me is cold.

"Vanya . . ." I begin, but sigh. The concept of platonically spooning might take hours to describe, so I motion him over and make gestures and throw out words until he finally gets it. He lies down beside me and puts his arms around me. Immediately I feel the heat from his body.

"Good?" he asks.

"Yes, good."

I have to admit, lying in Vanya's arms could not be used as a torture anywhere in the world. I hear his breathing.

"Cold?" he whispers.

"No, warm." I wonder if he's searching through his mind for some more *Fifty Shades of Grey* pillow talk. *You're here because I'm incapable of leaving you alone.* Well, that's true.

All things considered, it feels good to be here, in the arms of an obscure Russian hermit, under the stars, crickets sounds, and wind through trees.

I hear a rustle out in the dark. Immediately my muscles tense, and Vanya's arms tighten around me.

"Medved?" I ask.

Bear?

He giggles. "No," he says. "No bear. *Belka.*"

"Belka?" I ask. "What is a belka? Never mind, don't tell me. I don't want to know."

Just before I fall asleep, I remember *belka* means squirrel.

My eyes flutter open. I jerk in Vanya's arms, my heart racing. The little girl kneels in the cold ashes of the fire. She smiles at me and says my name again.

"On idyot."

He is coming.

twenty

I'm getting a bit tired of the Zen riddles of a phantom girl. Does she mean rescue is coming? Or some other stranger from down the river? It doesn't feel like a warning. More like a present, by the way she smiles. Unless she's an evil ghost and wants me dead. Which would suck. I almost tell Vanya about it, then decide against. I don't know how he'd feel about his little sister appearing to me. I know so little, even after all these weeks, about this family and their superstitions and beliefs.

We wake up face-to-face in the morning, our arms around each other, our lips very close, but we do not kiss. The spell of night and stars is broken. Back in the morning light, I see him again for what he is: a way out of this world. Maybe I should kiss him, get this going, because I probably have only a few weeks before the first frost comes, but something tells me not to spook him, to be a little more patient. It was only yesterday that I tried to ditch him for the rescue copter. I have to reel him back in slowly.

Don't get too eager, said *Cosmo. Men are hunters. Let them come to you.*

When we finally get back to the homesite, there is a big uproar as the family spills out, yelling at us in Russian. Even Clara seems agitated, hopping up and down and flapping her arms. Most agitated of all, to my astonishment, is Gospozha. The old woman rushes right past her son and makes a beeline for me. She reaches me, puts her hands out, and holds either side of my face. I look at her and I see fear.

"Ty v poryadke?" she demands.

Are you okay?

It was me she's been frantically worrying about.

I'm so startled that I don't answer her at first, and she asks again, in a louder voice, her hands cold against the sides of my face.

"Ya v poryadke."

I'm all right.

She looks at me for another few moments before the fear leaves her face, and her hands fall to her sides. She looks at Vanya.

"Durak," she snaps. I'm not sure of the translation, but the tone is unmistakable. Vanya's in trouble for keeping me out in the woods overnight, beyond her protection.

I'm still reeling at the thought that Gospozha would worry about me. Strangely touched by it. This same mothering has been given to me thousands of miles away from a far different mother. And yet, it feels the same. A bit frosty, a bit strict, but the same.

Vanya's trying to give his mother what must be lame explanations, but she's not having them. I stand off to the side, my hands clasped behind my back, being as quiet as possible.

Vanya talks back rapidly so that I catch only a word here and there—*fire* and *grave* and *girl*—but mostly I read his tone, at first pleading, then defiant, and then back to pleading. I have to admit, he is a bit cute when he gets worked up about something. His eyes get bright, and the part of his face I can see that's not covered with beard flushes red.

Guys flush around the world. Families argue. Sides are taken. It feels curiously comforting. My stepbrother has made these same gestures, flushed this same color, when attempting to get the latest version of Call of Duty.

Clara has calmed down. She comes up and leans against me. I put my arm around her shoulders.

Marat is also quiet, though still seething. I have noticed

his lips turn pale when he is angry, and he tightens his fists as though he's about to get blood drawn from both arms at once. He glances over at me and meets my eyes, then looks away, and suddenly I wonder if maybe Marat is jealous. Marat must be lonely, too. Marat has no scowly version of himself to hold at night or hump against a tree. He has no one. All of them are alone together.

Finally Gospozha brings the argument to a screeching halt with a single hand in the air. She's done with this. Her son and the strange and possibly trampy girl are back and uneaten, and around these parts, that's a pretty good day. Or at least her expression seems to imply.

That afternoon, when I'm finished digging potatoes and have just washed my hands in the stream, wiping them on the dirty towel my shirt makes, Clara approaches me shyly. I start to get up but she gestures for me to stay seated on the grassy bank. She hides something behind her back and that, too, is a universal gesture. She has a surprise for me, a gift.

"So you're not mad at me, Clara, for running off with your brother?" I ask in English.

She smiles, because the sound of English always delights her.

"What is it?" I ask in Russian.

She shakes her head, laughs.

"Ya dolzhna dogadatsya?"

Want me to guess?

She nods.

I have some Russian words I learned randomly that I still haven't found a use for out here. I use them now.

"Zmeya?"

A snake?

More laughter. The gap in her front teeth would have been closed with clear braces had she lived in America, but I think it's charming and even pretty.

"Oleniy rog?"

An antler?

A head shake and a giggle.

"A Taylor Swift CD?"

She cocks her head.

I spread my hands. "Ya ne znayu."

I give up.

Her smile spreads bigger. Her whole body trembles. The Siberian winters evidently preserved her love of surprises. With a great flourish, she whips out some birch drawings and sets the first one down on my lap. It's Vanya, a new portrait that shows his longer hair. The details are amazing. It's as though her hands didn't need her near-sighted eyes and had their own internal guidance system. I look away from Vanya's face. Look back again. A shiver runs through me that I choose to ignore.

"It's beautiful!" I tell her.

She beams. She has another drawing. She leans down, places it in my lap.

I look down at it. All my breath leaves me. My heart stops.

It's my father.

twenty-one

Clara walks away through the forest. I follow her, the drawing of my father in my hand. In my shock and bewilderment, I've left Vanya's behind on the bank, but I'm not going back for it. I want answers, and the faster I walk, the faster Clara walks. It's a game to her. I break into a run and she shrieks with laughter and begins to run as well. But it's not a game to me.

Of course I have put two and two together: the drawing and the words of her dead sister, *He is coming*. And this isn't just some new wilderness riddle I can carry back and write about without ever having to solve. This is my life. This is my heart. This is my faith, so long abandoned, that the world lives on.

That he lives on.

That the hours I spent wandering the hills where his ashes were scattered weren't wasted but simply the beginning part of the trail that ends here, in the other world. If this is magic, I want it. I will pay any price for it. My breath is heaving now as I gain on Clara. It occurs to me that she's letting me catch her. Suddenly she turns and stops so suddenly that I run into her and we both fall in the ferns. She's laughing. Then she notices I am crying, and she stops. Her eyes widen. She touches my tears as though to confirm them. Speaks to me in the language she was left to speak alone when her twin died. Begins to cry herself.

"Vse normalno," I reassure her, wiping my own tears on my shirt sleeve.

It's okay.

I wait until she's in the sniffle stage and then I begin, in slow, broken Russian, to ask about my father. I know she understands Russian and speaks it perfectly, but she's always chosen dove talk with me, of which I don't understand a word. And I need to understand and I'm not leaving this forest, even if a helicopter lands right on my head, until I do.

"Gde on?" I ask.

Where is he?

Her answer is confusing. She points to above her and in front of her, into the trees, into the sky, then sweeps her arms as if to say *everywhere.*

"Did he speak to you? Did he say something?" My Russian is hurried and rough. Verb tenses all wrong, words left out. Clara seems spooked by my intensity, because she draws her knees up close to her body and hugs herself.

"Please, Clara!" I beg. But it's no use. She won't answer me. She seems distressed now. Maybe in her world, giving me this present is a tiny, simple thing, the Siberian equivalent of liking an Instagram post, and I've gone and made a big deal about it.

I look at the drawing again. Ashes and birch bark have brought my father back to life. I can see so clearly not just his face but his essence. The man he was. The lawyer and husband he was. The father and the friend. His expression is peaceful, contemplative, as one would expect it to be on a stroll in a forest so far from the world.

And yet, how? Is remote Russia where dead fathers go? I think back to the hand that grabbed my wrist. The large footprints on the bank. Was he the one who saved me from drowning? But how could that be?

Suddenly I'm no longer worried about bears or freezing to death or bugs or my clothes coming unraveled without a single Forever 21 in sight. This is news; this is big news. This is the biggest story of my life, of anyone's life. Maybe I've come all the way to the other side of the world to learn that maybe our loved ones don't die. Maybe they are still here.

Maybe death is not the end.

Maybe that sorority girl did not kill my father, just put him in a different realm that I can reach somehow out here in the wilderness.

I must find him. And I'm not leaving here until I do.

part three

twenty-two

The birch bark picture is hot as fire in my hand. I can't put it down, so I take it and look for Vanya. Tonight I was going to kiss him. In the morning I was going to make my plea for escape.

But this can wait. My father is here, somewhere. I approach Vanya while he's working on the canoe with Marat. They have reached the varnish stage. I have no idea what stinky liquid they've siphoned out of the woods and are now wiping into the wood of the canoe with the rough cloth that used to be Sergei's pants. Now I believe, looking at them, that Sergei wouldn't mind giving back in this way.

Marat gives me a dirty look as I approach, but dirty

looks can't stand up to seeing my father again. I ignore him, whisper, "Talk by water," into Vanya's ear, and walk quickly away toward the stream, wading in fields of sunflowers, their hairy stalks brushing my arms.

I sit down by the stream and wait.

It's peaceful here. Everyone busy with their chores. I stare at the water and remember all I used to think about was how this water flowed into the river, and the river flowed back to the world. Now I'm thinking about the mystery that lives here, and I'm shivering with excitement and curiosity and wonder.

I hear footsteps behind me, and then Vanya sits next to me. Splotches of varnish cover his arms and the back of his hands.

"I have something to show you." I hand him the picture.

He says nothing.

"Vanya, this is my father."

His raised eyebrows are the only indication that he's surprised at all. He studies the picture some more silently, then looks at my face. Back to the picture, back to my face.

"Your eyes," he says. "Same." Gently he touches my brow line, then moves his fingers down my nose. I can smell the varnish on his hands. It's sharp and bitter and a little sweet. "And here and here. Same." He touches my lips as an electric energy rushes through me. "But here, different."

"I have my mother's lips," I say, and I know this can't

continue, Vanya stroking my face and and talking genetics, always hot, but I need to return to the subject at hand. "I think when I was drowning in the river, my father pulled me out. Is that crazy?"

He thinks about this and then shakes his head. "No. Not crazy."

"I never told you this, Vanya, but I see your sister. Zoya. She comes to me at night. She talks to me. She's not a dream. She's real."

He looks at me steadily. His eyebrows don't move. Nothing about his face suggests surprise.

"Do you ever see Zoya? Your father?"

He looks uncomfortable, suddenly. "They are dead."

"I know they're dead, but do you see them?"

He takes a piece of grass and twists it idly in his hands. He seems to be weighing something in his mind.

"Tell me!" I insist. "Do you see them? Do you touch them? How did Clara know what my father looks like? Is your family magic? Are they sorcerers? Is that why your family is afraid of being discovered?"

He shakes his head at the words, and I'm not sure if he's denying this or if he doesn't understand the English.

"Vanya. *Where is my father?*"

The growl comes from behind us, distinct and human. It's Marat, and he's none too pleased to see us sitting together alone. He starts yelling at Vanya and waving his arms. I growl back in frustration. He really needs to chill out and maybe smoke a bong. Vanya sighs and stands up.

"I am sorry," he tells me, and the two of them walk away together, Marat still lecturing him.

Since I haven't run off in some time, Gospozha must be starting to trust me, because she lets me go by myself to look for flint. But I'm not looking for a glint of precious stone. I'm looking for a glint of precious father.

Straining to hear his voice. Calling his name. Looking up when there's a shift in the breeze. The flint glimmers. My father stays hidden. Silent. But I know he's here. There is no other explanation. My reporter's mind is fading. Reporters don't chase magic. They chase the truth. And to be honest with myself, I don't care if it's the truth or a lie, as long as my father can be as real and present as the little girl who appears at night.

When the family is off working, I sneak back to the cabin and go through their ancient books. Straining to understand the Russian. Looking for a spell or an herb or an explanation that would help me find him. And yet, I find nothing.

Two days pass. My cast is off, revealing pale skin and an arm that feels weak but serviceable. I'm not sure bones heal that fast out in the world, and I wonder if Gospozha's potions, or her prayers, should get credit.

The canoe is finished.

And yet, I'm not ready to go. My seduction plan is still in place. But for now, the goal is not escape. I need Vanya to tell me the secret of where my father is.

I find him leaning up against a tree in the forest, reading *Fifty Shades of Grey*. He's halfway through. I dread what this has done to his vocabulary and his perspective on women. He hears the sound of my footsteps and looks up wild-eyed, like I'm going to make him lash me with an elk tail or something.

"How is your book?" I ask in English because, let's face it, he knows English much better than I know Russian.

He looks at me suspiciously, as though wondering why I'm talking to him now. "Good," he says. He's searching for a word. *"Weird."*

"Yes, it's not quite Cinderella," I answer.

"Cinderella?"

"Never mind."

He looks back down at the book. "Some words don't understand."

"Like what?"

He points a fingertip to the middle of the page and sounds it out carefully. "Cock ring," he says.

"Oh, boy," I answer.

He looks at me, "Oh, boy?"

"It's jewelry," I say at last. I reach around in my shirt and hold out my necklace. "Jew-will-ree. Only it's for . . . for . . . oh *God*."

"God?" His eyes brighten.

I have to redeem my culture here. I mean, I'm all for free love between consenting adults, but *all* love in America isn't like this. "No. Listen, Vanya. This is not how all couples act, do you understand? A man and a woman . . . sometimes very *sweet*, very gentle, yes?"

"Gentle," he repeats, nodding as I stroke the air. I come up close to him and stroke his arm. "Gentle," I say. "No hit woman." *It's now or never, Adrienne.* I'm still stroking his arm. I move up to his face. "Gentle," I say.

He drops the book. He touches my cheek. "Gentle," he says. Our faces are moving closer and closer. It feels so natural, after all this time, just a sweet, gentle thing a girl and a guy do when they are standing alone in the shadows and the time is right.

My lips touch his.

Gentle.

Sweet.

I kiss Vanya again. It happens by the plank table when no one is around. It happens in the forest. It even happens one night in the darkness of the hut while the family sleeps. It's risky, to be sure, with Marat in the same room, but also exciting. Vanya has started to give me more passionate kisses. There is some tongue action.

I ask him, again and again, about my father. At first,

he won't tell me anything. Then finally he says: "Let's go."

"Where?"

"I want to show you something." His grammar is getting better than my stepbrother's. He takes my hand and leads me down to the river, and we walk up the bank, past where Dan drowned. We visit his burial site, where the cross is still standing. We pull some flowers—orange and white—and drop them on his grave, then we continue on. The rains have not come; the water is calmer and shallow enough to cross over to the other side before we get to the bank where the others lie under the branches. It's been almost six weeks since they died, but the slight odor of death still drifts across the river, real or imagined. If I couldn't see Dan's grave with my own eyes or those bones scattered on the bank, I could almost think it never happened at all.

I hold Vanya's warm hand and let him guide me around rocks and over tree limbs, watching my footing, making sure that I am safe. Occasionally we stop and kiss, and he brushes my hair away from my face. I wonder if I look half-savage now. My hair is tangled; my skin feels dry. My hands are thin, the knuckles pronounced. My fingernails are chewed. My eyebrows, overgrown.

"I need a mani-pedi," I say.

"What is—?"

"Nothing."

I'm so tired of waiting. So tired of going hungry. So tired of hoping. I'm going to make him tell me today if I have to wring it out of him with my bare hands. He knows the secrets of this world. Of the afterworld, and I'm not going back to the cabin before I know them, too.

Hours pass. Vanya finally leads me away from the river, up the hill. The leaves on the trees are turning yellow. They must still be green in Colorado. My mother loves the colored leaves of fall. It's hard to picture her face. She seems caught in another dimension. When I imagine her voice, it is vague and ghostlike. Maybe it's a trick of the mind but here, in these woods, my father is more alive than she is.

We plunge into a thicket of larch. The forest is dense and overgrown here. We stop, and I gather some berries nearby while Vanya draws nuts and slices of dried potatoes from a sack tied around his waist, and we eat in silence.

Here the trees are three feet in diameter at the base. The forest looks like it's been standing undisturbed for centuries.

It's time to bring up my father, but Vanya brings him up first, surprising me.

"Your father," Vanya says.

"Yes?"

"How did he die?" It is something, over the years, that I learned not to talk about, once I realized that the counselors were not doctors and talking healed nothing in me, just made it real all over again, and that well-meaning friends could hear the story but not feel it, and that I had to disguise everything to tell it, the black despair and the terrible, unrelenting rage so pure and so immediate that the sight of a sorority bumper sticker would make me lose my breath.

So I shut up.

There was a peculiar satisfaction I got from keeping the story to myself because whatever reaction I got was not the right one. Maybe there was no right one.

And now, telling Vanya meant I had to explain so many things first. What my father meant to me. What a district attorney was. What a car was. What a sorority girl was. What an ICU breathing machine looked like. What a court of law was, and what it meant to have a justice system fail you.

There's no way I can make him picture these things. So I keep the story as simple as I can. Using words and gestures and a stick that was worn down to the nub before I was done drawing and redrawing things in the dirt, I tell him about my father. I say his name. William Cahill.

"Moy otets."

My father.

"Moy drug."

My friend.

As I get further into the story, my voice begins to rise, thinking of how he died because of someone else's stupidity and carelessness.

I draw a car.

"Devushka. Glupaya devchyonka."

Girl. Stupid girl.

I imitate drinking.

"P'yanaya."

Drunk.

He nods, but does he really get it, not having ever been drunk, not having ever driven a car or even seen one before in his life, does he get how *stupid*, how *utterly selfish* it is to do both at once? I lapse into English now.

"My father was jogging down the road, minding his own business, and she mowed him down like he was just some animal, some *thing*, do you understand, Vanya? How she took his life? How she took my life? My life was over then. I had to make a new life and the new life is nothing like the old one. It will *never* be like the old one, does anyone understand?"

I get more and more angry, throwing the stick into the trees, pounding on the dirt meant for drawing, because I am mad, furiously mad, ragingly angry, still just as angry as the moment it happened. And everyone has wanted me to experience that rage, tell them of it in the context of moving on from it, like talking about how much I love my home while I'm packing to leave. I still can't say the girl's name because I don't want to see her as a person, know her a person. I don't want to believe she has an identity beyond a faceless drunk driver.

I scream and he screams too. He hates her too, hates her purely and with intensity. Finally someone hates her, too, because of what she took from me, because her story beat mine in the courtroom and in the press. Because she still has a father and I do not. I kick trees. He kicks them too. Birch bark crackles and falls, collecting like paint chips at our feet. I scream at the clouds and he screams with me. He hates this girl too, this girl I cannot and will not ever name.

Finally I can tell the story that no one wanted to hear stripped of its politeness and religion and context and civility.

Finally it's mine.

I lose energy and sink to the ground. He lies next to me, puts his arms around me. He feels the story, the gravity of my loss. He has lost people too, and maybe he can't name what took them, either.

We turn to face the sky, watching the clouds drift by together. He doesn't have to tell me he's sorry. He doesn't have to talk about the people he has lost. We've both lost people. We both wonder why. I've never thought of him this way, really, someone who knows me more than my own friends who still have their dads, their brothers, their sisters. Who haven't known loss. Right now, it just feels right to watch the clouds together, and remember.

We have finally reached our destination. Vanya guides me through a copse of dense vegetation and trees, and we are suddenly out on the other end, looking down at a chasm cut out of the middle of the forest. I look around, amazed. It's the ruins of some ancient civilization. Crumbling stone columns, carved statues, steps made of granite. Half-fallen structures that must have served as homes. I can see, even through centuries of neglect and overgrowth, the circular grid in which the village was laid out.

I shake my head. "Where did the people go?"

"I don't know," he says. He tells me, half with words, half with gestures, the story of chasing an elk all day through the woods with his spear. The elk eluded him but brought him to this ancient place. We wander around the square, whose edges of rock we can still find among the plants and trees.

A statue of some large animal still remains in the center of the square, although it has no head and the front legs have crumpled, giving the feeling of a creature bowing to the passage of time. I reach out and touch the crumbly shoulder. The stone feels like it might turn to dust. I wonder if the ancient people still live here as spirits, if they come to Clara in the middle of the night and beg to have their faces drawn. I wonder if they still have town councils, and if in the middle of this council, my father has appeared, some strange spirit from the other side of the world with a graceful way of speaking, and if he has the same attorney job he had in life, giving opening statements here, his voice echoing in the ruins as it once did in court.

Standing in this place makes me feel that everything is believable and happening at the same time. Our miracles are another dimension's passing days. Our love is borrowed and returned to those who come before and after us. Everything we believe is something unreal, and everything magical is something we can taste and feel, if we only try. And what we think of as news is only what we think we recognize as true. The real news, the real happenings, occur beyond our discovery. Whole nations have lived and died right under our noses, and we don't know anything.

I turn to him, stare into his eyes.

"Vanya," I say. I've been cautious about asking for this. Afraid he would say no. But now, I take the chance. "I want to see my father. Tell me how to see him again."

He blinks, then looks back steadily. His shoulders square. "Do not tell Mama I help you. Do not tell Clara. Do not tell Marat."

"Oh, sure, Marat and I hang out all the time."

He raises his eyebrows. Vanya has not yet mastered sarcasm and may never.

"Sorry," I say. "I promise I won't tell anyone."

He takes a deep breath and looks into my eyes. "I see Zoya. I see Papa."

It's astonishing to realize that, standing here with the

285

sun on his face and stone monuments of some lost civilization crumbling around us, here in these shadows and light, it would seem stranger if he didn't see them.

"When?"

He falls silent.

"When?" I ask again.

"Clara knows when they are coming. Clara is special. Zoya was special."

"Special, how?"

"They see things others don't see. Like my father. He see things. His people in Moscow don't like. They call him a devil."

It dawns on me. The old man did have special powers. He really was afraid to stay in Moscow. Dan was right, again.

"My father leaves," Vanya continues. "He comes to the river. He tells me one day, 'I am dying.' Zoya was alive then. He says, 'Zoya and I will die.' I say, 'Why? You are strong. Zoya is strong.' But then winter comes. They die.

"But—four times now—I see them. Clara knows when it is time. She sees signs from the sky. We gather on the stones and we see them. We touch them. Zoya and my father become alive again, because we believe."

"When will this happen again?" I demand.

Vanya is thinking. He counts on his fingers. Finally he says, "Seven days."

"Seven days?"

He's nodding. "Moon will be full."

"I want to be there."

He shakes his head. "You cannot. You are not family."

"I'll be there."

"No." He says it firmly now. I have seven days to work on changing his mind.

When we leave, we are different. We know each other. There are so many things that we will never understand from the world each of us comes from, but those things aren't important. We have more important things in common: wishes and feelings and prayers and love for things you can see and things you can't.

I wonder if my father is watching us now. Wonder if he can reach out and touch my face.

Seven days.

We walk back slowly. There's a crackle in the air. A distant lightning without thunder or rain. This seems to make Vanya anxious.

"What's the matter?" I ask.

He shakes his head, indicating it's either nothing or nothing he wants to speak about. But I notice he hurries his steps, and so do I.

It's late in the afternoon by the time we pass the encampment where the dead crew lie and my stepfather's grave. As we get within a few hundred yards of the point where the family's stream feeds into the river, Vanya suddenly stops and stares at the tops of the trees over the mountains, then breaks into a run, forgoing the bank and rushing up the side of the mountain as I scramble to keep up with him, and we rush together toward the hovering plume of smoke.

twenty-three

We have no time to talk. By the time we reach the hut, we must grab what we can—brooms and birch bark buckets—and rush to help the family defend their home-stead from the fire that crawls down the mountains, through the dry woods, straight for their garden and every-thing they own. I have never fought a fire before. I have no idea how it can appear in one place and then another. How it can grow and fade and bite your feet and be beaten down and spring back again. Frantically we carry water from the creek in any container we have. We beat at the fire with branches and shovels. We scatter dirt on the flames. Soot fills the air, and the sun sinks in the sky.

Slowly, we inch up the mountain and the fire retreats,

only to swell again when a breeze comes up and fans it. The woods, dry all summer, are crackly with dead leaves and bark. It is a forest full of tinder.

Smoke burns my eyes and chokes my throat. My hands and arms turn black. It's like being inside a chimney. I grab a bucket from Gospozha and hurl it at the blaze. Marat shouts orders and the family moves into a line, Clara at the edge of the stream and Marat and Vanya at the front of the fire, and we pass the homemade buckets as quickly as we can. I'm exhausted, but we can't stop. We battle for hours as the sky grows dark and our only light is the fire trying to eat us. Gradually, though, it begins to fade, sparking up again and then relentlessly beaten back, and now it's finally just a line of embers and a forest full of smoke. Together we move through the trees, stomping on whatever glows red and threatens us when the wind brings reinforcement.

It's over. The fire is dead. My throat is scorched. Tears of pain run from my eyes. My skin is blistered. My back is in knots from lifting buckets of water. We start to go back to the campsite, but we are too exhausted to go more than a few feet, and collapse in the remains of the faded sunflowers, five ash-blackened creatures lying as though dead among those wilted blooms. We sleep that way, in the positions that we fell.

We awaken at dawn and look at one another. Clara smiles. Soot is caked in her nostrils. Her teeth are stained black. She points, laughing at the way her family looks.

One by one, we join in the laughter, even Marat. We all look ridiculous and we are all alive.

We finally get the strength to stagger back to the hut. Gospozha lights the stove and Clara grinds the grain with a mortar and pestle and I go to fetch the river water that, when heated and added to the mixture, will turn it into gruel. Vanya lights a fire in the pit outside among the stones, a friendly fire that knows its place and does no harm. As the gruel cooks, we wash our arms and faces and hair in the stream. When Marat washes his beard, black water drains onto his shirt in a spreading stain. We all walk back to the hut. Gospozha stirs the gruel until it is soft. A measure of salt from the dwindling supply is added to the gruel in an amount that I know means celebration.

"We kicked ass," I announce in English. No one understands, but it had to be said.

The meal is divided into five bowls. The family takes their positions on the stones, and I take my usual position on the stone behind them. They bow their heads and Marat gives a prayer of gratitude and relief. Just as I begin to take the first spoonful of gruel, Vanya sets down his bowl and stands up. He leaves the circle of stones and walks over to me. He extends his hand. I don't know what he's doing, but I take it, and he pulls me to my feet. His family has been chattering nonstop among themselves about the miracle of their deliverance, but now they fall silent as Vanya leads me back into their circle and sits me down next to him, on the stone where Grigoriy used to sit, or Zoya. The Osinovs stare at me. Clara's eyes are wide. Marat opens his mouth to say something. His mother shoots him a glare and he closes it again.

We all eat together.

The days until the miracle pass slowly.

I can't stop thinking about what Vanya said about his father, about mine. I'm not feeling so good lately. My skin is peeling. I have sores on my feet. My teeth hurt. I know I'm missing some essential vitamins and minerals that could be found at any GNC, if any were local to the middle of nowhere.

Marat's nose is blistered, as are Vanya's hands. Gospozha thrusts a clean needle through the blisters and presses on them until they drain.

And we go back to work. We have to. When we look up, we see the first snowfall on top of the mountains. We have firewood and pine nuts and buckets and buckets of potatoes to gather. Vanya manages to kill another rabbit. It doesn't last long.

My arm feels weak but serviceable. Summer is passing, in a way that summer does everywhere—getting warmer and warmer until the day it will collapse and fade. More and more, I'm beginning to understand the gist, if not the details, of the family's conversation. I know they worry about Marat's last unsuccessful hunting trip and the effect the dry summer is having on the crops.

A bear has been hanging around the main river. They wonder if it's a sign of something, an omen. They see things in the sky: objects, lights. I know they are not pleased with this year's potato crop, and they dread the coming winter. Marat accidentally damaged the family Bible while trying to turn a page. The fragile state of the family book disturbs them. It is all they have of the word of God.

Gospozha is a mystery. She is very thin and yet incredibly strong. I've seen her run through the meadow with a full pail of water and not spill a drop. She's an avid fisherwoman but catches very little. She hums through her nose. She is a teller of stories, and as I listen, night after night, I start to understand that many of the stories are the same story told a different way.

There is Vanya's birth, which was difficult and almost killed her. There was the time Clara wandered away as a little girl and was not found for two days and yet was smiling, curled up somewhere, living on berries. And the terrifying tale of the time a white wolf jumped at the old man and would have landed on him had Marat not killed him with a spear through the heart. She is obviously revered and adored by her family. Marat is the leader, but she can cancel that leadership anytime she wants and put him in his place, take his car keys, so to speak, and show him who's boss.

Marat is still scowly and unfriendly to me. Also, he's super opinionated. When Clara reads aloud from the Bible, Marat will correct her from across the room. Evidently there are right ways to harvest and pray and hunt and whittle, and Marat is certain he knows them all. And yet, he is tender with his sister. He never goes to sleep without kissing his mother good night. And I have seen him fish meat from his own bowl with a spoon and dump it into one of the women's bowls. He even puts up with Clara's playfulness. While the rest of the family, heads bowed, listens to one of his interminably long family dinner prayers, Clara will open one eye and spider her fingers down the table and up his arm. Eyes still closed, he will patiently catch her hand to stop it and hold it steady, his prayer never missing a beat.

It is clear he still doesn't like me and considers me a danger. Sometimes he'll point at me and then point out the window into the sky while spewing in Russian. *They're going to come for her and discover us.* His meaning is clear even if every word is not.

And Vanya. I woke up last night and sat up against the wall. Saw that he was awake and looking at me across the dark room from the floor where he lay next to his brother.

And we just looked at each other over the the sleeping bodies of the family. And a warmth went through me, down my arms, into my hands. All this time, I've been pretending I like him. Using him to get back to Colorado, back to my father. But what if I do really feel something for him?

Three days now, until the moon is full.

The nights are getting cold. In the daytime, the sun fills less of the canyon by the river, and fishing is a shadowy business. I've learned to cast nets, a chore that both the men and women share. Nine times out of ten, they are empty when I bring them up. Vanya communicates to me—in that hybrid language we call Vandrienne, Russian and English and gestures and expressions, a language choking on the dust of trampled grammar but in which meaning is miraculously preserved—that in the old days, the fish were plentiful but somehow they went away. They are like ghosts now, and their silvery fins are greeted with joy and respect. Every bit of them is eaten. The head and the flesh and even certain organs. The skeleton and fins are boiled into a soup stock.

I am growing even thinner. My clothes hang on me. Gospozha gives me a length of rope to hold my pants up. One day, I open the door and find the women sewing something at the table. Clara spies me and shrieks, and they quickly put the item away. I'm guessing they are making me a dress, and though it doesn't seem like it would be very warm, I'm touched by the gesture.

I can't talk to the women about the usual things: What kind of purse goes with a belt, the annoyance of the shampoo always running out before the conditioner, the folly of trying to find a hunter-green shirt when it's not in fashion this season. The fact that the aluminum in deodorant might kill you but it just works so well. Music, movies, politics, global warming. How could they know that in the thirty years since their vanishing, the population has doubled again?

They don't know that Princess Diana has died or about 9/11, the rise of the internet, the stock market crash, the housing market bubble. The world as I know it is outside their understanding and experience.

But basic things join us: the need for food and warmth and stories, appreciation of flowers, the craving for salt when salt is scarce. The need for love. The habit of making work go faster by singing. The desire for solitude and for company. The appreciation of summer beauty. Reverence for the dead. And occasionally, laughter. Once in a while, I do something that makes them inexplicably laugh, or they do something that makes me laugh, or someone laughs and it spreads fast. At those times, we need no language. Everyone understands it. People laugh when they are safe. And that's how I suppose I'm beginning to feel here. It's the real world that seems dangerous.

Clara and I have wandered far from the hut, looking for a certain wildflower that her mother likes to boil into a poultice that seems to ease the stiffness in her knees. I've seen the wildflower from time to time, but now the season seems to be fading, and we walk farther and farther downriver in search of them. We reach a meadow covered in white flowers, with apparently nothing to offer except the beauty of blooms, because Clara doesn't pause to collect them. Clara takes my hand as we wade through them. She's not very talkative today. She seems content just to be out in the woods with me.

I'm thinking about Vanya. The way he looks at me. Studying me up close. The thought of him is still confusing, half-formed. Like other things. Maybe I'm not getting the right vitamins, because my mind is playing tricks on me. Shadows move, take vague human shape and disappear. Last night when I was drawing water from the river, I thought I felt a hand on my shoulder. I looked around and no one was there. I'm not sure what is real and not real, and that includes my attraction to Vanya. I've been away from everything so long, zero communication, no email, no text. No nothing. Have I gone crazy out here?

Halfway through the meadow, Clara freezes and drops my hand. Her eyes grow wide, and my heart begins to pound. There's an electricity in the air, like the kind you feel before a great clap of thunder.

Is he here? Has Clara led me to him at last?

"Daddy?" I murmur.

Clara looks at the sky and I watch, too. We wait.

Then I see it.

It's not the spirit of my father descending from a cloud to give me comfort and astonished joy.

It's a helicopter.

Instead of relief, I'm filled with panic. I have to get away. They can't find me, not yet. Not before the full moon and the ritual. Clara and I rush toward a large bush near the edge of the meadow, diving into it, branches breaking and quivering around us. We lie on the ground, spooning, making ourselves small, very small, each of us holding our breaths as we hear the sound of the blades grow louder, lingering over our head.

Finally the sound of the helicopter fades, and we are left in silence. Clara and I crawl out from under the bush. She looks at me, wide-eyed, releasing a stream of quizzical coos. I'm guessing she has never seen a helicopter, or an airplane, for that matter. I try my best to explain in limited Russian. I clear a place on the ground and draw a stick figure of the helicopter and the people in it.

I try to tell her it's okay. The helicopter is gone, and we are safe.

But are we? Maybe the smoke from the fire has alerted someone to our position. Maybe they are coming back. But they can't. Not yet.

The full moon is two days away.

She takes my hand, and we keep walking. We find the medicinal flowers half an hour later, at the next meadow over. Clara seems subdued, troubled. She barely speaks as we walk home together. I think she will give the family the news of the strange sighting as soon as we are through the door, but instead she puts the flowers in her mother's lap and accepts her smile of approval.

It is only later that I realize that Clara isn't stupid. She knows that the helicopter full of people might be searching for me and to tell her family this would not be good news to them.

I wait until nightfall, crawl over to Clara, and whisper, "Thank you," into her ear. Her eyes open. She pats my cheek. Her eyes close again, and I crawl back to my corner of the room.

Was the helicopter even real? Or just another apparition?

Day 6.

Tomorrow the full moon rises. Tomorrow is the ritual. The one I've been left out of. I beg and plead with Vanya in the woods, hidden safely in the middle of a group of red-berried bushes. Finally he bursts out, "I can't help you! I do not decide! My mother decides!"

"What?" I gasp. "Why didn't you tell me earlier?"

He looks guilty. "I like the kisses," he admits.

I snort in disgust and stand up. "You are a typical man, Vanya. And that's not a compliment."

He looks at me quizzically. "What is 'typ-i-cal'?"

"Look it up."

I storm away. The truth is, I haven't regretted the time I've spent kissing Vanya. Far from it. In fact, other than the desire to see my father, I've found my other preoccupation is Vanya himself. His insatiable curiosity. The way he puts English words together. His accent as he says them. The way he makes toys out of sticks for his sister and cocks his head to listen to his mother. The way he and his brother fall into rhythm as they chop wood together.

The kindness in his eyes.

His laugh, so clean and pure, it would work in the streets of Boulder, or on a lifeboat, or in outer space. It would work anywhere.

His smile.

The touch of his lips.

Perhaps I'm losing my mind.

Or falling in love.

Or both.

In all my time here, I have not had a single private conversation with Gospozha. There's still something unreachable about her, intimidating. And I know she knows about Vanya and me. She's his mother. She knows everything.

Tonight, when she quietly leaves the cabin, I follow her. Find her in the middle of the meadow, her back to me, gazing out into the trees. Somewhere in the dark, in that direction, lie the graves of her husband and daughter. I wonder if she's thinking of them.

I head out to her, wading through sunflowers, the moon almost full over my head. The air moves through my shirt, makes me shiver. She doesn't acknowledge me when I reach her. Says nothing as I stand beside her, my arms crossed, my breath making mist. I almost lose my nerve and head back to the cabin. But I force myself to speak.

"Moy otets zdes'."

My father is here.

I look sideways at her. For a long moment, she doesn't react. Then, slowly, she nods.

"Ya khochu uvidet' yego."

I want to see him.

No reaction now. Complete stillness. I hope she is not silently calling her owl to come kick my ass. I try to keep talking, in Russian, but I stumble. So many words I don't know. And so I talk in English, hoping that the magic that seems to hover all around us will enter my words, my voice, make it all understandable. "I know some things about your family. That you left Moscow years ago because you had special powers and no one understood you and people were afraid of you. And now people are still afraid of you. I'm not afraid of you. I understand you. I know that you have lost people and found a way to find them again."

I say the names of her loved ones. Say them with reverence.

"Grigoriy. Zoya."

With each name, she closes her eyes and then opens them.

"I know they're coming back tomorrow night. Vanya told me. My father died seven years ago. I think he is here now. I want to see him, too."

And then I say his name.

"William."

It shivers in the air. It was his name and saying it means hearing his voice and watching him tie his jogging shoes. Saying it hurts and helps.

"Please let me see him. Just one more time. I believe."

I say the last two words in Russian. "Ya veryu."

She says nothing. I'm not even sure she's understood. I don't know what else to say. I want to add, "Pozhaluysta"—*Please*—but it seems wrong. Like begging. Finally I walk away.

I'm heading back to the cabin, head down, when she calls my name. "A-drum."

I realize I've never heard her say it before. She pronounces it like Clara does.

I turn around.

She looks at me for a long moment.

"Khorosho."

Yes.

◈

Clara wakes up all excited and talks to her family, too fast for me to follow.

All day long, I go about my chores with a gathering sense of bewildered excitement as I watch the family. They're different. Lighter. More prone to laughter. Marat seems just on the edge of his first good mood. He blows cheerfully on his flute. I wince. He never gets better.

Near nightfall, as the air chills and the owls come out and the full moon rises, Clara returns from the forest with a small sack that the family keeps glancing at all through dinner. Clara keeps jumping up and looking at the sky and streaming some kind of live dove news that seems to further animate the family. I have no idea what's going on, and no one will tell me.

Later that night, Marat lights the fire outside while Clara dumps the contents of her sack into a boiling pot of water on the stove. Gospozha stirs the pot; I lean in for a glance. The water smells earthy. I wrinkle my nose. Gospozha waves me away. After several minutes of a hard boil, she removes the pot from the fire and sets it aside to cool. Clara runs to the window again. She can barely contain herself. She throws her arms around her mother's neck.

The tea is poured off into bowls. We carry them to the men, who are sitting on the stones, then join them with our own bowls. There is barely any wind tonight. The fire burns evenly, warming our faces. This is a tame fire, not like the wild fire that almost ate our lives. It's like fighting a ferocious wolf in the woods and then going home to pet the dog.

Everyone looks at Clara as though waiting for a sign. I glance sideways at Vanya. His face is intense. Finally Clara nods and lifts her bowl to her lips. The rest of us follow her, drinking the liquid, which tastes terrible, like dirt. We look at one another. We wait.

The firelight curls, straightens. My head feels light in the center, as though that part of my brain has turned to froth. My eyelids flutter. The fire is now blue at the edges. It's half a fire and half a body, moving and dancing.

I notice everyone is looking up at the night sky. I look up, too, and gasp. A brilliant yellow light undulates like a snake; from this light springs a red light. Like waterfalls of colored mists, they play together. The murmurs of the family around me prove that I am not imagining this, that everyone sees the same thing. Clara reaches her hands to the sky. We all do, as the lights spread out as though they have wings now, then fold back into one another. Purple emerges. Orange. Green.

Under this light, I feel joined not just with the family, but with the woods and the sky and the world. It's all the same fabric now, something where nothing is lost and no one is strange. It's an eternity of the familiar expressed in colors. I speak to the people around me in the circle, in a language of silence. I understand them perfectly, their fears and their longings and all the things they've dreamed about with me in the darkness of the hut. I know them, and I am not alone. I'm one of them, one of everyone and everything. The lights above us descend. The fire reaches out for them and then we are all enveloped in colored light.

Clara turns and cries out. I follow Clara's gaze and then I see her.

It's the little girl with the rosy-lipped smile.

Their sister, my sister.

Just behind her is an old man. He is thin. His beard is full, but his hair is cut short. His back is straight; his steps are light and easy.

There is nothing about their appearance that would indicate they're anything but flesh and blood. They look like they've been out for a stroll and now they are coming back home.

"Zoya!" Clara cries. "Papa!"

The family shouts out ecstatic greetings and rushes to them, surrounding them. They are jubilant, embracing. I stand there, dazed, watching them. It's not that I believe. I don't have to. I'm here. I'm a witness. This is fact, as surely as it's fact that I am alive, that I move and breathe. The miraculous is as real and basic and crucial as a pile of salt or a threaded needle.

I don't have to believe or not believe. I am right here, experiencing it. I'm a part of it, a part of everything.

Zoya notices me. She breaks free of the family and comes to me and holds her arms out. We embrace. Her body is solid, and has the scent a little girl would have after running in the woods, sweaty and warm and alive. I can feel the beating of her heart as I hold her against me, the rest of the family making a circle around us. Clara cries with joy and the mother is reaching out to stroke Zoya's hair, whispering, "Moya malyshka, moya malyshka."

My baby, my baby.

I am not afraid. This feels natural. An ordinary visit on an ordinary night.

The little girl whispers into my ear, *He is here*, in a language made of all the languages, and she turns me around.

My father is standing there in front of me.

He is alive.

He is that same exact man taken from me when I was ten. He's wearing the same jogging shirt and shorts. His hair is as it was that night, growing out, the top a little curly.

For a moment I stand frozen in place. For so long I've waited for him, hoped for him, and now it seems too good and real and natural to be true.

"Dad?" I whisper.

He smiles. "What did I miss?"

Tears run down my face. "Everything." I rush to him and throw my arms around him, feeling his stubble against my cheek and the warmth and substantiality of his body as he holds me.

"Adrienne," he whispers. "The messes you get into." That lighthearted voice has not lost its tone in seven years. It's traveled thousands of miles to tease me.

"Is it really you, Daddy?" I ask him, ear against his heartbeat, nose against his shirt that smells of his jogging sweat. I'm afraid to let go. Afraid that I'm only holding cold night air in my arms and I'll realize that at any second. And I can't bear it. I can't bear to wake up in this moment alone and cold in Siberia without him.

"It's me," he reassures me, and he's still real and still warm.

I release him and look up at his face. "I have so many questions. So much to tell you."

"I already know."

"But where have you been?"

"With you."

"Here?"

"Everywhere."

He strokes my hair and kisses my forehead. He whispers in my ear. "You've found me again. Now go home, Adrienne. Go home to your family, or you'll die here this winter. There's not enough food for you. There's not enough food for them with you here, either. Go home, because you have a story."

"The story of the Osinovs?"

He shakes his head. "The story of you."

"Me?" I'm puzzled. "I don't understand."

He smiles. "Your story is forgiveness."

I'm dumbfounded. "Forgiveness? Of what?"

Somewhere the other family members are still embracing, rejoicing. But now my father and I are locked in our private conversation.

"Say her name," he says. "Say the name of the girl who killed me. Because I forgive her. And everything is good."

This is the last message I expected.

"But Daddy—"

His voice is kind, but he's not asking. This is an order. "Forgiveness is your story."

twenty-four

The next morning, I wake up in the hut, staring at the ceiling. I'm not sure at first if I imagined it all. I blink. My eyes adjust to the old beams of the ceiling. The family stirring, the light coming in.

No, it was real. It happened.

Our loved ones are gone, but only gone in a way that water is gone when it turns to vapor. The people in the small hut share a sleepy contentment. I'm filled with a peace I haven't had in years. I saw my dad last night. He spoke to me. He was alive and no one can tell me different.

Clara goes with me to fetch the water, holding my hand. I want to tell her about the night before, how it made me whole again, and thank her so much for the gift of my father, but I sense that this is something not meant to be spoken of by light of day, so I say nothing. Instead we sing the Rolling Stones song I taught her, "Ruby Tuesday."

Clara understands the melody if not all the words. "Goo . . . dy ooby dooday, oo koo put a nae don oo . . ."

The air is crisp and cold. I am the happiest that I can ever remember being since my father left me.

But he didn't leave.

This is the truth I've found out here, with this family and with this girl.

"Ya schastliva, Clara," I tell her as we dip the water.

I'm happy.

She looks at me, eyes wide. Smiles. Answers me in a sweet burst of dove talk, and we walk back to the hut together.

As the sun goes down, my good mood fades. The potatoes are small. Some animal got into the stored nuts. And the fishing net was pulled in full of fish, whose weight broke the twine, and they all escaped. It's time for me to leave. And I'm beginning to realize something.

I might be falling for Vanya.

Maybe I never realized it fully before, but now that it's time to go, it hits me. It's not like in America where we can text and FaceTime until one of us takes a plane to the other. This is a different world I'm going to. And it's quite possible when I leave that I will never see him again.

I know now that my father is with me always. But Vanya is here, in the wilderness, in the legend of the Osinovs. And I can't stand the thought of leaving him.

His family isn't stupid. They know about us just as certainly as they know a wolf is nearby, or a squirrel is on the roof, or it's about to rain. How could they not? Today at breakfast Vanya and I held hands openly in front of the family. Marat looked on with clear disapproval but said nothing. He and I have an unspoken agreement to leave each other alone, and that is fine with me. In another world, Marat would be living in another state with his family and we'd talk perhaps twice a year and exchange terse Christmas cards.

According to my original plan, now is the time to go to Vanya and ask him to secretly take me back down the river in his new canoe.

But I am done with secrets. Maybe because of all my work trying to gain the family's trust—the help in the garden, the searching for flint, fighting alongside them to defeat the fire—I have a place at the table now. I have a voice, and I'm going to speak for myself.

That night, after dinner, whatever dinner it was, there and then gone in a few moments, I speak.

"Ya khochu chto-to skazat."

I want to say something.

My voice is calm, but my heart thumps. The family looks at me, surprised. It's still strange that I'm sitting with

311

them and not off in a chair. And now I want to actually speak. What next, my own room?

I go on, in broken Russian, hoping the words are in the right place, in the right tense. Knowing they probably are not, but hoping the family will understand.

I used to be afraid of you. I didn't understand you. But now you've become my family, and I love you.

The family is motionless around the table. No one says a word. Vanya's eyes blink when I say, *I love you.* I look at him when I say it. Hold my gaze on his face.

Then I go on.

I have another family that I love. A mother. A brother. They are looking for me. And I must go to them. Winter will be here soon. There is not enough food for all of us. I might die. You might die.

Vanya and Marat exchange glances.

I need to leave here. I need Vanya to take me back down the river.

"No!" Vanya cries suddenly, but his mother holds up a hand to him. A tear suddenly darts down Clara's cheek.

You are my family. You are my secret. I will never tell the secret. I will protect you. I am a reporter, but I will lie for you. I promise you. I swear to you. They will never find you if you let me go.

No one says anything for a long moment. Finally Vanya reaches across the table and takes my hand. Clara cries silently. Gospozha nods. I look at Marat, expecting an outburst of anger and disapproval.

He looks at me and shrugs.

It's the closest thing to a smile that he will ever give me.

I'm leaving. Not under the cover of the night, not breathing hard and looking over my shoulder. I'm leaving because my new family wants the best for me, and for them. So why am I devastated?

I look around the faces at the table and burst into tears. I get up and rush from the cabin, run through the field of dying sunflowers, find the creek, shiver under moonlight, hugging myself, still crying.

Vanya comes up behind me.

"What's wrong?" he asks.

It's time for the truth. He deserves it. I turn and face him.

"Vanya, I love you."

He looks absolutely stunned.

I reach out and touch his face. "Love is a very easy thing in America. Because you already have enough food and enough clothing, and you're not about to burn up in a forest fire or be eaten by a bear. So I guess I didn't recognize I loved you at first. I was too busy surviving. And you know what, my grip on reality is definitely slipping. Or maybe reality itself isn't all that real. But yes, I love you and that's the truth."

I'm not sure how much he's followed, but he leans forward. Our kiss increases my shivering.

313

"I love you, too," he says when we pull away from each other. "Adrienne, don't go."

"Well, if you love me, you have to understand that I need to go home. I have a mother. I have a brother. I have a life. Winter's almost here, Vanya. And you know what I said at the table is true. There's not enough food."

He is silent. I think I hear a faint growl moving in his throat as though what I just said is an animal he can scare off.

"Vanya, do you understand?"

"I can keep you alive," he answers stubbornly. "I see moose tracks. I see deer tracks. . . ."

"I don't care!" It's our first fight as a couple, on the subject of my very survival. "Vanya, touch my arm."

I offer it to Vanya. "You feel the bone, don't you? When I came here, there was no bone. Now I'm skinny. More bones will show."

"Okay," he says at last. "I will help you go back."

"Thank you." I put my hands on the sides of his face, draw him forward, and kiss him tenderly. That particular combination of soft lip and scratchy beard seems suddenly impossible to replicate, even among the hipster baristas of downtown Boulder.

"Adrienne," he whispers. "I want to go with you."

twenty-five

We speak about it far into the night. It makes no sense. And yet we can't let it go. Of course, we tell no one about this new twist in the plans. His family would never agree for him to go with me. And I can't really blame them. What sense would it make to send their brother and son out into the world that had been so cruel to them?

We're leaving tomorrow.

Clara and I work the garden alone. Since Gospozha is out of earshot, we sing a forbidden song. A little number by Adele. Vanya and Marat are off hunting, trying to make up for in meat what we lack in starch. I unearth a large potato and let out a shriek of joy. Clara smiles, claps her hands, and goes back to digging and singing. Her interpretation of "Someone Like You" is truly an original. The words, of course, are incomprehensible, but she's got the tone down. She knows heartache. She knows loss.

I have spent the past few hours picturing Vanya riding on a plane, experiencing television, navigating a subway, fondling a perfect orange at the supermarket, catching a foul ball in a catcher's mitt he has just tried to eat. It's all entertaining and ridiculous and heartbreaking and I don't care. And what will I say? *Oh, everyone's dead, and meet this Russian boy I stumbled upon in the woods?* It's impossible to think too far ahead and not realize our plan's a bit irrational. And yet, I've embraced stupidity, and hope, and things I can't see. And if a reporter is just about the facts, I make a pretty bad reporter. Sydney Declay would be ashamed of me, but to be honest, her name sounds as foreign and strange now as that perfect orange.

I'm going to miss this world. I'm going to miss this family. The rye grass waving. The new fall flowers blooming. Sunlight and birds and the simple tools: hoes, rakes, axes, even a crude hammer. This family is so resourceful. And I've led a really, really easy life.

I want an easier life for all of them. When I see Gospozha patiently sharpening a needle against a whetstone, I think, *Never mind that. I can get you a hundred bright, shiny needles. Or hell, a Nordstrom gift card.* The candles they patiently make from deer hide and animal tallow when they could have light with a flick of a switch. They could sleep on

Sleep Number beds. They could go to movies. They could get their teeth fixed. They could have heat in the winter. They could meet people. They could love people. They could slide across the floor in their socks. They could sleep late and marry and rest and play Uno and have access to medicine and stand in front of the freezer door and eat ice cream out of a carton. They could have neighbors to look down on.

And yet, I understand why they stay. The magic of their solitude. The comfort of their rituals. The strength of their loyalty and love. For better or worse, this is their home now. It will always be their home.

And what if they did return to society? Would they run into a bunch of people who judged them, misunderstood them, were afraid of them as I once was? Why would I think the rest of the world would treat them any better than I once had?

Clara stops singing. Her voice trails off and she looks at me, worried. I close my eyes to hear her speaking to me. I don't understand a word—I probably never will—but the message is clear. She is worried that I don't look happy. I take her hand and smile at her, then let go, and we go back to our song.

It's dark in the hut. Around me the family breathes. It's begun to feel like music. And after tonight, I'll never hear that music again. They are just another variation of a family, like every family I know. They just have less food and more magic.

I want to crawl over to Vanya, put my arms around him, hold him. Maybe I'm selfish. Maybe he'll be miserable. But I can't stand the thought of him living out the rest of his life here, craving language, craving company, scribbling out his thoughts on a notebook that is already almost full. Thoughts that no one will get to read. I think about the notebook, all those neatly written words on a page. Wondering what they say. The letters blur and I drift off to sleep.

I wake up with a start. It's Zoya. She's not smiling. Her arms are crossed. She's even more real to me now since the ritual. It's less like a dream and more like a family member just walked through the door.

But it's a different Zoya. She doesn't smile at me. And when she speaks, she doesn't whisper the words. She screams them, so loud I think her family will wake up.

GO NOW!

twenty-six

This is my last day, and I am going to spend it looking for the final gift. One of the few real gifts I can give them, with my beady eyes and 20/20 vision. I carry the old pickax in my hand. A sack is tied around my waist.

I didn't tell anyone. I just left.

The brothers are out hunting, and Gospozha and Clara are working on a new dress with the dull needles I threaded for them. After I'm gone, who will thread their needles?

The woods are crisp and cool. This is the season when the hardier flowers grow. One of them has a bloom so enormous I can barely cover it with my hand. The petals tickle my palm.

I keep thinking of Zoya's words last night. *GO NOW!*

319

She must know I'm going to leave and possibly take her brother. She must be angry with me. I didn't tell Vanya about seeing her last night. I'm afraid her words might mean something to him, tickle some superstition in him that would make him change his mind. And I can't change my own mind. I have no choice, unless I want to stay here and wither and freeze and later, flowers on my grave, visit Vanya in his dreams.

Up ahead I see a glimmer among the rocks. Flint. Looks like a good chunk of it. I walk over, kneel, start chipping at it with the pickax. It's even harder than it looked when Vanya did it. He got chunks but I'm just getting chips. This is hard work. Even though the air is cool, sweat forms on my face. I swing the ax over my head.

Go now.

I freeze, look up. The little girl is nowhere in sight, but her voice is loud and clear. I'm getting scared. I claw at the fragments of flint, and I'm hurriedly stuffing them in the sack when she shouts it.

GO NOW!

I look around wildly, heart pounding. Then I hear the words again, but now it's my father's voice shouting, *GO NOW!* He bursts from the woods from the clearing, no longer the calm, peaceful father I saw the night of the ritual, but urgent, wild-eyed, screaming, *GO NOW! GO NOW! GO NOW!*

A growl behind me. I whip my head around. Fifty

yards away, the bear barrels toward me. I drop the pickax, scramble to my feet, and run straight for the woods, the bear gaining on me, roaring now, my arms and legs puffing, losing my breath, fleeing as fast as I can, my ears ringing from the cacophony of the roar and the two voices shouting, *GO! GO! GO!*

I'm at the edge of the woods now. My shoe catches on something and falls off, and I plunge into the trees, vines raking my face, the woods growing dark and thicker. The bear is right behind me, his roar has heat, and I throw myself into a stand of slender trees, trying to find shelter.

The bear bats at me through the trees. His claws rake the air inches from my chest. He's furious and foamy and determined, and I scream as the creature pushes on the trees holding him, the trees begin to give, and a set of claws comes out in slow motion and catches me just below the thigh. I hear my skin open. I feel blood pour down my leg.

I fall back as the bear takes my leg in its mouth, but it's so violent, so swift, that it's painless. I don't even know earth from sky from tree anymore. It's all part of a pattern.

Then I hear another growl, just as furious and distinct. Marat's.

The bear releases me, and I struggle to stay conscious as I hear the bloody battle going on between man and beast. My blood soaks the ground around me. I don't hear the bear's roar, or Marat's.

Confusion.

Vanya's rushing footsteps; he's got me now. Arms around me, saying my name, begging me in Russian to look at him. His face comes into focus, then fades out again as he strips off his shirt and ties it tight around my leg. I come back again, turn my head, and see that the bear is gone, blood covering stumps and ferns.

I see Marat's bloody spear.

I see Marat.

He seems to be sunk into the ground, but I blink and see that half his chest is gone. So much blood but barely any on his face. He's looking at me with calm, still eyes. I've never noticed the color of his eyes. They are hazel.

"Don't look!" Vanya urges.

But I can't help it. I look at Marat until his brother lifts me in his arms and carries me away.

twenty-seven

I wake up in the bottom of the canoe, smelling familiar varnish and facing the night sky. I thought it was morning. Why is it night? The canoe suddenly hits something, half spins, and rights itself. It bucks and shakes. I'm not sure if I'm dead or alive or somewhere in between, because I'm not afraid. I feel calm, as though the wild river is part of me and I am part of the wild river.

I heard Vanya's voice, angry. He is shouting Russian curse words. Trying to navigate the rapids. I want to tell him it's okay, but I'm too tired. Instead I stare up at the stars. They are calm although the water is rough, and I think of them switching places: rough, swirling currents of stars and the water beneath me still as glass.

I don't know how much time passes before the boat stops rocking and simply glides along. Vanya's breathing is ragged.

"Vanya?"

His face appears above mine, upside down. "Adrienne."

"Where are we going?"

"To people," he says simply.

I look down at my leg. It's wrapped tight in different-colored bandages. I recognize Sergei's sleeve. The fabric of Lyubov's sweatpants.

"The bear," I murmur.

"Yes. The bear hurt you very bad."

My leg doesn't hurt so much as throb, as though trying to expand past the bandages.

"Marat?"

Vanya doesn't answer me. His oar dips into the water, dips again. I try to sit up so I can see, but Vanya makes me lie back down. His voice is gentle, sorrowful. "You are hurt bad," he says.

We don't talk. We don't need to. My mind has cleared a little, and I have done some very slow and basic math.

Vanya's the man of the family now. His mother and sister can't survive without him. He has to stay in the forest with them. He has to stay a legend. He has to stay a ghost.

We have no future tense.

And so we share the canoe and share this understanding

in the final hours during the long trip to Qualiq. He paddles all the next day, the next night. The water is swift and pushes us onward. I sleep off and on, and in my dreams my two families mix together. Marat plays computer games with Jason. Gospozha shops for produce with my mother. Dan takes Clara by the wrists and swings her around and around.

It's not yet dawn when the canoe scrapes land. Vanya has brought the nut-gathering backpack with the boat, my backpack. I have no idea what I could take with me that isn't shattered, lost, or bloody, but I appreciate the gesture.

Vanya takes me in his arms and carries me through the darkness. Dogs begin to bark. He must hurry or soon he will be discovered.

He sets me down by a doorstep of an old cabin. Lifts my head tenderly and puts the backpack under my head.

More dogs join in the barking.

"You have to go," I tell him. We don't have time to say, *Goodbye* or *I love you* or *I'll find you someday.*

He pounds loudly on the door.

"Go now," I say.

I'm at the hospital in Moscow. A series of machines from the twenty-first century got me here. A motorboat. An SUV. A private plane, handing me off like a bucket

325

of water traveling to a fire. They have sheets here. And electric lights. And a team of doctors that saved my leg, although I won't be able to walk for a month or so.

I really want a pretzel.

And I would not be sure that any part of this actually happened, except for the scars I'll have for the rest of my life and for the knapsack I wouldn't let anyone take away from me. Inside the knapsack are two items: Vanya's notebook and a stone.

I don't know what the stone means. Maybe, *Don't forget me.* Maybe, *Things are actually very simple.* Maybe, *I want this back someday.*

I'm not near a laptop, or a cell phone, or any device at all, but to hear the nurses talking, it's quite the worldwide story: how I went into the forest with my father, his crew, and a guide, and showed up nearly two months later, bear-clawed and half-alive, on someone's front porch in Qualiq.

Men who wear official-looking uniforms have been in and out of the room, asking me questions. And they have so many. But I haven't said a thing. Because I don't know what to do. Tell the truth and prove Dan was right? Or lie and let his legacy suffer for no reason?

A nurse comes in. "Sydney Declay called for you again," she says. Sydney Declay is amazing. All calls are screened at the front desk. But somehow hers keep making it up to the nurses' desk over and over. The nurse adjusts my IV. "Do you want to talk to her?" she asks.

I shake my head. She leaves and I look over at the knapsack. It's not her story. It's not mine, either.

My mother and Jason fly to Moscow to see me. They've been briefed on my rescue and on Dan's death. Although I know they are coming, it's still a surprise when they enter the room, moving slowly through the doorway, still blinking, shell-shocked and jet-lagged and in the first stages of grief.

I'm still sedated, and my head swims a little when I lift it to see them. It's almost a dream as they approach me. They both look so tired and worried.

My mother gets to me first. Embraces me tightly. My time in the woods has sharpened my senses and I sniff not only her cologne but her hand cream as well and the new sweater she's worn without washing.

"Adrienne," she begins, and starts to cry, won't let go.

I cry, too.

"I'm sorry, Mom."

"Sorry for what?" she manages.

"Sorry for everything. Just sorry that it happened." She lets me go, fishes in her purse for a Kleenex. "Dan was brave," I add, and she starts crying again. Jason cries, too. Now both of them are hugging me, and we are all crying. My mother looks a few years older. So does Jason. They lean over my cot, giving me that awkward hug people give when one person's standing and one is lying down. The nurse hovers nearby, watching the IV drip like a hawk.

I have a family and they have me.

They have me.

They have me.

twenty-eight

The leaves are turning color in Boulder. A blanket of snow covers the mountains. I haven't gotten out my skis yet. I haven't been doing much of anything. I'm waiting for next spring to go back to my senior year of high school. I just wasn't ready for it yet.

We're all trying to adjust to life without Dan. We did give him a memorial service, in an overflowing church. I think he would have appreciated so many of his colleagues and friends being there.

I got up and spoke for Dan. I told everyone at the service the story of how he died. I told them what I told the reporter for the *New York Times*—that Dan was right, that there was a family. But I tell the story in my own way.

Some would call it a lie.

But, you see, I had no other choice. I had to clear my stepfather's name. I had to protect the Osinovs. There was only one way I could do both.

So maybe I'm not a reporter, after all. Maybe it's enough, right now, to be a sister and a daughter and a friend and figure out what I'll be later on in life. There's still so much to learn.

What I wanted to tell them was that Dan is still here. I didn't see him that night; he did not come back to me. I'm not sure why. But I know Dan exists in a place that's just beyond our modern senses. In a belt of colored light, under a full moon. He's with us.

We are all together, the living and the dead. It doesn't matter who believes me. I believe me.

Dan taught me that's all that really matters.

I spend a lot of time drawing, and writing. I walk in the woods, snow crunching under my feet, and think about the Osinovs. I wonder if they're cold. If the summer harvest is sustaining them. I get the Russian news and I always look for the weather in Siberia, marveling at how they can survive year after year. I wonder if Gospozha still nods when she speaks, if Clara is still singing modern songs in her own strange way. I wonder if Marat has joined the loved ones who visit them all when the sky turns colors, if Marat will let Clara run her fingers up his arm like a spider.

If he smiles at that.

If he knows I love him, too.

I hope so.

I hope the time is right for magic, for the bowl of tea to be passed around, and time to collapse, and loneliness to dissolve and joy to be found, the pure joy of reunion.

And of course, I think of Vanya. Beautiful Vanya. It is fair to say that I am brokenhearted over him. Just before I go to sleep and I'm fading out into a world that includes all worlds and all possibilities, I feel his arms around me. I hear his voice. I write to him, long letters on notebook paper that I put away in a drawer. There is no address to send them to. There is no map to his footsteps. And unlike the frost, half-melted, that makes the trees in the drunken forest lurch, his memory is solid and whole and eternal and will always hold me up straight.

People have finally stopped asking me questions. Requests for interviews have been denied so many times that the news outlets have given up, and the fan club on Instagram that sprang up overnight for me and earned one hundred thousand followers just went off-line.

There were no photos, no updates to post. No explanations. No exclusives. Just that one interview that was as much of the truth as I could possibly tell.

My story does not belong to the world. It does not belong to me or even to the Osinovs. What I have learned is that we are all the same story, and in this story we love

331

and we hate and we pray and we sing and we search for food and shelter. We want our fathers to come back, real and solid and breathing again, and embrace us, as our fathers wanted for their fathers, and their fathers, and their fathers. We love certain colors. We wonder what is up in the sky. We wish for things and we believe in magic, and when that magic fails, we don't understand. We enter people's lives and bring them joy; we also bring them sorrow. We forgive and we do not forgive, and we in turn are forgiven and are not forgiven. We do things we cannot take back. We perform heroic deeds that no one ever sees. We fold laundry and we play in snow. We try to comfort one another. We wish the summer days were longer. We wonder what it means to be alive.

The girl who killed my father is almost thirty years old now. She's started a foundation to educate college girls about drinking and driving. She speaks at high schools around the country.

She says my father's name.

William Cahill.

I know this because I came to hear her speak, sat in the back row and listened. She cried when she told the story, after all these years. I still wanted to stop her before she hit my father. Still wanted that magic to work, even in a story.

I emailed her later. Told her who I was. Invited her over to my house, the same house she'd brought so much sadness into. I don't know what I'm going to say to her. But I know that I will be kind to her and understanding. I know that I will finally say her name.

A knock on the door.

I open it.

She's standing there, looking nervous.

"Hello, Lisa," I say. "Come in."

I myself am part of a family. I have a wife, a son, and a daughter. We are not a perfect family. But studying the Osinovs made me understand what families really mean.

Dr. Daniel Westin
New York Times article

Do you think I don't want to believe? Who doesn't want to believe?

Sydney Declay
Washington Post article

It is true the Osinovs existed, that we found proof before the crew died and my stepfather drowned in the river. The proof was irrefutable: the remains of their cabin, their graves, some scattered bones, and tucked into an old cabinet near what used to be the hearth, the diary of the second son. We will never know what killed them: the elements, the cold, wild animals, illness. What we know is that, like all families, they sought sanctuary. I hope they found it.

Adrienne Cahill
New York Times article

Love is very simple. And I love her.
Vanya Osinov

from the book *A Voice in the Forest:*
The Letters of Vanya Osinov
published posthumously, translated from the Russian

Acknowledgments

Thanks go first to Mollie Glick, überagent, whose early faith launched my YA path. Thanks to Claudia Gabel and her ferocious talent for finding and shaping a story.

Thanks to Katherine Tegen, Rebecca Aronson, Stephanie Guerdan, and all the gang at Katherine Tegen Books.

Thanks to Heather Daugherty and Helen Crawford-White for the home-run cover.

And Bess Braswell, Ebony LaDelle, and Rosanne Romanello for getting this novel into the hands of the readers.

Also thanks to Jon Howard, Robin Roy, and Dasha Tolstikova, as well as Mariana Olenko and especially Yelena Makarczyk, whose knowledge of Siberia greatly informed this book.

Thanks always to Polly Hepinstall and Becky Hepinstall, tireless readers, supporters, and friends.

And a shout-out to the Cool Kids: Rachel Johnson, Kelley Coleman, Anthony Grieco, and Joe Whyte.